any place
but here

also by sarah van name

The Goodbye Summer

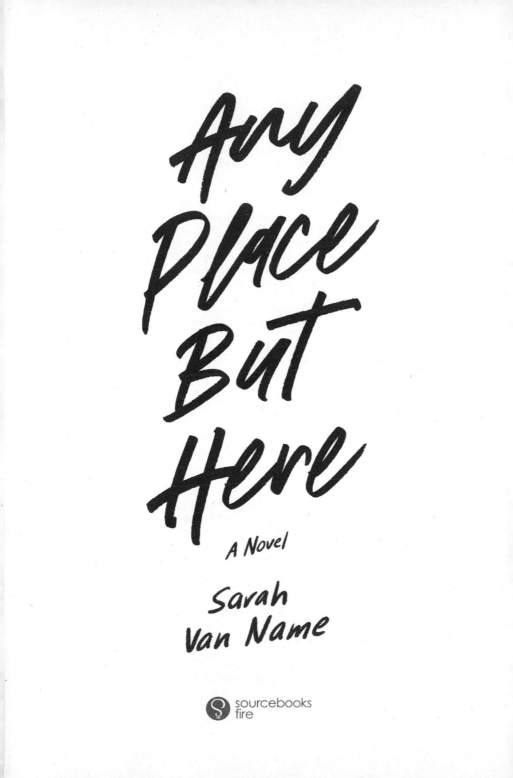

Any Place But Here

A Novel

Sarah Van Name

sourcebooks
fire

Published by Sourcebooks Fire, an imprint of Sourcebooks
P.O. Box 4410, Naperville, Illinois 60567-4410
(630) 961-3900
sourcebooks.com

Library of Congress Cataloging-in-Publication Data

Names: Van Name, Sarah, author.
Title: Any place but here : a novel / Sarah Van Name.
Description: Naperville, Illinois : Sourcebooks Fire, [2021] | Audience:
  Ages 14. | Audience: Grades 10-12. | Summary: Seventeen-year-old June
  feels she is nothing without her best friend, Jess, but everything
  changes after she is expelled and must attend a Virginia boarding school
  where her grandmother teaches.
Identifiers: LCCN 2020053482 (print) | LCCN 2020053483 (ebook)
Subjects: CYAC: Identity--Fiction. | Best friends--Fiction. |
  Friendship--Fiction. | Grandmothers--Fiction. | Boarding
  schools--Fiction. | Schools--Fiction. | Bisexuality--Fiction.
Classification: LCC PZ7.1.V353 Any 2021 (print) | LCC PZ7.1.V353 (ebook)
  | DDC [Fic]--dc23
LC record available at https://lccn.loc.gov/2020053482
LC ebook record available at https://lccn.loc.gov/2020053483

Printed and bound in the United States of America.
VP 10 9 8 7 6 5 4 3 2 1

For Ben:
a novel, of all things

one

I arrived in northern Virginia on January 1, the metaphor of the fresh start laid out in front of me as bright and wide as the river itself. But it had been predestined. The moment that decided it had occurred four weeks earlier, in the bathroom of the cafeteria where Greenmont held its annual Jingle Bell Ball.

Jess and I were squeezed together in the last stall, downing whiskey in gulps from the bottle she'd tucked into her jacket pocket. I was already dizzy and giggling from what we drank before we came, and she had the slow kind of smile that meant she was drunk, too. We were whispering about nothing and trying to keep quiet. And it was all okay—it was fine. We had done this before.

But then I leaned hard against her, which pushed her against the door of the stall, and I guess we hadn't latched it tight enough, because it fell open and she fell down. The whiskey fell on top of her, what little of it remained sloshing into her cleavage and the bottle clattering onto the tiles. Of course, both of us started cackling.

"Jerk," she said, giggling, not even trying to get up.

"Klutz," I retorted.

Which would have been fine, too. All of it could have been fine. Except right then, Mary Elizabeth Marcus opened the door to the bathroom and held it open, gaping at Jess on the floor. The bathroom opens to the dance floor because of course it does. And a few yards behind Mary Elizabeth, Mrs. Beckett, the tenth-grade American history teacher, while scanning the room for illicit teen sexual activity, saw a student collapsed on the floor and rushed in to help.

I looked in the mirror, and I swear I saw my future self: a little taller, a little sadder. *You are about to be so thoroughly fucked,* my future self said to me. And as Mrs. Beckett knelt beside Jess and picked up the whiskey bottle, I knew there was nothing at all I could do about it.

They didn't expel me, because short of committing a felony, it's hard to get kicked out of Greenmont; they don't like to have expulsions on their record. Natalie Harmon and Carson Xiu had gotten caught having sex in the boys' locker room during a football game; Jordan Pugh had spent several months selling drugs in the hallways; Annie Kolkow had said some horrifying things online. None of them got expelled. They were *asked to leave.* And that's what happened to me, too. They *asked me to leave.* Which meant I wrapped up the last few weeks of the semester sitting in the back of my classes, scribbling dark lines of pen until they ate through my notebook paper. Making A's on all my assignments and still seeing the disappointment in my teachers' eyes when I handed them in.

They didn't expel Jess, either. They asked her to leave, just like me. Then her parents gave a "significant gift" to Greenmont's Annual Giving Campaign, and all of a sudden, they were asking her to stay. When we walked out of school on the last day of the fall semester, the December sun shining brightly on the sidewalk, only one of us was walking out for the last time.

That's how I ended up going to Oma's on New Year's Day. The whole family drove me up, as if they were seeing me off to war rather than dropping me off at a familiar apartment four hours away. The twins were unusually quiet for most of the drive, Bryan's face buried in a book and Candace's thumbs moving furiously over her game console. As we passed the sign welcoming us into town, Bryan looked up, his eyes somber.

"I can't believe this is your home now," he said. "You'll never be around anymore."

"Stop being melodramatic," I snapped. "I'll be back for the summer. And spring break. At least."

"That's right," Mom said, her voice slightly strained. "Four hours is nothing. We can come pick you up any weekend."

"Exactly," I said. But I stared out the window, too. A Walmart, a tire repair place, an Italian restaurant, a pawnshop, endless antique stores. The sun was sparkling over the patchy remnants of an early snow. Bryan was right. Until college—assuming I could even get into college, switching schools like this midyear—this was my home now.

"I still don't get why you have to live here," Candace said quietly.

"Me neither, Candace."

But I did get it. I was being made to leave because of Jess, and the irony of it, the unfairness of it, still made me ache. It was both of our faults equally, but still. Last night, our last night together for months, we had sat together in the park, and I'd held her close as she sobbed *I'm sorry, I'm sorry, I'm sorry.* All I wanted was more time with her, and she was the reason, according to my parents, I had to go away.

"We've had this conversation," Dad said. "We are not having it again."

The car fell silent. My throat burned, but I dug my fingernails into my palms, and I didn't cry.

My grandmother was waiting for us at the gate to the condominium, eating an apple and beaming. As we parked in a visitor spot, she tossed away the apple core. Bryan was the first out of the car to give her a hug. I was the last.

"June," she said, opening her arms to me. "You've really gotten yourself into a pickle, haven't you?"

"Hi, Oma," I said while hugging her. Mom, pulling a suitcase out of the trunk, shot me a glare. I had received a comprehensive guilt trip from my parents the night before. *Your grandmother never expected we'd have to ask her to do anything like this,* she'd said. *You should be very, very grateful.*

4

"Thank you for..." I started.

Oma pulled away and raised her eyebrows.

"Everything," I finished.

"You're welcome," she said. "We're gonna get you sorted out. Now, how much luggage do we have to deal with?"

Her condo was exactly the same as it had always been: A long rectangle that stretched along a continuous window looking out at the river. The front door opened into an expansive, open kitchen and living room; the skinny guest room and skinnier hall bathroom were in the middle; and her bedroom was on the end.

Then there was the dog. Eleanor Roosevelt barreled toward me, howling in delight, and wriggled around my legs in spasms of joy. The twins dropped their bags immediately to pet her. I pushed past her, my parents trailing behind me, to drop my things in the guest bedroom.

I shoved my bags into the closet, taking a moment to stand apart from the sounds out in the hall: the twins laughing, my parents complaining about the drive, the dog's nails clicking on the hardwood floor. I leaned against the wall and looked around. This would be my room for at least the next five months. The walls were painted light blue. There was a framed painting of a beach on the wall and a tall window. It was a small space with little furniture to crowd it, just the bed and its nightstand and an enormous, empty chest of drawers.

Ellie dashed in and did a lap before jumping on me. She was a big dog, seventy or eighty pounds of eager yellow mutt, and she licked me on the neck before I was able to push her away. Candace followed her in, breathless.

"Come look at the river, June!" she urged, then ran away again. Ellie galloped after her.

"I know what the river looks like," I said to the empty doorway. But I got up and followed her anyway.

My whole family was gathered in the living room, bags discarded in a pile on the floor. The river stretched out in front of them. Oma kept the condo warm, but near the window, it was colder. I stood beside my mom and let her put her arm around me, though it felt awkward and heavy.

"Wow," Dad said.

"It's so beautiful," said Mom. "I know I say that every time we visit. But it's true."

"Sometime, I want to go out on a boat," said Candace.

"You can't do that now," Bryan said.

"I know. I'm not stupid. I mean when it's warmer."

"We can do that," said Oma. "When it's warmer."

Mom squeezed my shoulder, but I said nothing. One by one, they drifted back toward the living room and kitchen to get glasses of water, use the bathroom, flop onto the couch. Ellie walked among them, ears perked and tail wagging, waiting for someone to pet her. But I stayed by the window. The water was gray and wide and glittered with an otherworldly light. Even from five stories up, you could barely see the opposite bank. Oma joined me there, crossing her arms.

"If you're anything like me," she said, "you'll wake up one

morning after living here a while and think, what a stupid river."

I felt myself smile, just a little, before swallowing it away.

But Oma hadn't noticed, or if she had, she didn't say anything. "Dirty and brown and cold," she continued. "Practically useless for fishing, from this part of town anyway, and making the air cooler when it's already winter. But then the next morning, you'll wake up and you'll feel like you've never seen anything so beautiful. It just takes your breath away. You feel..." She paused to choose her next words. "Immeasurably lucky."

She looked right at me. Her eyes were dark gray, like newly poured concrete.

"Every morning, you get to choose how you look at the river," she said. "I recommend feeling lucky."

"I'll keep that in mind," I said.

"Do," she said. "Because you can't choose whether to look at it or not. You're here now, for better or for worse."

She walked away from me, her stocking feet padding quietly on the floor, and I heard the coffee grinder start whirring. The river beneath me was both brown and blue, both dirty and bright. The light from the sun hurt my eyes. But I didn't want to turn my back on it. So I just kept staring, trying to make a choice.

———

My family had a three-day stay planned. School started on Wednesday, January 4, in both the twins' middle school and my new school here, St. Anne's. After they left, of course, I would be staying in the guest bedroom, which Oma told me I should think of as mine. Until they went home, though, my parents were sleeping in the double bed in that room, the twins were sharing the pull-out couch, and I was on an air mattress.

It seemed to me deeply unfair that despite being the only one who would actually live here for several months, I was sleeping on a mattress that deflated throughout the night so I woke up flat on the floor. But when I tried to protest while unpacking with Mom, she just shrugged.

"Tough," she said. "It's only for a few nights, and your dad has back problems. This makes the most sense."

"Make Candace and Bryan sleep on the air mattress," I retorted.

"It's a twin mattress. There's not enough room."

"Then buy another mattress!"

"June," she said, a note of warning in her voice. "You know how much we were spending on Greenmont before you got yourself kicked out. St. Anne's is going to cost us, too, even with the faculty discount from your grandmother. Do you really want to suggest that we take on unnecessary expenses right now?"

A flood of words rose inside my throat, but I shut up. Instead of screaming at her, I slammed the dresser drawer closed, and when I turned around to pick up the bundle of socks from my suitcase, she had left. In the living room, Candace and Bryan yelled as they played video games.

During the three days we were all there, Oma and I didn't spend much time alone together. Not that we ever had. I loved her, and I knew she loved me, but we had never been close. She visited us at Thanksgiving and Christmas, and we spent Labor Day weekend with her, along with two or three other weekends throughout the year. But we didn't talk about each other's lives in a real way. She didn't know what I liked to read or who my friends were; I didn't know how she spent her time, apart from teaching and going on walks with Ellie.

I didn't even know where to begin, and during those long, cold days before school started, it seemed that neither did she. We played board games, watched movies, and cooked dinner together, but my parents or the twins were always with us.

It wasn't until the night before school started—after the rest of my family had packed up their things and not mine, after Mom had teared up standing in front of the dresser she had helped me unpack, after Bryan lost his book and couldn't find it for twenty minutes, after Eleanor Roosevelt had started howling in anxiety at all the activity, and after they had finally driven away—only then, after all of it, were Oma and I alone. Having waved them off from the balcony together, we came inside and sat on opposite ends of the couch. I texted Jess, recounting the day's events. Oma picked up a book, opened it, and put it back down. Outside, it was only four in the afternoon, and the sky was already darkening.

"Should we order Italian food, maybe?" Oma suggested.

"That sounds good," I said. I felt a wave of tightness, breathed, let it go. At home, there was a place called Cucina; Jess and I would go sometimes on Friday during happy hour, dressed up in heels and dresses, and linger for hours over a basket of free bread and a plate of arancini.

Oma passed me a folded paper menu from the end table drawer. I gave her my order, and she called it in. While she was speaking, I texted Jess. **looks like dinner is night-before-school penne alla vodka.**

She instantly responded. **I feel physically sick I miss you so much.**

same, I said, relieved. Sick, I wanted her sick. I wanted her to hurt if I hurt, wanted the two of us to share everything.

Later that night, after a quiet dinner, I went to bed with my phone lighting up the guest room walls. When I fell asleep, it was still there beside me, inches from my nose, my lifeline back to her.

two

You know when you're walking around in the summer, and the heat is so oppressive that you can barely breathe, and the sidewalks are so hot, it's all you can do to take another step? You can tell that everything and everyone feels the same, bled of color, sick of being awake.

But then you feel a tension rising in the air. A heavy cloud appears overhead out of nowhere; a cool breeze drifts through. And when the rain comes, it is apocalyptic. You don't make it inside and you're drenched. You look down to see your shirt sticking to your skin. You're cold for the first time in months. When the storm passes, a few minutes later, you feel reborn. The whole world does.

That's what Jess was to me. I was the ground; she was the rain. I wasn't anything until she woke me up.

We met the summer after ninth grade. We went to the same high school, so I knew of her; maybe she knew of me. I had seen her in the hallways, usually alone. But we never talked until we showed up at the same YMCA day camp. It was full of athletes, girls who would try out for soccer and field hockey come autumn, girls who liked to run. I had never run a mile of my own volition in my life. The first day, I sat on the grass beside the field, holding my ankle as if I had rolled it, eating a bag of pretzels.

Jess came up from behind me and sat down beside me. She squinted out at the soccer field, where the blue team had just scored a goal. "Soccer is the worst," she said.

"Yeah. Well," I amended, "sports are the worst."

"Correct," she said. She looked at me sideways. "Can I have a pretzel?"

"Yeah." I held the bag out to her. She took one and placed it on her tongue, carefully, like a communion wafer.

At the time, her dark-brown hair hung loose halfway down her back. Six months later, I would sit behind her in a chair in her kitchen and cut it into a horrible bob that her mom would insist she get professionally corrected. But that first day, she had to keep tucking it behind her ears because she refused to wear it in a ponytail, even though the air was already sweltering. She was wearing purple shorts that would have been several fingers too short for our school's dress code, and a tiny amethyst sparkled from her nose.

We ate the bag of pretzels together in silence. On the field, the red team scored two goals in quick succession. After I had taken the last pretzel, Jess crumpled up the bag and stuffed it into her pocket. She turned toward me and squinted.

"My name is Jess," she said, sticking out her hand in an awkward motion.

"June," I said. I shook her hand. I had to reach across my body to do it. It was the second or third time I had ever shaken anyone's hand in my life. "Short for Jessica?"

"Technically, yes," she said. "But really, no. Just Jess."

I nodded. "I'm just June."

"That makes sense," she said. "You look summery. Do you wanna go over there and climb one of the magnolias?"

The magnolias stood in a line at the edge of the soccer field. In front of them was a small white sign that said DO NOT CLIMB.

"We're not supposed to," I pointed out.

"Hmm," she said. "But it's *very* hot out is the thing."

I couldn't help but smile. "That's true," I admitted.

"So let's go."

When we were discovered an hour later, hidden halfway up the magnolia in the cool green light, we had become irrevocably best friends.

Jess liked to say she corrupted me. Or she'd call me her student, her protégé. She'd do it while flinging one arm around me and reaching the other up to play with her hair. It was always to impress someone else; she never said it when we were alone. "Have you met my beautiful pupil, June?" she would say to the boy, because it was always a boy. "I've taught her so much. Haven't I, June?"

I would nod and provide one of a few tried and tested responses. "And yet there's so much to learn," I'd say sometimes, or maybe, "She's a very good teacher," or maybe I'd just smile, looking away or down at my shoes.

It was a good routine. Not the words so much, which were an absolute cliché, but the delivery. We always looked mysterious. At least I thought we probably looked mysterious, which was what mattered to me. And it always ended with the boy's attention focused on Jess, which was what mattered to her.

It was a good routine because it was true; the best things always are. Before I met Jess, I had never kissed a boy or gotten anything pierced or taken even a sip of alcohol. I cursed, but rarely and timidly. By the end of that summer, I had started dating my first boyfriend—Jess's neighbor's cousin—made out with him exactly six times, and broken up with him when he went home to Indiana at the end of the summer. I had gotten two ear piercings, one of which would close within months. I cursed like a sailor. And I drank everything Jess could find for us, squeezing my eyes shut and bracing for the burn as I swallowed it down. One day that August, when the two of us were drunk and sunburned at the pool near her house, she said I had graduated.

I thought then that we were worldly—otherworldly. That we were the two most badass girls who'd ever stepped foot into any room, that we had broken all the rules there were to break. I was sure of it, even if I wouldn't have said it aloud.

Later, though, Jess started seeing Patrick, and things changed. Mostly, we just hung out with him and his best friend Ethan, but sometimes we ran into his or his brother's other friends at shows or when we were driving around on the weekends. And I knew for sure that I was wrong about me and Jess. We were not worldly. There were more rules to break, thousands more that Jess and I would never touch. Drugs I didn't know the names of and didn't understand. Getting into cars while wasted and high. I left those meetings knowing I had been a good girl at heart the whole time.

I never tried to explain this to my parents: how much worse it could have been.

But they wouldn't have understood it. If anything, it would have made them worry more. So I let them think I was a delinquent, and alone together with Jess, we detailed the ways in which we were good. *We don't smoke,* she said, leaving off the fact that it was only because smoke made her sick to her stomach. *We don't do drugs,* I said, leaving off the fact that we had tried a few. *We don't steal,* she said. *We've never hurt anyone,* I said. *We're still in our right minds,* she said. *And we always will be.*

We always talked like that after we got in trouble. We'd sit somewhere holding hands and figure out a way to make the punishment better.

"At least we're together," we said until, this last time, we weren't.

———

I have never been an early riser. Almost no one in my family is; except for Candace, the lone inexplicable morning person, all of us could happily wake up at ten every day. But I was awake hours before sunrise on January 4, my first day as a student at St. Anne's, and no matter how many times I visualized relaxing each part of my body, I couldn't fall back asleep.

I texted Jess. **you up?** No response. It was 5:30. If she was keeping to her normal schedule, she'd wake up at 6:45 or 7:00 to slide into school just in time for first bell at 7:30. Here, the bell didn't ring until 8:00. If this place even had bells. I didn't know.

I padded into the kitchen and flipped on the light switch before realizing I also didn't know how to make coffee here. At home, we had a normal coffeepot that made enough for me and my parents to have a cup or two every morning. But Oma's mechanism of choice was a French press, nestled in a corner of the counter. I had never used one of those.

I felt shaky with nervousness. The first day of a brand-new school, and I was going to have to get through it without coffee. Without my brother and sister. And without Jess.

I heated a cup of water in the kettle on the stove, stirred some honey into it, and sat in the big blue chair under a blanket. In the black of the early morning, the floor-to-ceiling window was more like a mirror. I could feel the chill bleeding in through the glass. If the sun had been above the horizon, I could have seen St. Anne's from where I was sitting. It was inescapable, visible from every window in the apartment, pressed right up against the river's edge.

I had looked at it enough to visualize it even in the dark: a series of clean, redbrick two-story buildings with gray slate roofs, stretching maybe half a mile along the road that ran beside the river. On the side facing the road, there were small grassy gardens with magnolias and oaks that approximated college quads. (The website had a photo of girls studying there that might as well have been a stock image, but I found it oddly compelling nonetheless.) The whole thing was surrounded by a low brick wall, setting it apart from the rest of the tiny town.

I had only stepped foot on campus once. Apart from that, the closest I had come was holding Bryan's hand as he walked, as if on a balance beam, atop the brick wall on our way to the antique store my parents liked.

Oma had offered to take me on a tour, but I said no. Starting January 2, I had seen the students trickling back in. Some had piled out of St. Anne's vans fresh from the Richmond or DC airports; others, like me, arrived with their parents and siblings in cars that departed lighter than they'd come. All of them, unlike me, entered the dorms shrieking with delight to see their friends. It was bad enough being the granddaughter of a teacher. Worse if the first time they saw me was wandering the halls with Oma, lost, bewildered, and small.

I texted Jess again: **miss you.** No response. It was still barely six. Maybe her mom would make her get up early and she would text me back before school. Probably not. It unsettled me to think of us on different schedules.

I heard a rustling behind me and turned too quickly, splashing water on my hands and cursing. Oma stood a few yards away in her old-fashioned robe, head cocked and smiling. Ellie walked in behind her, yawning, and lay down on her dog bed.

"I thought I was going to have to pull you out of bed by your hair," Oma said. She leaned on the edge of the couch. "Your parents warned me about your sleeping habits."

"They're normal sleeping habits," I said, a tad too defensive.

"I am a big fan of mornings. Especially first day of school mornings. Something about them. And of course with you here, it's extra special."

"I was going to make coffee," I offered. "But I didn't want to wake you up. And I don't know how to do a French press."

"Oh, I'll show you." She got up and started toward the kitchen, then turned back, brow furrowed. "I forgot. Do you want breakfast? I never eat it, but I tell all my girls they should."

I shook my head. The first day of junior year, Jess had picked me up and we'd gotten McDonald's together, barely making it to school on time. The day had been too hot, the air yellow and alive, and I couldn't remember anything tasting as good as our biscuits had tasted. No second-semester first-day breakfast could match that memory.

"Well, that's probably for the best. I'm out of eggs," Oma said, going to the kitchen. I heard the grinding of the coffee beans start and then stop. "We can go grocery shopping tomorrow. You can tell me what you like."

I sipped from the cup of sweet water. It had cooled down, and it tasted like nothing at all. I looked at my reflection in the window and tried to imagine myself on the campus.

My one visit before today had been to the garden. Every teacher at St. Anne's was required to run an extracurricular activity in addition to teaching. This was nothing new to my grandmother. At past schools, she had been in charge of literary magazines, community service organizations, and once, with disastrous results, a volleyball team. As an experienced teacher, she was used to getting her pick of after-school clubs. But when she accepted the job at St. Anne's eight years ago, the only option open was gardening.

As Oma told it, she had never had a green thumb, but she was game to try anything. So she checked out some books from the school library, spent the summer at garden stores, and, in the fall, greeted the five girls in the Garden Club with an abundance of theoretical knowledge and absolutely no practical skill.

It took two years before their first twelve-by-twelve-foot plot grew enough to harvest. But as of this year, the Garden Club membership hadn't dipped into the single digits in many semesters, and they had eight plots. Oma could have retired years ago, but she had stayed, and I thought the club was probably a big part of that. Apparently, she was popular among the girls of St. Anne's.

I was not planning on joining the Garden Club. The closest I came to gardening was caring for my cactus, who was named Rosemary. I had received her as a birthday gift from Candace a few years ago. "Because you're very spiky," my sister had said, not even ten and already a smart-ass.

I rolled my eyes, but I set Rosemary on my bedroom windowsill in the sun and watered her every week or two, just like the internet said, and she grew. Not very much, not very quickly, but

19

still—growth. She was a tiny miracle. On hard days, when I'd gotten a B or my parents had yelled at me or Jess had been in a bad mood, I liked to open my window, feel the air on my face, and just look at her. *I'm very spiky*, I would think to Rosemary. *That's not such a bad thing*, I'd imagine her retorting.

"June?" Oma called from the kitchen.

I got up to join her. The lights in there were harsh and bright, and after looking out at the dark river for so long, I squinted.

"This is the French press," she said, nodding to the machine in front of her.

"I know what it is." I leaned on the counter. "I just don't know how to use it."

"Don't be snippy. I'm just telling you where things are. The kettle stays on the stove, and the coffee is in the pantry, top shelf. Grinder is here. You grind the beans first, which I've done, and then you boil some water, which I'm doing now…"

I watched and listened as she walked me through measuring the water, letting it cool, measuring the beans, and waiting. We stood there for a minute. I hopped up on the counter to sit, which drew a startled look from Oma.

"Should I not…" I trailed off and scooted to the edge of the counter, ready to slide off.

"No, no," she said, waving a hand. She laughed a little. "It's just that I don't think anyone has ever sat there before. I'm too old, I guess."

"You're not that old."

"Old enough."

A shrill timer went off, and I bumped my head against the edge of the cabinet. I rubbed it as I looked down at the old-fashioned little egg timer on the counter, jumping and jittering as it rang. Who used a physical timer?

Oma, apparently. Unbothered, she switched it off and slowly pressed the coffee.

"And see, now, you just pour it from here into a cup…" She poured until it barely reached the brim and stepped back, satisfied. "Exactly the right amount."

"There's only one cup," I pointed out.

"Oh, sugar." She frowned. "Well, that's true."

"I don't need any," I said, though I desperately wanted it.

"I can tell that you do. Well, I'll take this one, and it'll be good practice for you to try to make a cup yourself. I'm going to go shower and get dressed." With that, she picked up the mug and left me alone with the grinds and the mysterious glass mechanism.

I struggled through the French press process as the shower came on in the master bedroom. After five minutes, I was rewarded with a cup of coffee: too thin and tasting mostly of water, but better than nothing. I wrapped my hands around it and brought it to my new bedroom, where I set it on the bedside table and sent Jess a picture with the caption **this coffee is the worst.**

Again, no response.

And then, her name and **why the fuck are you up so EARLY**

I felt a grin splitting my face. **couldn't sleep,** I responded quickly. **I hate that I'm not there.**

meeeeeee toooooo, came the instant response. I imagined her bleary-eyed in bed or having just gotten up, stumbling around trying to find an outfit in the dark. As if she was reading my mind, she said, **tell me what you're wearing today.** I texted her a picture of the outfit hanging on my closet door: black leggings and a long gray sweater.

you need to make much more of an impact than that, she said. **those girls don't know you like I do. they don't know you're a star.**

what are you wearing? I asked her.

I looked at my outfit again. A dress felt like too much for the first day, and besides, it was so cold that I would've had to wear the leggings underneath it anyway. I didn't want to seem like I was trying too hard.

oh, you know. probably my gray sweater and leggings.

I laughed aloud. **you're the best,** I told her.

no, you. now I gotta shower. talk to you later beautiful

The water shut off in Oma's bathroom. I took a sip of my coffee. It had gone cold. Eleanor Roosevelt padded into my room, jumped on the bed beside me, licked her lips, and yawned. *Beautiful,* said the word on my screen. I touched my face, trying to feel the beauty there.

three

It was dark as Oma and I walked from the entrance of the condos to the parking lot. The path was only really wide enough for one, so I walked on the grass, frost crunching under my boots. It was still nighttime, or at least it felt like it, gray light just starting to harden the air around us and cast its reflection on the river. I shivered. My torso was warm enough, but I had forgotten my gloves, and there was a hole in the sole of my left boot.

Oma exhaled heavily, her breath crystallizing in front of her. "It gets warmer," she said, as if defending northern Virginia. I did not feel that sentence merited a response. Oma didn't speak up again.

I had started a distance tracker on my phone as soon as we stepped through the front door of the condominium, and when we finally reached the classroom building, I stopped it: half a mile, eleven minutes. It had felt much longer in the cold and silence. I tried to imagine walking it every day for the next semester, instead of Jess picking me up in her cozy car filled with empty sour-candy bags. It made me want to melt straight down into the earth.

But I didn't have that option. Instead, Oma opened the door, and I stepped gratefully into the heat. I looked around as I shrugged off my coat. We were in a foyer with an administrative office and a few overstuffed chairs. In front of me, an enormous bulletin board was covered in colorful paper and pictures of smiling girls. I took a few steps forward to look down the hallways to the right and left. Doors, some open to classrooms and some still closed, alternated with lockers all the way down both halls. The lockers were mounted halfway up the wall, leaving a space underneath them with hooks for backpacks. At the ends, stairways led up to the second floor.

"Ginger should be around here somewhere," Oma said from behind me. "Normally, she gives new students their schedules…"

"It's only seven fifteen," I pointed out. "School doesn't start until eight."

"Well, the lights are on, so she's definitely here. I guess she's just not *here*." Oma put her hands on her hips. "Come see my classroom then? You can wait there until she gets back."

"Yeah, okay. Then I think I might walk around a little bit." I didn't want to be in my grandmother's classroom when the other girls started arriving. Thankfully, because she taught ninth and tenth grade, I would not be Oma's student.

Oma led me down the hall to the right and unlocked one of

the closed doors. I absorbed the room while she started unpacking her bag and setting up her laptop. There was a bookshelf full of textbooks and another of historical fiction, a gigantic world map, a projector screen, a whiteboard, and two big windows looking out at the river. The sun was finally up, and the light on the water looked cold and beautiful.

"You're welcome to come in here any time you want," Oma said, sounding as awkward as I felt. "I have fourth and sixth periods free. Plus lunch, of course."

I hated the implication that I would have nowhere else to eat, but I said, "Thank you."

"So you're going to go explore?"

"Yeah. A little."

"Well, give me a hug." I walked over to her desk, and she enveloped me close, her wiry arms wrapping tight around me. My parents would always hug me before the first day of school, but usually the first day of school was in August, and they would take pictures of me and Candace and Bryan with our backpacks. This wasn't August, and they weren't here. Instead, it was my grandmother in the winter, so the hug, which should have felt familiar, was something new. I pulled away.

"I have a meeting after school," Oma said. "You have your key to the condo?" I patted my bag. "Okay. Well, I'll see you later."

"Have a good day," I said.

"You too," Oma said. She looked like she might say something else but then shook her head and turned away.

I wandered down the long, empty hallway, up the stairs and

across the building and down again, where I finally ran into Ginger the admin, who had been looking for me. She gave me my class schedule and a map and showed me to my locker on the second floor. I waited until she left to pull out the picture of me and Jess from my bag and tuck it into a corner of the locker door.

Girls were starting to filter in, yawning, texting. They came in pairs and trios and leaned against the wall or sat underneath the lockers, and though I saw a few curious glances, none of them talked to me. I busied myself looking at my schedule. It was the same every day, except for the period before lunch, which was an SAT prep class on Monday, photography on Tuesday and Thursday, and study hall on Wednesday and Friday. I was thankful for the study hall. With all the AP classes I was taking and a new school that I had been assured was at least as academically rigorous as Greenmont, I needed the extra time for homework. I was thankful, too, that there were no required religion classes. Despite the name, Oma told me, St. Anne's was pretty secular; according to her, the only time I'd have to listen to a religious speech was at an Easter gathering in April.

From the very first bell, the day was a blur, interrupted only by lunch, during which I sat under my locker alone, texted Jess, and tried to start on some reading for AP U.S. History. Teachers introduced me to their classes, handed out syllabi, gave lectures, assigned homework. Girls stared, smiled, didn't smile, introduced themselves, ignored me. I didn't mind them ignoring me. I did not expect to make friends.

I had thought school would be different without guys around, and it was—in a way I couldn't quite put my finger on—but it also wasn't. There were loud girls, quiet girls, cliques, couples, jokes, flirting, gossip. There were the athletes and the artists and the kind of girls who seemed to do nothing except be beautiful. It was the same as Greenmont in these ways. A different school, but still just school.

By the time I got to my last-period physics class, I was ready to return to my new room and fall asleep for hours. The beginning of the class was the same as the others: an introduction, an awkward raise of my hand, a few jokes between the teacher and the class, an outline of our next few weeks. A lecture on the physics of a ball rolling down a hill took up the next twenty minutes.

"And now," Mrs. Talpur continued, "let's go through our working groups for this semester. We're switching them up from last semester." There was a mixture of reactions from the class, a few girls clearly annoyed and others pleased. "Group one: Feng Parker, Natalie Jenkins, Beatriz Weber. Group two..."

I wasn't sure what a working group would entail. I looked around the class as I waited for my name, which didn't come until the very end. "Group six," Mrs. Talpur finished, folding the paper in her hand. "June Jacobsen, Claire Isaac, Tabitha Kim. Find your lab benches, please, and decide who will take notes for today's activity."

I picked up my notebook and moved to the lab bench labeled six, which was at the end farthest from the door. Two girls who had been sitting next to each other behind me followed. One was a tall white girl, with long curls and deep brown eyes empha-sized with lots of eyeliner. The other was smaller and Asian, her straight black hair cut short, wearing a green striped sweater. The taller one walked close on the heels of the shorter one, and they spoke quietly, smiling, their heads tilted toward each other in mutual deference. I lifted a hand in greeting as they sat down.

"Claire," said the taller one.

"June," I said. "I'm new. As you heard."

"That's a great name," said the shorter one. "I'm Kitty."

"Tabitha became Tabby, and then…" explained Claire.

"Like the frivolous one in *Pride and Prejudice*," Kitty said.

"Sure," I said. "Are you also a big fan of womanizing soldiers?"

Kitty laughed. "If anything, I *am* a womanizing soldier."

I smiled despite myself as Mrs. Talpur explained the activity, which involved rolling a ball down a wedge of wood at the bench and calculating its speed. I had aced physics the previous semes-ter at Greenmont, but my success was all memory. Jess and I had quizzed each other on formulas and answered practice word problems until we could do well on tests, but the principles had never really clicked.

Claire grabbed the wedge and the ball from the basket of supplies at the back of the table. I looked at them helplessly.

"I'll be note-taker," Kitty said, seizing my only chance at contributing to the group.

"She has perfect handwriting," Claire said as Kitty labeled a page *January 4 Ball/Wedge* in neat block letters.

"Physics is not my best subject," I said. I didn't want to be the girl who was bad at science, but they would find out soon enough. "I'm good at math. I just…don't understand how the numbers relate to the physical objects."

"Well, you are in luck, because Claire is a physics genius," Kitty responded promptly.

"It's true."

"I don't want to just copy off your work," I protested, but Claire cut me off.

"I don't mind, really. Although I appreciate the thought." She handed me a stopwatch. "Here, time this. Three, two, one…" She released the ball she had been holding at the top of the wedge and let it roll down into her cupped hand. It took just over two seconds. I showed the timer to Kitty, who jotted down some notes.

"So," Kitty said as Claire reset the ball. "Are you rooming with Natasha?"

"Who?"

"I thought she was the only one without a roommate this semester. Because Evie left. Right, Claire? Unless we got another new girl, too."

"Yeah, Evie went back home."

"Oh," I said, finally understanding. "No. I'm just a day student."

Both of them looked up at me. "Interesting," Claire said.

"Why interesting?"

"Well, St. Anne's doesn't take day students anymore."

"Except for special circumstances," Kitty chimed in.

"Right. Which has us wondering what your special circumstance is."

"My grandma teaches here," I answered, feeling more than a little self-conscious. But the confusion on their faces cleared up as soon as I said it, and they nodded in unison.

"I forgot about the teachers' kids," Claire said. "Time me again?" The ball rolled down, I clicked the timer, and Kitty's pencil scratched on the page.

"Yeah, there are a few girls like that," Kitty said. "Although you're our first granddaughter, I think. Who's your grandma?"

"Marie Nolan. Ms. Nolan, I guess. History, downstairs? Tenth grade?"

Kitty laughed, a loud and unexpected sound. "Hell yeah," she said. "I love Ms. Nolan."

"She's the best," Claire said.

"She's very strict."

"But fair."

"Yes. I miss her. Mrs. Keller isn't nearly as good."

"Not even close."

"So..." Kitty looked at me with open interest. "Does your whole family live with her? Why are you just starting this semester?"

I wasn't sure where to begin. I had tried all day to hide inside a tough shell, to be spiky like my cactus. It had worked until now, when the camaraderie and curiosity of these girls had thrown me off guard. "I—"

The bell rang. Relieved, I started packing up my things as Mrs. Talpur yelled something about recording our results and finishing the activity tomorrow. My phone buzzed in the pocket of my bag. Jess had finished school twenty minutes ago and, judging by the number of buzzes, had been texting me ever since. I tossed my bag over my shoulder, already mentally out of the room, and Claire said, "To be continued."

"Yeah, for sure."

"See you tomorrow," Kitty said.

"See you," I said, and then I moved as quickly as I could out of the classroom, down the stairs, and out the doors. The cold hit me like a wall as I stepped outside, but I welcomed it. With my head tucked against the wind, I walked quickly across the brown grass, hopped over the low wall, ran down a steep hill, and was in the parking lot of Oma's building. It was a lot faster if you didn't walk on the roads and sidewalks.

I spent the next hour in my bedroom, texting Jess and avoiding Eleanor Roosevelt, whose desperate need for attention felt less cute today. **I had to eat lunch with just Patrick and Ethan,** Jess texted me. **I missed you.**

I missed you too, I responded. **I didn't eat lunch with anyone.**

omg. did you eat in a toilet stall like in the movies?

no, under my locker. the lockers are high up on the walls here.

weird.

The history textbook for the second semester of AP U.S. History was the same one I'd used at Greenmont, so when Jess said she had history reading to do, I pulled out my textbook, too. I didn't actually have an assignment yet, but my class here was a little ahead of where we'd been at Greenmont. I read and texted her about history. After a while, she stopped responding. Dinner, maybe, or Patrick.

At five, the light was almost gone, Jess hadn't texted me back in ages, and Oma still wasn't home. I closed my history book and took my phone and the novel I was reading to the chair beside the window. The river was dark and still. By the water near the dormitories, though, I saw a little spark of movement.

I got up and stepped closer to the window. It was three people, walking down the hill to the small strip of beach, fluffy blankets wrapped around their shoulders like capes. Claire and Kitty and a boy; the boy had unruly curls and a smile I could see from five stories up. They laughed and nudged one another, playful. Halfway down the slope, they stopped to point at something near the dorm, and I saw the two girls embrace and kiss, then linger before continuing to walk, hands entwined, the boy a little ahead of them. When the three of them got to the sand, they sat down on the ground huddled together in a soft shivering little clump. I watched them like a silent movie until the air got so dark I couldn't see them at all, and then I was looking at my own reflection.

four

My anxiety did not wake me up on the second day of school. Nor did the alarm I'd set on my phone; I had forgotten to plug it in, and it had died in the middle of the night. Instead, I was greeted by a dog licking me full in the face, an experience so shocking and unpleasant that I shrieked in fury. When I managed to sit up, I saw Oma standing in the door, giggling.

"I fucking closed the door so this wouldn't happen," I said, wiping my face.

"Well, you weren't awake yet, so I opened it," she said mildly, not commenting on the curse. "I'm leaving in ten minutes, which means you need to leave in half an hour, and I didn't want you to be late. Of course, if you *do* want to be late, you can go back to sleep."

She shut the door. Eleanor Roosevelt leapt onto the bed and cocked her head at me.

"Fuck," I said into the empty room.

After plugging in my phone to charge, I got ready and left the apartment in twenty-six minutes. My hair felt like it was freezing into icicles on the walk over, and I made a note to myself to shower at night from now on. I texted Jess **I am so fucking cold** and received a response almost immediately: **I am in history class and the heat is on very high so I am not so much cold as sleepy. but my heart is cold without you.**

I'll take it, I told her. I tucked my hands inside my jacket pockets and hurried up the hill to campus. Without Oma to supervise me, I jumped the wall and cut across the grass.

This morning, I was not early, so I was not alone. Girls emerged from the dorms by themselves or in pairs, yawning and texting and making their way to class. I recognized a few faces from the day before, but it still felt like a group of strangers. On the bright side, they seemed sleepy enough that they weren't looking at me with any kind of curiosity, which was a relief. In English, I sat quietly as the other girls talked about *A Tree Grows in Brooklyn*, answered when the teacher called on me, and otherwise focused on waking up.

At fourth period, I had to leave the warm cocoon of the main building to go to the arts building for photography, my Tuesday-Thursday elective. I was not especially excited. I was not a creative person, but starting in the middle of the year, my elective options were limited. At least photography was a one-semester class, so I'd be starting at the beginning with everyone else.

The art building was a labyrinth, and I slipped into the last remaining seat just as the teacher was quieting down the class. I had my notebook open before I noticed the person next to me. That person was a boy.

St. Anne's was an all-girls school. My parents had made it clear that was one of the reasons they wanted me here, even though I had never gotten in trouble because of a boy. But here was a boy, definitively masculine, with pale skin, dark curls, wide shoulders, and something familiar that I couldn't quite place. A few of the other girls were also looking at him askance, but most of them seemed unbothered.

"Welcome to photography," said the teacher before I had a chance to figure out where I had seen him before. "For those of you who don't know me already, I'm Erica. I know a few of you have taken some version of this class with me already." Erica was a slight, short-haired Black woman with a commanding voice. She smiled at a few people she clearly knew. Oma had explained that she changed the class projects each semester, so like orchestra or choir, students could take her class multiple times if they wanted. She continued, "Here or elsewhere, how many have done any shooting with a film camera?"

A handful of girls raised their hands, as did the boy next to me, but I was stuck on her phrasing. A film camera?

She nodded. "Good. Well, we're going to start with the basics." She grabbed a large, sturdy box from a table at the front of the room. "Grab a camera and pass the box around. They're all basically the same, but pick one you like the feel of. You'll be using it for the rest of the semester."

When the box got to me, it was half-empty. I looked in, helpless. All the cameras seemed the same. I picked out one that was marked with a little gold star sticker, flaking off at the edges. It felt both heavier and more fragile than I had expected. I passed the box to the boy next to me, who promptly slid it to the next girl. Maybe I looked surprised, because he caught my eye.

"I've got my own," he said. He pulled a camera out of his backpack. It looked like the one I had just chosen, but it had been better cared for and had a slightly bigger lens. It was attached to a worn leather neck strap. "I'm Sam," he said.

"June," I said. "I'm guessing you've taken this class before?"

He nodded. "Last year. But I had the camera before then."

"And are you also a new student here?"

He smiled. I liked his smile. It started small, as if he was giving into happiness with reluctance, and then split into its full glow. "I go to Stevenson High. But we don't have darkrooms there. Or any photography curriculum, really, so I worked out a deal to take just this class at St. Anne's. Study hall before and lunch after give me enough time to get back and forth." He paused. "I take it you are actually new, though?"

I started to answer, but Erica interrupted, her voice rising over the conversations that had started up all around the classroom.

"Okay. Let's talk functionality. You see this wheel on the top of the camera here?"

Over the next forty minutes, Erica walked us through how each element of the camera worked to capture an image on film. She explained how to tweak the f-stop and shutter speed, after explaining what an f-stop and shutter speed were. She talked about the focal length of a lens and what ISO meant when you were using different kinds of film. I took notes frantically; I had heard some of these words before but never understood what they meant. Finally, she passed out film and led us through the process of loading and advancing it, getting the camera to show the little 1 in the window that meant it was ready to shoot a picture.

"You cannot open the back of the camera until our next class, or you'll ruin the film," she emphasized. "I know it is tempting. Do not open it. On Tuesday, we'll go over how to do that safely, and we'll start to talk about developing. For the weekend, you've got two pieces of homework. The first is to read the first two chapters of your textbook. That should reinforce what we talked about today, and it'll give you a good point of reference for questions.

"The second is to shoot the rest of this roll of film. You can take pictures of anything. People, still lifes, landscapes, whatever you want. Don't worry too much about the subject matter. The only requirement is that you write down the settings you used for each picture. After we develop the film and you see what you shot, the notes will help you understand how your choices contributed to the image." She glanced at the clock. "We've got a few minutes left and some good light in here. Go ahead and shoot a few frames."

For a moment, everyone sat motionless, no one wanting to be the first to move. But then a girl on the right side of the class got up, and the silence broke. The room was large, clearly used for painting and other visual art classes, and some girls went to a corner where canvases were stacked and a mobile was hanging, while others ducked out into the window-lined hallway.

I stayed seated. I looked down at the camera in my lap. Was the aperture the same as shutter speed or f-stop? The film she had given us was ISO 400, but were there other things about the ISO that you needed to consider? I flipped back a page in my notebook. It was not helpful.

Beside me, Sam was also sitting with his camera in front of him, but he looked decidedly less nervous. He raised the camera to his eye, pointed it downward, adjusted a few dials, and clicked. I glanced at where he was pointing, but it looked like nothing, just the floor.

"Are you not walking around?" I asked him.

"I will eventually," he said. "There's plenty to see right here."

I craned my head to look at the screen on the back of his camera. But of course, there was no screen on the back of his camera, so I turned the motion into an awkward stretch, which he must have interpreted as me trying to get his perspective on the floor.

"You want to see?"

I didn't know what I would be seeing, but whatever. "Sure."

"Look through the viewfinder right there," he said, pointing at a spot on the floor. "Sort of at the intersection of those tiles. From where I was sitting, here."

He scooted his chair a little to the right, and I followed suit. I put the camera up to my eye. It was blurry. Tentatively,

I turned the lens until the floor became clear. It looked like a floor with some stuff on it. It was not an interesting picture. I moved the camera, and my head along with it, to the left and right experimentally.

And then I got it. It was like looking at a Rorschach inkblot: just a splotch until it wasn't. One hexagonal tile spawned other hexagonal tiles, which opened out into the shapes of the items on the floor: a backpack slouched in the top right, just touching the spindly legs of a desk, which led down to a stray piece of paper. A sweater, arms reaching out of frame, in the bottom left.

I imagined it in grayscale, as Erica had suggested. The sweater, textured black; the paper, bright white. It was kind of an interesting picture.

"Okay, now…" I heard Sam say from beside me. Hearing his voice was like listening to a telephone call, my eyes occupied with the camera. "Wait. I'm sorry."

I set it down and turned to him. He looked as if he'd just dropped something on the floor—childishly guilty, embarrassed. "Sorry for what?"

"I should've asked. Do you want help? I thought you were a beginner because you said you were new here, but I shouldn't have assumed. That you were a beginner. Or that you wanted any help. I mean—" He gestured around the class. "It would be almost too much of a cliché for me, the one guy in the class, to be explaining the subject matter. I…am so sorry."

I laughed. "I most definitely do need help, so yes, please. I promise it's welcome."

"Okay, if you're sure." He grinned, still a little flushed. "But tell me if it becomes unwelcome. I won't be offended."

He explained the light meter, and I experimented with changing the aperture and the shutter speed. I felt the concepts that Erica had explained clicking into place as I turned the dials back and forth. It made sense, mostly. I sat back in my chair.

"The first picture feels momentous," I said.

"It's not." Sam raised his own camera, fiddled with a couple of settings, and snapped. I looked where he'd pointed his viewfinder. Just the whiteboard and a framed Ansel Adams print. "I guess it's a little more important than it would be with a digital camera, because you are using up film," he amended. "But I think you just have to jump in."

In my pocket, my phone came alive with buzzing. I took it out: Jess, complaining about Patrick, saying she wanted a drink, telling me she missed me, asking if she should ask her mom for a new coat. I set it down on the desk, watching the texts roll in. Lunchtime was a little earlier back home.

"Who's that?" Sam asked.

"My best friend," I said. I stood up and put the viewfinder to my eye, aiming it vertically down at my desk, where my phone lay bright and crooked next to my notebook. I adjusted the shutter speed and aperture until the light meter was balanced right in the middle, and I clicked. When I put the camera down again, Sam was smiling.

"Done," he said. "How do you feel?"

"Accomplished."

"Nice. Congratulations."

From the front, Erica called, "Folks, class dismissed. Enjoy lunch."

I packed the camera carefully into my bag, cushioning it with a scarf. Before I left, I paused and responded to a bunch of Jess's texts all at once: **Patrick loves you, I love you, that coat is great.** The class cleared out around me, and Sam put away his camera. His messenger bag had a special compartment for the camera and its various accessories, and I couldn't decide whether to be jealous or roll my eyes.

"See you next class," he said, raising a hand. "Happy shooting. I hope you enjoy it."

"I'll let you know," I said. "You too."

"I always have a grand time," he said. "It was really nice to meet you, June."

"Nice to meet you, Sam."

He left, turning back and smiling one more time before he disappeared around the corner.

five

I liked photography more than I had expected, and I was glad that Jess had texted me. But the morning had been dulled across the board by lack of coffee. I headed to the cafeteria in search of it. At the cafeteria at Greenmont, you could buy premade Starbucks Frappuccinos, which were expensive and too sweet but better than nothing. I was hoping for a similar situation here. But when I got to the cafeteria, the line was almost out the door. I waited for a few minutes before tapping the girl in front of me. She looked up from her phone and turned around.

"Do they have coffee?" I asked.

She shook her head and returned to her phone.

I left. My sandwich would have to be enough.

no coffee in the cafeteria, I texted Jess. **this place is going to kill me.**

I had gotten maybe halfway back to the classroom building when I heard someone yell, "Hey!"

I stopped. It took a minute before I saw where it had come from: the gazebo in front of the arts building, down the hill near the river. Claire, from science class, was waving inside it. I looked around, but there was no one else outside. I raised a slow hand in her direction.

"Yeah, hi!" she screamed. Her voice sounded as if it were taking ages to travel through the air. "Come here!"

I switched directions, walking fast down the grassy slope toward the gazebo. As I got closer, I could see two other people huddled inside as well, sitting on the bench under an enormous plaid blanket: Kitty, who was not a surprise to me, and Sam, who was.

I stepped into the gazebo, and Kitty stuck out one hand for a weak wave before retracting it back into the flannel cave. Sam nodded. Claire stood in the middle, wearing a hat and gloves and puffy coat, holding a thermos, red-cheeked and triumphant.

"Hello," she said. "June, yes?"

"Yes. Claire?"

"That's me."

"What's up?"

"You looked cold."

"It's not really warmer in here," I said.

"That is correct," Kitty said between clenched teeth.

"True," Claire said cheerfully. She gestured to the blanket.

"You remember my girlfriend Kitty from yesterday, and this is my cousin Sam."

"We just met in photography, actually, but I did not know you guys were related."

"Guilty," Sam said, smiling.

"Lucky," Claire corrected.

"Can I ask why you're outside?"

"I have the same question," Sam piped up.

"And I have an answer," said Claire. "This year, I made a New Year's resolution to spend more time in and near the water. More time outside. We spend way too much of our lives stifled up indoors, and I want to take every opportunity to get some fresh air." She breathed in deep, as if emphasizing her point, and Sam pointedly rolled his eyes. Kitty, silent, looked as if she very much wanted to be inside.

"So...that means you eat lunch outside?" I asked.

"We will once it gets warmer. For now, our lunches are inside. And we will go get them soon. But we're doing part of lunch out here every day," she answered.

Sam pulled out his phone. "Five minutes left," he reported.

"Thank God," Kitty said. "I am from *Florida*. I'm not built for this."

"I made them promise to do at least ten minutes," Claire explained. There was silence. It really was freezing. No one said anything for a minute, and I got the feeling it was time to go.

"Well," I said, starting to turn away. "Enjoy."

"No, wait!" Claire said.

"Yeah," Kitty chimed in. "I wanted to hear more about why you're here. We got cut off by the end of school yesterday."

I hesitated.

"I'll let you have some blanket," Kitty said.

She raised the edge and waved it at me like an invitation, and I relented. I scooted in, and she let the heavy fabric fall down on us. I was immediately warmer. "Thanks," I said.

"Thank *you* for joining us," Claire said. "So come on. Tell us more. Tell us why you've come to Saint Annie's."

I took a breath. "It's not that interesting."

"By telling us that, you have made it infinitely more interesting," Claire said. "We're not going to judge you."

"They're definitely going to judge you," Sam said under his breath.

Claire ignored him. "Only if you've committed a violent crime or something."

"I did not commit a violent crime, and I certainly wouldn't tell you if I had."

They didn't press further, so I didn't say anything else. I looked out at the river, calm and cold, and back at each of them in turn. Claire was squinting at the trees and buildings on the hill above us, her cheeks red, hair frizzing underneath her wool hat. Kitty was inspecting something on her phone under the blanket, maybe the timer—surely we had only a few minutes left. But Sam, who hadn't even asked the question, was looking at me with a frank, unguarded curiosity, as if I were a problem to solve.

The silence stretched on and on, during which time I went

through a litany of emotions: defensiveness, annoyance at them for asking, and finally annoyance at myself for making a bigger deal out of it than it was. I said, shrugging, "I live a few hours south of here, in North Carolina." Kitty and Claire looked up at me again. "I got expelled because my friend and I got caught drinking at a dance. I wanted to just go to public school at home, but my parents thought I was going to keep getting into trouble if Jess was around. I think. I don't know for sure. They didn't exactly give me a full and reasoned argument. Anyway, they sent me here."

I picked at a thread at the edge of the blanket. My phone buzzed, and I resisted the desire to take it out of my pocket. The river washed lightly onto the sand and back out again, like water sloshing in a bathtub.

"I'm not a delinquent or anything," I said into the silence. "It was just alcohol. Jess got to stay at school, but that's because her parents suddenly became big donors."

"Jess is your friend who you were drinking with," Kitty clarified. She had put her phone in her jacket pocket.

"My best friend," I answered. "Yes."

"Well," Claire said after a long moment, "I would say that was about seventy percent as interesting as I had hoped." She grinned. "Thanks for telling us."

"Don't be an asshole, Claire," Sam groaned.

"I'm not," she protested. "I'm just saying—"

"I had my money on you being a witch sent away to hide while your powers develop," said Kitty.

"I was thinking pregnant," Claire added.

"A pregnant witch was our best guess, is what we're saying."

"A witch could use a changeling to get a baby. She wouldn't need to get pregnant herself," I pointed out. All three of them stared at me for a moment, and then at the same time, Claire started laughing and Kitty's phone alarm went off.

"Thank *God*," Sam said. He and Kitty got up and started folding the blanket. I helped as much as I could. At this point, it seemed rude to walk away. And besides, if I had told myself that I didn't want friends here, I had been lying. I wanted someone to hang out with at lunchtime, gossip with before class, share notes with when it came time for tests. I just didn't have my hopes up for anything too serious. Before Jess, I'd only ever had surface-level friendships, and I didn't expect anything deeper here. I wasn't good at making good friends. Jess was once in a lifetime.

We walked back up the hill together, Claire chattering about the proven benefits of spending time outdoors, and went back to the classroom building. Inside, they sat down underneath their lockers, and when I sat down with them, they didn't object.

Still, I waited to pull my sandwich out of my bag until they started to eat. Last year, there had been a month when Jess decided she was going to stop eating lunch because she wanted to lose weight, even though she was and had always been perilously thin. It was an awful few weeks. Claire and Kitty didn't strike me as that type, but you never know, and being the only one with food at lunchtime would have been worse than eating alone.

Fortunately, each of them quickly unpacked their lunches. I

grabbed my PB&J and pretzels in relief. I was finishing the first half of my sandwich, listening to Claire explain how your body adjusted better to cold the more time you spent in it, when Sam reached to grab a handful of her crackers and knocked over a thermos.

"Shit, Kitty, I'm sorry." He set it upright and pressed a few napkins into the carpet.

"No big deal," Kitty said. "There's always more coffee."

I stared.

"*Where?*" I asked.

"In my room," she said slowly. "You look like you've seen a ghost."

"Maybe an angel. My grandma only has a French press. I have not yet made a successful cup of coffee. All I want is a standard coffee maker. Or to have a McDonald's within walking distance, but I know I'm not going to get that."

Claire screwed up her face. "McDonald's?"

"Their coffee is good," I said, maybe a little too forcefully.

"Okay, but you should actually try Harold's," Kitty interjected. "Or if you ever want to stop by my dorm room, you're always welcome." She did not know what she was offering. "But I make pretty average coffee. Harold's is incredible. I don't know how they do it. They order the beans from this place in California that they will not reveal."

"We've tried," Claire sighed.

Sam shook his head. "I can't believe y'all drink that stuff."

"You don't like Harold's coffee?" I asked.

"I love their food. I don't drink their coffee. I don't drink any coffee. It's so *bitter*."

"That's the best part," I said.

"It's gross."

"You're wrong."

"She's right," Kitty noted.

I did know what he was saying. I had not started drinking coffee of my own accord. My parents drank it, and every time I'd tried a sip as a child, I'd hated it—which was probably appropriate. But the first summer of Jess was also my first summer of coffee. She loved it, and on weekends, we would hike the mile and a half from her house to McDonald's, the cheapest source of caffeine we could find. I spent my allowance on iced coffees that were half creamer and a quarter sugar, weaning myself off the additives slowly, getting to the point where I could drink it black like her. Now, I couldn't have it any other way.

"Oh! Did I tell y'all about the recital Ms. Hammond is making me do this semester?" Claire asked Sam and Kitty, and the conversation switched tracks smoothly. I finished my sandwich and listened to them talk about Claire's piano recital and the three colossal pieces she was supposed to memorize for it. When Claire started trying to convince Kitty to try out for the track team, I listened to that, too, and I listened when Sam described the elaborate historical role-playing debate his history class was putting on.

I listened, and they spent at least as much time explaining context to me as they did talking to each other. It was like getting caught up on a television show I had missed three seasons of.

"Claire is an incredible pianist. Beautiful."

"Kitty would beat every school record we have if she would just try out for the team."

"Claire won a piano competition for all of eastern Virginia last year. But I can't listen to Beethoven any more. Not like he was big on my rotation anyway."

"Kitty gets up to run in the morning all by herself. Because she *wants* to."

"Sam's history teacher is really into hosting events where you have to dress up like famous historical figures. We think he does Civil War reenactments on weekends."

I recognized the rhythm. It was friendly and it was also showing off. *Look how well we know each other.* In Kitty and Claire's case, *Look how well we love each other.* Jess and I would do this to strangers at parties sometimes, but never to people at school. With someone you saw every day, the danger of inviting them into your friendship was too great. Banter like this could make a person feel included.

After the bell rang, I texted Jess. **people here are not 100% terrible. I had a good lunch!** She responded a few minutes later, so I had to pull my phone out of my pocket secretly while my math teacher had her back turned. **good!!!** she said. **I swear to god if you replace me, though…** To which I responded, of course, **never.**

We talked on the phone that night, which she generally disliked, but—

"I'm doing this for you," she said, her voice bright and fuzzy over the miles. "I hate talking on the phone, but I love you."

"I love you, too. Let me tell you about my photography class."

"Great, and let me tell you about Patrick's new car, because God knows it's the only thing I've been hearing about for the past week. It's his grandparents' used minivan. How much time can we spend discussing it? And yet he will not shut up."

I explained the photography and the cold and the lack of coffee and the strangeness of living with Oma. I complained about Ellie, who was sitting beside me on the floor while I talked to Jess, and about Ellie's fur, which thinly coated every uphol-stered surface.

I mentioned Sam and Kitty and Claire, but when Jess went off on a tangent about her parents' wildly inconsistent disci-plinary methods—grounding, except when she could negotiate it, and taking her phone but then giving it back—I didn't pull the conversation back to my new friends. After I hung up and turned over in the dark, I still wasn't sure why. Maybe I didn't want to make her jealous. Or maybe I was worried that she would find fault in them from afar, and I would need to back away from them as quickly as I had approached.

———

The next day, I forgot my physics book, so I went back to the condo to pick it up and eat my lunch there alone. I made a silent pact with myself to never forget a book again. Not only was it freezing, but once I got home, Eleanor Roosevelt followed me everywhere, begging for treats, unused to having people at home during the day. The sensation of being home in the middle of a school day was equally peculiar to me, and I wandered around the few rooms with the dog at my feet, opening cupboards and flipping light switches on and off.

I got back to school with a few minutes to spare before my next class, and Kitty waved at me in the hall. "Claire made me stay outside for twelve minutes today," she told me in a low voice. "It was terrible."

"I sympathize," I said. "I had to run back home and grab a book. Wind was in my face both ways somehow. At least it's supposed to be nice tomorrow." The weather forecast had predicted a tiny upswing in temperature and clearer skies.

"Thank God," she said. "Actually, you know what—" For a moment, she looked unsure of something, and then she shook her head as if to clear it. "Yeah, Claire won't mind. Do you want to get brunch with us tomorrow? We're going to Harold's. Celebrate the first weekend of the New Year, et cetera."

I hesitated. "Are you sure? I don't want to intrude."

"Yes, definitely," she said, sounding much more certain. "Claire and I specifically have a New Year's resolution to make some new friends. See you at noon?"

I laughed. "In that case, yes." I wondered briefly why the resolution was necessary, not entirely sold on being a project. But I couldn't fill a whole weekend's worth of silence with Oma, just the two of us in a home tailored for one. At least now I had one thing to do on Saturday.

The rest of my classes that day were difficult enough that

I didn't have time to dwell on whether Claire and Kitty really wanted me to hang out with them. I was behind the curve in Spanish and had trouble understanding the way my new math teacher taught precalculus, though I had been doing well in precalc at Greenmont. In physics, instead of getting into our groups, we had a long and complex lecture. I shouldn't have worried about filling time with Oma. I would need to spend most of the weekend catching up.

On the walk back home, the sun sat low and bright in the sky, glittering off the river and the tops of parked cars. The air felt infinitesimally better, the start of the warm front the news had promised. I opened the gate and paused. Half of the empty courtyard was yellow and sparkling in the sunlight, the other half shadowed and gray. It was beautiful, like a garden in a storybook. A concrete bench sat in the middle, split in two by the sun.

Erica had said, "It doesn't matter what you take pictures of for this week's homework. It can be anything that catches your eye." I pulled out my camera from where I had tucked it at the bottom of my bag the day before. I lifted it to my eye and moved the dials in the ways I had learned, but depending on where I pointed it, the light meter told me it was either too bright or too dark. *Areas of high contrast can be difficult to capture,* my textbook had said. I got as close as I could to the center, chose the side with the light, and snapped.

six

"But…surely it couldn't be…"

"Yes. The gardener was his half brother."

"Which means…"

"Which means motive, Matilde. Motive enough to kill."

On-screen, Matilde staggered back, and Oma murmured, "I knew it."

It was Friday, and we were watching a twentieth-century British crime drama, which was, I had learned, Oma's favorite genre of television. I was not opposed to it. At home, I generally watched whatever the twins did, which meant either action movies or weird, emotional cartoons. *Murder at the Manor* was a welcome break.

I was also texting Jess, who was with Ethan and Patrick at a belated New Year's party at Melanie Lane's house. According to Ethan, it was better I wasn't there.

I hate every single person in this room, he said to me.

I WISH YOU WERE HEREEEEEEEE, popped up a message from Jess simultaneously.

I really wish I was there, I said to both of them in separate messages.

you don't, I promise, Ethan typed back quickly. Jess didn't answer. I pictured them. They would be on either side of Patrick, Jess pressing her body into him from the right. She would be laughing, her drink clutched precariously between her thumb and middle finger, going joke for joke with the other people in their circle. Ethan would be on Patrick's left. He'd be standing back from the group, staring at his phone, brushing his dark hair away from his eyes. In addition to texting me, he was probably texting his friends from Eagle Scout camp while ignoring the rest of the room.

I did not miss Patrick. But I missed Ethan. When Patrick and Jess had gotten together, I had considered the idea of a crush on Ethan, but it had never fully materialized. Patrick and Jess had liked each other instantly; as soon as Jess brought him to lunch one day in our second semester of sophomore year, I knew they would date. I couldn't understand what she saw in him, but it was clear that no number of gentle hints about Patrick's lack of personality would make a difference to their love.

Ethan Martinez had tagged along to our cafeteria table that day, more earnest and not as cute. A good guy, though. A nice guy with actual interests. He was on the swim team, had decent taste in books, and understood math better than anyone I knew. He and Patrick had been best friends since they were five. With Jess and Patrick connecting us, we spent enough time together that we grew pretty close. I would have happily dated him except that I didn't want to. I suspected he felt the same way about me.

Jess, however, desperately wanted us to get together. I think she liked the idea of true double dates instead of what we did when the four of us hung out now—namely, the two of them hanging all over each other while Ethan and I sat on opposite ends of the couch. We never talked about it as a group. But when it was just me and Jess, we talked of nothing else.

"He's into you," Jess would protest for the millionth time. I was sure this wasn't true, but she made up signs from whole cloth. He asked me if I was cold on the first chilly day of autumn. He told me he liked my haircut. Hanging out at Patrick's house on a Saturday night, he let me choose the movie. "You just have to give him a signal."

"If he's getting a signal that I don't like him that way, that is accurate," I told her.

"But he's *so great*."

"You date him, then," I'd retort, and she would give me a look, and the topic would change.

Lord knows what kinds of conversations Ethan was having with Patrick. Sometimes I would catch Ethan's eye and try to communicate wordlessly: *I'm sorry. We can be friends. This is good the way it is.* Maybe the message got through, because he never asked me out. But Jess also never stopped trying. Until we got

us that you should be able to pick up right where you left off, but…"

"Mostly, yeah. It's hard to get used to new teachers. And new teaching styles. My math teacher is awful. But I'm not behind. Ahead, if anything." I omitted history and Spanish. I would do some flash cards and extra reading, and by the time our first quizzes rolled around, I'd be fine.

"Good," Mom said, ignoring my flat voice. "Are you—"

The call froze. I sat up in bed and scooted forward, and my parents' faces appeared again.

"Sorry, call cut out. What did you say?"

"I asked, do you want to plan a weekend visit in February, or do you want to wait to come home until spring break in March?"

I hesitated, and Dad jumped in. "Obviously, we can't come up and get you every weekend, and your mother and I agree that it's best for you to stay there and get settled through January, but after that…I mean, we'd have to coordinate around the twins' schedules, but—"

"Spring break is fine." I wanted to be home every weekend. I wanted to be home *now*. But I knew what the twins' schedules looked like, and between them and me, I knew who would come first. The negotiations would take time and phone calls and angst, and they might not even go my way. Spring break, at least, was an entire week.

"Okay," Mom said. Her smile wobbled and glimmered on the screen. "Well, we miss you tons."

"Tons," Dad echoed.

I focused on my own face rather than looking at theirs. One long second passed, two, three. "I miss—" I started to say, but Mom spoke at the same time.

"We have some news here," she said. "Candace, do you want to—"

The camera shook, briefly pointed up at the ceiling, and centered again on my sister's beaming face. "I got the lead in the middle school musical!" she shrieked. "A seventh grader never gets it, and I got it. And I get *two* solos."

"And—" came Bryan's voice. Another camera shake, and he joined the frame. "I got reelected to second semester student council! And in an even better position than secretary! Vice president. I'm gonna try for president next year."

I could feel the energy through the screen, and I smiled even as a lump grew in my throat. "Y'all are the best," I said. "I'm so proud of you."

"Thanks," they chorused.

"What weekend are you coming back again?" Bryan chimed in.

"Yeah, we miss you," Candace said. "Are you gonna come back for the musical?"

"You gotta tell me when it is first," I teased. The lump grew, pressure, pain.

"Umm…" She paused. "It's April sometime. I don't know. Mom is gonna tell you. Here."

"Love you!" Bryan yelled from off-screen as the phone was passed from hand to hand.

"Yeah, love you!" Candace screeched. At moments like this,

it was hard to remember that she had the best singing voice I'd ever heard. But she did—clear and perfect as a spring day, ever since she was little. I could barely carry a tune, and Mom and Dad didn't have any musical talent whatsoever, but Candace was better than the girls we saw in singing competitions on TV, better than the radio.

My parents' faces appeared again, but they were still looking at the twins, who were doing something on the other side of the room. I could hear their mutters and giggles in the background, the familiar, half-spoken twin language I had known for most of my life without ever being a part of it. I felt like I was going to vomit.

"Isn't that amazing?" Mom said, grinning, her eyes focused above the camera. "I'm so proud."

"I'm glad they're having a good start to the year," I said, smooth and friendly. I didn't want to fight with my parents. I didn't even want to be on the phone anymore.

"Do you have plans tonight?" Dad asked, finally looking at me again. There was a little tension in the question. At home, on a Friday, I would have had plans.

"No," I said. "Just staying in with Oma. Watching TV."

It was the answer he was looking for. He smiled.

"We're glad you're doing well, too," Mom said.

Off-screen, Candace yelled, "Mom, you said you'd play a game with us!"

"Sorry," Mom said and laughed. "Pun intended. Seems like we've gotta go."

"Talk soon, June," Dad said, hitting the rhyme like he did every time we ended a phone conversation.

"Okay," I said.

"I love you," they said, one after the other.

"Love you, too," I answered, and the screen went dark.

So proud. They had not asked if I missed being home. *We've got some news here.* They didn't ask about my photography class, though I was sure they had seen it on my schedule, and they knew it would be something new for me. Of course they made sure I was still making good grades—which they had no reason to doubt; I always, always had—but they didn't ask if I was happy. They must have known I wasn't.

I fell back on my bed, my head resting on the edge of the unfamiliar pillow, and stared at the ceiling. A hairline crack in the plaster whispered its way out from the wall. Outside the window, the air was black and quiet. I suddenly needed to be out of the apartment. I got up, startling Eleanor Roosevelt, who had snuck in with me and was dozing next to my bed.

She followed me into the living room, where Oma had resettled herself in her chair and opened up a book. Oma looked up when I came in.

"I need to go for a walk," I said. I felt breathless, trapped.

She looked surprised and opened her mouth, then closed it again, before speaking. "Where exactly do you plan to go?"

"Just—" I gestured vaguely. I didn't have anywhere in mind. "Along the beach. Not far. I'll be back soon."

"For what reason?"

"To get some air."

"You're not meeting anyone?"

I stared at her. "Who would I meet? I don't know anyone here."

"June," she said, closing her book and tucking a bookmark inside. Eleanor Roosevelt looked at me, looked at her, and then curled up at her feet. "You can't just leave. It's almost ten o'clock, for goodness' sake. I didn't think we were going to have to talk about a curfew so soon, but your mother brought it up with me, and I think after sunset—"

"Jesus Christ."

Oma did not berate me for cursing as my parents would have, but she did give me a piercing look that I disliked. I took a deep breath and let it out before speaking carefully and slowly. "I'm sorry. I'm not going anywhere or meeting anyone. I'm just feeling a little…claustrophobic. I would really, really like to take a walk. Alone. Please."

She considered me for an uncomfortably long time. "Half an hour," she said finally. "No more. Be back by ten thirty."

"Fine. No problem."

"And—" She set her book aside and rummaged in one of her large sweater pockets before coming up with her phone. "Let's swap phones, shall we?"

I was so taken aback that I just stood there for a moment, unmoving. "What?"

"Well," she said, her voice reasonable, "one of the great blessings of mobile phones is being able to call for help if something goes wrong. And I'm not going to send my granddaughter out into the night, even for a short while in a safe town, without a way to call for help. But if you are lying to me—" She gave me that look again. "It'll be a little harder to do whatever you're thinking of doing."

This was not a technique my parents had ever tried. They had taken away my phone plenty of times, but they had never switched with me.

Oma held out both hands, one empty, her phone in the other. "Come on. Let's have it."

"This is weird," I said.

She shrugged. "It's this or no walk until we earn some trust together."

I gave her my phone. "It's locked," I told her. "So you can't look at my texts."

"Oh, same here," Oma said.

I didn't know what to say to that.

She turned back to her book. "Ten thirty," she said without looking up.

I left.

The windowless halls of the condominium building were silent and bright. I took the five flights of stairs down to the lobby and stepped out the door. The frozen air outside was a welcome shock. I took in one deep breath, then another, before hurrying down the path to the beach.

Beach was a generous term. Maybe twenty feet of damp brown sand, crunchy with rocks and sharp shells, separated the river from the edge of the grass. You couldn't go barefoot here, even in the summer, when you might want to. On the rare visits when my family went swimming in the river instead of in the condo's pool, we wore flip-flops. If you lost them in the water, you had to run back up to the soft grass dodging the worst of the rocks, praying you didn't get cut.

Now, the sand clicked and snapped under my sneakers as I set out toward the school. I trained my eyes on the line of water to my left, brushing gently against the shore. It was silky and black except where it reflected the moonlight. I took my hands out of my pockets and let myself feel my own shivers, luxuriate in them. The cold returned me to myself.

When my parents had sat me down at the kitchen table and told me they were sending me away, they had laid out their reasons as if they were building a wall brick by brick: solid, inarguable. "We don't want to do this," they had said. "But…"

The closest public high school had gotten mediocre rankings for the past several years. (True, but not a reason; Oakview had a billion extracurriculars and AP classes. I would have had a good education there, and they knew it.)

They wanted me to have a closer relationship with my grandmother. (Might have been true, but again, not a real reason. Besides, Oma hadn't made the request, and who were they to say what she wanted?)

Jess was a distraction and a bad influence. (Jess was witty and thoughtful and brilliant. She was my best friend. The only person completely on my side.)

I was setting a bad example for my siblings. (It didn't matter what kind of example I set. At the age of twelve, the twins had more ambition and stronger senses of self than most full-grown adults.)

The status quo was not working. (I think by this my parents meant that they had tried various disciplinary actions to change my behavior, and my behavior had not changed. This, at least, was true.)

"We don't want to do this," they had said, but after that phone call, it felt very much like they wanted me gone. It must have been easier at home without me. They didn't have to worry about Candace and Bryan breaking curfew or drinking or fighting with them. The twins' friends were easy, well-behaved but distant, because Candace and Bryan were each other's best friends.

I couldn't blame my siblings. They really were great: smart and creative and charismatic, funny and weird and sweet. They were never disappointed in me. They always assumed I was doing my best. Even when they were so annoying that they enraged me—which was often, with all that energy—I loved them in a way that made me want to sweep them up and carry them on my shoulders.

I knew they missed me. I just wasn't sure if my parents missed me, too.

A few yards of rocks separated the stretch of beach in front of the condos from the beach in front of the school. I clambered across them, stepping carefully in the dark from one flat plane to another, balancing occasionally on a sharp point, feeling it dig into the rubber of my shoes. On the other side, the sand was the same. I kept close to the water as I walked.

I pulled out my phone to text Jess and realized it was not my phone before putting it back in my pocket. 10:10. I would have to turn back soon. I thought about coming back to the condo late, just to see what would happen. But to what end? I had nothing to gain. Nothing was keeping me outside except my own restlessness and a loneliness too big for my body.

Campus was quiet. Up on the hill, two girls jogged from the athletics building to the dorms, one holding a volleyball under her arm, the pair of them lit up golden in the glow of the streetlights. Some other girls hadn't closed the curtains of their dorm rooms, and through the window, I could see puzzle pieces of their lives: here a band poster, there a bookshelf. A girl leaning close to a mirror and touching her face. A girl talking on the phone and laughing.

I got as far as the arts building before turning back. I cut through campus and walked back toward the condos on the low stone wall, placing one foot in front of the other like a child. It slowed my progress, and to make up time, I ran the last little bit. By the time I got in the elevator, I was out of breath and coughing from the cold.

"10:28," Oma said, looking up from her book as I walked in. She smiled, seeming genuinely pleased. "Two minutes to spare. How was your walk?"

"Good," I said, still breathing hard. We exchanged phones. I checked to see if Jess had texted me, and indeed she had: **I wish you were here to make me leave this stupid party.** "How's your book?"

"Excellent," she answered.

I stood there for a moment, uncertain of the next step. Typically, my parents started asking questions as soon as I got home after being out at night, which I then deflected or answered minimally until they decided to fight about it or let me go to my room. But Oma seemed to have no questions. In fact, it seemed that what she really wanted was to get back to reading.

"Thank you," I said at last. "I feel better."

"Good," she said. She paused for a moment, then continued, "You know, I'm here if you ever—you know—want to talk, or—"

"I know," I cut her off. She looked a little relieved, and I wondered for a moment how my mother could have come from this woman. In appearance, they were clearly related; all three of us, in fact, looked like carbon copies of each other at different ages, the same dark-brown eyes, the same square jaws. But if my mother had learned to parent from her mother, Oma must have been very different as a younger woman.

"I'm going to bed," I said, though just as I was turning to leave, a thought occurred to me, and I turned back. "I forgot to tell you," I said, "I'm going to have brunch with some girls from school tomorrow. At Harold's. I don't think I need a ride. When I looked it up, it seemed like a short walk." I paused. "That's okay, right?"

Oma raised her eyebrows. "Of course. I was actually going to suggest we go out to lunch tomorrow, but if you already have plans…"

"We can go another time," I said quickly, but Oma didn't

look offended that I had made arrangements for my weekend without her.

"Which girls, if you don't mind my asking?"

"Claire and Kitty..." I realized I didn't know their last names, but I didn't need to—Oma nodded. "We're in the same science class. And I had lunch with them a few days ago." I didn't mention Sam. I had never gotten into trouble because of boys at home, but my parents didn't trust any of the guys that Jess and I spent time with, no matter how many times I told them that Patrick was basically a walking mannequin and Ethan was great. Besides, Sam wasn't part of our brunch plans, so I didn't feel I was lying.

"Sure, I know them," Oma answered easily. "I had both of them in my class last year. Really nice girls. Smart. A little..."

"A little what?" I was ready for her condemnation, but it didn't come.

"Insular is what I was going to say," she continued, "but that sounds bad, and that's not the way I mean it." She looked thoughtful. "They really only had eyes for each other is what I mean. I'm glad they're branching out."

"I'll tell them they have your approval," I said, and Oma started laughing.

"Lord, no need. They don't need to hear anything more from me. The two of them passed my class with flying colors. I wish them only the best."

"Well, I'll tell them that," I said, smiling. "Good night, Oma."

"Good night, sweetheart."

Sweetheart. She had called me that ever since I was a little girl, and it had always struck me as old-fashioned and funny, the kind of thing a grandmother says only for the sake of being a grandmother. But tonight, the word and the way she said it—gentle, as if she were holding it in her hands like a baby bird—made me want to sit down next to her and tell her everything. The phone call and the suffocation that followed. All my anger and fear and the emotions I had not sorted out yet. I wanted to tell her things I didn't even know about myself, and come to know them in the telling.

But only for a moment. It passed, and I didn't speak, and I went to bed.

seven

I woke up the next morning to the sun shining brightly on my pillow. It was so nice to see the sun that I didn't even mind the light waking me up. It had been such a gray week that I had assumed the room was naturally dim. But no—I would need to ask Oma to buy curtains. I took a shower, got dressed, and stepped outside to the balcony, hoping the air had given up some of its chill. It had not. But the wind had calmed, and the sun on my skin had a faint, promising warmth, and that was something.

Oma was in the living room, reading with Ellie. "You off to brunch?" she asked.

"It's not till later. But I have to shoot a roll of film for my photography class. I was thinking I'd walk around a little and do that beforehand. Explore." I hadn't really been thinking that until this very moment, but I did have to take some pictures, and I didn't want to take all of them here. I shuddered at the idea of showing my class a collection of photographs set exclusively in the home of their old history teacher.

Oma nodded. "Sounds good. Text me when you're headed home, okay? We don't need to swap phones this time," she added, smiling. "As long as you're back before it gets dark. I was thinking of making eggplant parm tonight."

"Yeah, of course," I said. "But there's something I want your help with first."

Oma stood beside me while I made French press coffee for both of us. She corrected me as I went, stopping me from grinding the beans too fine and showing me how long to wait for the water to cool before pouring it into the glass. Still, though, when we took our first sip, it was not quite right. She narrowed her eyes.

"Usually it tastes better than this," she said. "Maybe it was all the stopping and starting we had to do."

"This is better than I did a few days ago. I'll get it eventually. This helped. Thank you."

"I'll think on it."

I brought the coffee in my thermos as I left the condo and set out in the approximate direction of Harold's, which, according to the map on my phone, was a little more than a mile away. I held my camera by my side as I wandered, but I didn't see anything worth photographing. The air was cold and quiet. No one was out and about at this time, not that I would have felt comfortable aiming my camera at a stranger. I passed a crooked street sign that I thought might look good silhouetted against the sky; when I held the camera up to my eye, though, it just looked flat. There was a lawyer's office with a red door, and I was about to click the shutter when I realized that in black and white, you wouldn't be able to see the difference between the door and the brick walls around it.

After ten minutes of walking, I hadn't taken a single picture, and I was starting to question whether *any* photography was interesting.

But this was just homework. I knew how to do homework. My phone told me there was a park nearby, so I turned left on the next street and resolved to take at least ten pictures.

Thus far, I had walked on the same street that my family always drove coming into town, so I was familiar with most of the buildings, even if I had never looked at them closely. But this street was new to me. It was narrow at first, but a little ways down, a wide, grassy median split the two lanes like an island.

I walked down the double yellow line in the center until I reached it. The brown grass was soft under my boots. A few trees stood on the median, branches bare of leaves, and underneath the trees were some large, misshapen rocks.

Not rocks. Headstones.

I took a step back and nearly fell off the curb. I glanced around quickly, but no one was around to see me spooked. I walked the length of the median, looking more closely at each grave. All the headstones were low, curved, and simple, the edges rough with decay and the letters smooth and indistinct. The newest, from 1924, had a crude etching of a dove on the top; the oldest, from

1893, had crumbled half away. All of them shared the same last name.

I let myself imagine for a moment that I believed in ghosts. I didn't, and even if I had, it was hard to get too emotional about a family of strangers a century ago. But it was inescapably eerie.

I knelt and framed the first gravestone in my viewfinder, turned the dials until the light meter was satisfied, and clicked. I did the same with the others, reading them as I went and ending with one where the inscription was still legible:

Beloved daughter. Blessed are the pure
in heart, for they shall see God.
Matthew 5:8

"I never would've thought to take pictures here."

A male voice, off to my left. I put the camera down, cautious, but it was only Sam, standing on the sidewalk and grinning. He had his own camera slung around his chest like a necklace and his hands jammed into his coat pockets, and he looked pleased to see me. I stood up.

"This is weird, right?" I said, gesturing to the graves. "A cemetery in the middle of the road?"

"It is weird," Sam admitted. He came across the street to join me on the median, but not before checking both ways for cars, a needless, childlike motion that made me smile. "But it's always been here. There's another little cemetery in the convenience store parking lot up a few blocks," he said, nodding in that direction. "I have no clue why."

"Maybe this was a family's backyard once, and their house was torn down, but they didn't want to move the graves."

"Yeah, maybe." He wasn't standing too close to me, which I appreciated. He wasn't tall, but he was solidly built, and I was acutely aware of the emptiness of the road around us. Of being alone in a place I didn't know well, with a boy I had only just met. "Or maybe there was a church."

"There are so many churches around here already."

"Maybe it was a very small church," he proposed, and I laughed.

"The classic five-person church," I said.

He shrugged and smiled. "I'm Jewish. I wouldn't know. But it is something interesting to photograph, I'll give you that."

"Yeah." I looked around the road. I was avoiding meeting his eyes. Every time I did, it felt as if he were seeing me one level deeper than I wanted him to. I nodded at the camera resting on his chest. "I take it you're also out here for our photography assignment?"

"I would probably be out here with my camera even if we didn't have the assignment, but yeah." He pointed up the road and to the left. "There's a park up there where I was planning on going. I don't have any great ideas, though. Usually on Saturday mornings, I walk around until I see something I want to take a picture of. That could've been these headstones, but..."

"Beat you to it. And actually, I was on my way to that park when I stopped here, so in some ways..."

"You beat me to that, too." He grinned. "Okay. Well. Do you have any interest in walking around with me and doing some of this assignment together?"

"Sure." I felt an edge of excitement at the back of my neck, and I told myself to calm down. "Oh, except that I'm having brunch with your cousin and her girlfriend at noon."

He nodded as if this was not surprising. "Harold's, right?"

"Exactly."

"Yeah, they love that place. They say the coffee—"

"Oh, believe me, I remember the coffee discussion. That's critical." He screwed up his face like he had eaten a whole lemon, and I laughed. "I know. You're not a fan."

"I don't get it. But come on. We'll wander that way. You've got an hour or so." He cast a sideways glance at me as we walked. "The blueberry waffles are great, by the way. At Harold's."

"I'll keep them in mind."

We walked to the park, and then we kept walking, turning left, turning right, sometimes looping around blocks in a complete circle. I had no idea where I was, so Sam led, though I kept an eye on my phone to make sure I wasn't in the middle of the chillest kidnapping ever. But everything was fine. He was walking me to brunch, albeit in a long and winding path, pausing to stop and take photographs.

At first, I couldn't tell what he was looking at. On a sidewalk with shabby little houses on either side, I saw nothing until he squatted down and pointed his camera at a tabby cat paused in its exit from under a porch. A few minutes later, he snapped a close-up of a pile of newspapers on a lawn, the newsprint on the bottom blurry and wet from dew. I hadn't even noticed them.

The longer we walked, though, the more it started to make sense. Not his photos exactly—some I never would've thought of myself, and others I doubted would turn out well. But I liked the idea of every view containing something of value. I started aiming my camera at anything that caught my eye without worrying too much about the quality of the final image. A burnished brass knocker shaped like a dachshund on the door to a chiropractor's office. A mailbox that someone had hit with their car, crushed and splintered in the middle, barely standing up. A puddle striped with gasoline shimmer.

"Is this supposed to be meaningful art?" I asked Sam at one point.

He shrugged. "Does it matter?" he answered, and I accepted that on this day, it didn't.

The photography required us to stop and start often, which let us drop our conversation and pick it up again after a short break. It could have been awkward, but I found the pattern a relief. It meant that there was no pressure to be speaking constantly.

I learned that Sam was an only child and had grown up here, in a house a few miles away. Claire's mom was his mom's sister, and they had been close since they were young, though they'd only gotten to be real friends after she came to St. Anne's. He liked books but was a slow reader. He liked video games but not as much as his friends. He played no sports and no musical instruments. "This is my instrument," he said, patting his camera affectionately before making a face and saying, "That was corny as hell. I'm so sorry."

I gave him a little more of the story that had led me here. I told him about the meetings with the school, my talks with my parents and Jess's talks with hers, and the twins' reaction to my going away. I left out the hard parts, which were—like all the most important things—in the details. I talked about Jess and how much I missed her. I did not tell him about the night in December after everything was settled when Jess and I sat together on the swings in the park, sobbing and shivering and holding each other's hands. I told him it was a weird adjustment to live with my grandmother, but I didn't mention the call last night or my walk along the beach.

Sam was a good listener. He paused after I finished each sentence, as if waiting to see if I would keep talking, before he said anything himself. He asked good questions. A couple of times, he shook his head in sympathy or said, "That really, really sucks." But otherwise, he just listened. I hadn't told the story to anyone before. Oma had gotten it from my parents, Ethan had seen it all happen, and Jess—well, Jess was the story.

By noon, we were a block away from Harold's. Sam was on his second roll of film, and I had one shot left on my first. We rounded the corner and were greeted with a small, square building of electric-blue concrete. Sam gestured to it as if presenting a band on a stage.

"Here we are," he said. "The only five-star breakfast in town."

I raised my eyebrows. "Five stars from whom?"

"It speaks for itself."

As we approached, I could see the painted lettering on the side of the building, HAROLD's in thick white letters above the windows, and below them, five sturdy yellow stars. I put my camera to my eye and took a step forward, a step back, until the corner of the building was centered in the frame, the stars cascading down the bottom edge. *Click.* I advanced my film for the last time.

"Success," I said. "Done."

"Congratulations. How's it feel?"

"Good. I think. I mean, I'm not a good photographer, but this was a fun morning. Thank you," I added.

He looked down at his shoes or at his camera, I couldn't tell. I thought for a moment I might have said something wrong, but then he said, "Anytime," and he sounded so shy and pleased that I knew I was fine. "I'm not that great at it either, and I've been doing this for a while. But I love it. Glad you're at least having a little bit of fun."

"You were not invited to brunch!" The yell came from behind us, and we turned in unison to see Claire and Kitty walking toward us. For a panicked moment, I thought they meant me—that Kitty had not, in fact, told Claire that she'd asked me to come—and I was ready to run.

But Sam rolled his eyes and said, "Calm down, Claire. I'm not here to crash. June and I were both out doing our photography assignment this morning. We ran into each other."

"A likely story," Claire said cheerfully. "Hey, June. Are you good with hugs?"

"Hi and yes," I said.

"Excellent," she said, and she gave me a tight embrace, squeezing me around the shoulders. Kitty greeted me the same way. They traded hugs with Sam before all of us pulled back to stand in a circle, Claire bouncing a little on her toes.

"Shall we breakfast?" Kitty asked.

"Yes, please," I said. I couldn't have walked more than two or three miles with Sam, but I was still starving.

"Come on, y'all," Claire said, starting toward the restaurant.

"See you later," Sam said.

"No, you're here now. Come on," Claire called over her shoulder.

"I thought I wasn't invited!" Sam said, grinning and following her.

Kitty hung back to walk with me. "He does this all the time," she told me. "Crashes our brunch. He's lucky I like him."

"So it's not weird to have your girlfriend's cousin around all the time?"

She shrugged. "Nah. It's really a pretty small percentage of the time we spend together, and they're best friends. And I like him."

We stepped inside Harold's, and I shrugged off my coat. The alcove was small and loud and pleasantly stuffy, lit only by the sun streaming in through the windows. The walls were covered with vintage ads and photographs of people posing with food. A harried-looking man stood at a host stand, phone tucked between his shoulder and his ear. As we walked in, he held up three fingers, then added a fourth as his eyes flickered to me, and he raised his eyebrows in a silent question. Claire gave him a thumbs-up, and he pointed to his right wordlessly.

I followed the others into the main dining room, which was ringed with windows and much brighter, though just as loud. We sat down at the only empty booth, Claire and Sam on one side and me and Kitty opposite. It still had a few half-empty water glasses and crumpled napkins, but no one seemed to mind.

"We are seriously lucky," Claire said, grabbing an enormous laminated menu.

"Yeah, we almost always have to wait on the weekends," Kitty told me.

An older woman appeared at the edge of the table, briskly clearing away the remainder of the last meal. "Welcome back, y'all," she said.

"Thanks, Leah," Claire said. "How was your Christmas?"

"Oh, good. Relaxing. We were closed for a week, you know." She pointed at each of us in turn. "Coffee, coffee, no coffee..." She got to me. "Coffee?"

"Yes, please," I said fervently.

"This is June. It's her first time at Harold's," Kitty said.

"Leah. Nice to meet you," Leah said, smiling. "Welcome to town."

"You too. And thanks."

"I'll be back in a sec," she said before disappearing.

Claire gave the menu a cursory glance, and then put it back down. "I don't know why I'm looking at this. I already know exactly what I want."

"Same," Sam said.

Kitty, however, was still reviewing her menu, her eyes carefully scanning each and every item. "I like to try something new every time," she explained to me. "They have so many options."

"I maintain that is a wild way to live," Claire said. "Why take a chance when you know for absolute certain what the best thing on the menu is?"

"What's the best thing on the menu?" I asked, looking up from long lists of breakfast and lunch plates.

"Waffles," said Sam at the same time as Claire answered, "Pancakes." They looked at each other and burst into laughter. Kitty shook her head at her menu, smiling.

Leah returned to take our orders—Sam and Claire had their usuals, I got some kind of biscuit and grits combination, and Kitty selected a plate of meat, eggs, and breads called the Banjo Special. Then Leah grabbed a pot of coffee from a nearby cart and started filling our mugs. I scooted mine toward me as soon as she walked away and inhaled the steam. The smell alone was bitter and fresh, a holy blessing.

"Wait'll you taste it," Kitty said, blowing on hers.

"I didn't like coffee until Harold's," Claire added.

"Yeah, I converted her."

"How long have y'all been together?" I asked, lifting my cup to my lips before realizing it was still too hot.

"Fifteen…sixteen months?" Kitty answered, making eye contact with Claire.

"Over a year," Claire said.

"Seems like forever," Sam commented, not unkindly.

"But we want to hear more about *you*," Kitty said, nudging me with her shoulder. "We know why you're here. But that's all. What do you like, what do you hate, does your grandmother yell at you for using your phone at home like she does in the classroom..."

"I like being outside, when it's not freezing. I like reading. Back at home, I mostly study and hang out with Jess." I took a sip of my coffee. It scalded my tongue, but I could tell even through the sharp heat that it was as good as it smelled. "I hate...um, I hate team sports. Celery. Hypocrites," I added, thinking of all the girls who had whispered about me and Jess getting caught when they spent every Friday night drunk on their parents' wine. "Oma does not police my phone behavior at home, no. But hey, can I ask you something?"

"Those were excellent answers, so sure."

"You said the other day that you had a New Year's resolution to make friends. Is that—" I looked among the three of them. I wasn't sure where I was going, already starting to regret the question. "Don't get me wrong. This is great. Thank you for inviting me to brunch. This coffee is unbelievable—"

"Another convert," Kitty said triumphantly.

"It wasn't a hard sell. But I honestly did not expect to even speak to anyone here for the first month. So..."

"Here it is." Claire had been rummaging around in her tote bag as I talked, and she extracted a small spiral notebook covered in a print of leaves and ladybugs. She flipped about halfway through before turning it around to show me the page, her finger on the words at the top. There, in neat block script, was written, *C + K's New Year's Goals.*

"Number one: Make new friends," Claire said. It was indeed at the top of the list. Immediately underneath it were a few bullets (*not just Sam's friends; who/how???*) and then the list moved on to number two, *spend more time outside.* The page was crammed with writing, and I couldn't help scanning it. Number five was *be less stressed.* Number seven: *figure out college.* Claire closed the notebook and tucked it away before I could read everything.

"The issue," Kitty explained, "is that we spend all our time together, which is great, but we realized last year that we didn't really have anyone else to hang out with at school. Only Sam—"

"Who barely counts."

"Hey!"

"Well, he isn't at school most of the time."

"We both get along fine with the girls there." Claire picked up the narrative. "Like, my roommate is great. But I wasn't that close with anyone before Kitty started here last year, and as soon as we got together, I think I just..."

"Did not make an effort to have friends," Kitty finished. "I didn't, either."

"You are both far too weird to have friends apart from me," Sam said. Kitty threw a small container of butter at him, which he caught deftly.

"Make space." The waitress appeared with a tray overflowing

with food and started setting down plates as we scrambled to move our water glasses.

My egg and cheese biscuit was preternaturally fluffy and at least four inches tall, and my grits bowl could've been a meal on its own. As much as I missed McDonald's breakfast biscuits, I couldn't pretend they held a candle to the plate in front of me. After my first bite, I took out my phone to send a quick picture to Jess, who was, if her Saturday habits held, still asleep. **this biscuit is the best thing I've ever eaten**, I texted, then put my phone away. These three rarely seemed to have their phones out, and I didn't want them to judge me for always being on mine.

"It's perfect," Claire said, swallowing and breaking the sudden silence.

"Mine too," Sam echoed.

"This might be my favorite thing here," Kitty said.

"You get something new every time, and you always say that."

"Well, it's true every time."

"Here, June, try some pancakes. You have to."

"Honestly, the waffles are better. Here—"

We all traded food around, forks crossing over each other in midair as we dropped bites on each other's plates. It felt comfortable and familiar, and when the conversation started up again, I wasn't as worried about judgment. Sun streamed in through the window and my glass of water, making the surface of the table shimmer. Someone made a joke and I laughed. I made a joke and they laughed. Leah kept filling my coffee cup until I was shimmering too, shaking from the caffeine, the kind of stomach-ache that felt good.

I read an old book once that said the best way to get to know someone was to break bread with them. That was what came to mind—that old-fashioned phrasing—at this table. I passed around my grits bowl like an offering; half an egg appeared in front of me from Sam, the yellow yolk spilling from its center. Claire sliced a cinnamon roll into four equal pieces and placed them on a paper napkin in the center of us. Kitty tore off a piece of buttered toast, slipped it onto my overflowing plate.

eight

Sam went home after lunch, citing homework and a nap, so Claire, Kitty, and I wandered back toward school together. The air was a little warmer and the streets a little busier, and I wore my coat unbuttoned as we walked. An antique store had opened its doors and set out some old pieces of furniture. We passed a few other groups of girls our age, and Claire and Kitty waved to some of them.

"How many girls go to St. Anne's?" I asked as we approached the campus.

"Um…" Claire scrunched up her face. "I guess four hundred or so? About a hundred per class. Not that big."

"Big compared to my old school," Kitty said. "I went to a Montessori school until last year. My class was twenty people."

"My school before this was about the same size," I said. "But I went to public school until high school. I miss being someplace bigger."

"Why?"

I shrugged. "I don't like how everyone knows everyone else in a smaller place. At least at home, Jess sort of took all the attention. Here, everyone knows I'm new. I feel like everyone is looking at me."

"They're not," Kitty said bluntly.

"It's truly not that big a deal," Claire said. "It's just that so little happens here that almost anything feels like an event." We reached the campus wall, and she turned to me. "Do you want the campus tour, now that we have some decent weather to walk around in?"

"Oh, Oma told me what all the buildings are."

"I bet we can do better."

"Are you sure?"

"Yes, of course. What are we going to do, homework?"

I had no counterargument, though I was thinking with some anxiety about my pile of reading back home. *But there is tomorrow*, I told myself. If I was at home with Jess right now, we would be at the park or Patrick's house. I wouldn't be doing homework. Or I would be, but I would be with her, TV on in the background, bowl of Goldfish crackers in front of us, barely productive enough to justify all the distractions. As I followed Claire and Kitty past the wall and toward the farthest building, I felt a wave of homesickness so strong it made me nauseous.

I checked my phone. Jess had responded, finally. **omg I am hungover and that looks amazing. I think I am going to make Patrick come over and make pancakes. it's really for the best that you were**

not here for this party last night. it was not good and I do not feel good now.

I typed back, **I recognize that but I DO miss you,** and she responded immediately, **I miss you too. is it mean to say I wish you were hungover so you could sympathize with me?**

not mean, I said, smiling, and she didn't respond from there. I put my phone back in my pocket, because Claire was talking.

"So, from left to right, you've got dorms, classrooms, cafeteria, arts, admin, library, gym." She pointed at each building in turn. "Those first four you already know. Except I should tell you that every third Thursday of the month, dinner is Italian Night, and it is *great*. Most of the food is only fine, but Italian Night is the absolute best. They have these amazing meatballs, I don't know what they put in them—"

"I probably won't be around for dinners," I reminded her.

"Oh, true. Well, I'll get you a guest pass for Italian Night sometime, because you can't miss it. Anyway, that's all for the cafeteria."

"Their salad bar is pretty good," Kitty piped up.

Claire gave her a pitying glance. "No salad bar is good. Alas."

Kitty looked somewhere between annoyed and amused, but Claire didn't notice. We were on to the next building, cutting across the grass toward the far right side of campus. To our left were Oma's eight Garden Club plots, neatly arranged in two rows of four, empty tomato trellises standing up like scarecrows.

"You've seen the arts building already, right?" Claire asked.

"Yeah, for photography class."

"I spend a lot of time in the practice rooms there," she said, nodding. "The pianos are shitty, but so it goes. Sometimes I get to practice with the baby grand in the band room, if they leave it unlocked. Anyway, next is admin building, and that holds no interest for us. The library, however, is wonderful."

Kitty swiped her card, and we entered the library.

Outside had been quiet, but inside was quieter. Rows of books, interrupted by long wooden tables, stretched the length of the enormous room. There was a second floor, too, open in the middle with an ornate wooden balcony.

"It's open from 7:00 a.m. to 11:00 p.m. every day," Claire said, a little less softly than I thought appropriate. "The best place to study. Or to be alone." Based on what little I knew of Claire, I was surprised that she ever wanted to be alone, but she seemed sincere. After waiting a minute to let me look around in silence, she cocked her head toward the door.

"They have a really good fiction selection, too," Kitty added as we stepped outside and headed toward the gym. "Most of the time, if you want them to order a book, they'll get it. Which is nice, because the local library is too far to walk."

I nodded, but I wasn't worried about fiction. "I have a lot of books on my list already," I told Kitty. "My best friend gave me a whole bunch to read while I'm up here." She had sent me with a tote bag full of novels and poetry and instructions on which to read first. They were lined up on my windowsill in priority order, a little ribbon of color that reminded me of home.

"This is Jess?"

"Yeah."

"I like her," Kitty said.

"Me too." I couldn't help smiling.

We moved on. The gym was big and flat and opened onto an outdoor basketball court and a beach volleyball court, both currently deserted. Concrete stairs sloped down the hill toward the water, and on the beach, there were a few smaller buildings and hutches.

"For the boats," Kitty said. "Kayaks and canoes. It's way too cold now, but when it's warmer, they'll set them out during the day."

"I promise I'll take you out in one before the end of the year," Claire said. "It's great. Now, I wanted to show you the gym because it's part of the tour, but there is nothing exciting about it. To me, at least. Especially since phys ed isn't required here after tenth grade, thank *God*."

Kitty said, "I know you said you don't like sports, but do you run or anything?"

I shook my head. "Never. The only consistent exercise I ever got was when I played tennis for a few summers when I was a kid. But I was terrible. I think my parents wanted me to stick with it, but..."

"For some of us, it's not meant to be," Claire finished.

"Yeah. No one in my family is athletic. My younger siblings both play basketball, but it's the one thing they're not amazing at."

"How old?" Kitty asked.

"Twelve. They're twins."

"Wow," Claire said, raising her eyebrows, but I didn't volunteer any more. I felt a lump in my throat. I was missing most of basketball season for both of them. At the last game in December, Candace's team had won, and I had rarely seen her so happy, jumping around with her teammates, even though she hadn't played more than a few minutes.

"You like sports, right?" I asked Kitty, partly to change the subject and partly because I really wanted to know.

But she shook her head. "Not team sports. Just running."

"Why? What about it appeals to you?"

Kitty didn't answer immediately. Claire led us away from the gym, toward the far edge of campus. After a minute of walking, Kitty spoke up. "A lot of things, I guess. Runner's high is real. You get into a kind of trance after a few miles that I love. And I like that it's entirely self-contained. Only you, nothing else. Nobody else. I don't really like team sports because they require a whole bunch of people to work as—"

"A team?" I suggested.

Claire laughed, and Kitty's thoughtful expression split into a smile as well. "Yeah. But with running, I get to just go out and do it. As many miles as I want to go, as fast or as slow as I need that day. There's no one relying on me and nobody to compete with me. I can try to beat my own times for a mile or a 5K or a half-marathon, but no one else is going to care."

"I care," Claire said with gentle indignation.

I saw a flicker of frustration cross Kitty's face, but Claire was looking ahead, and she couldn't have caught it.

94

"I know, but that's not what I meant," Kitty said. "You don't get a lot in this world that is one hundred percent your own, under your own rules. With my running, I get to control it. Completely. That's what I love the most."

Quiet overtook us again. The mood had changed with Kitty's unexpected sincerity, but she did not apologize for it, nor did Claire try to soften the impact.

This right here, as the breeze picked up and we all shivered deeper into our coats, was the moment I felt our friendship snap into place, like a dissonant note that had finally caught the right frequency. I had felt that sensation almost instantly with Jess, when she accepted my gift of a pretzel on the side of the soccer field; not before or since had I resonated with anyone in the same way. This was not the same, not exactly. I had only known them a few days, after all, and I did not have that soul certainty I'd felt with Jess—that we were linked for good, no matter what. But I knew it then as we walked down to the river in silence: This was right. We would be friends.

We walked through the classroom building before Kitty and Claire showed me their dorms, the part of the school I had been most curious about. They turned out to be both more and less exciting than I had hoped. We visited Kitty's dorm, East House, first. The first floor had a movie room, a shared kitchen, and a study space, all of which were full of shabby furniture and bulletin boards papered over with flyers. After having signed out to go to Harold's, Kitty signed in with the residential supervisor, Rebecca, and I introduced myself as Marie Nolan's granddaughter.

"Good to have you here," Rebecca said, expressionless.

"Rebecca may be a cyborg," Claire whispered to me as we walked upstairs. "It's extremely hard to tell."

On the fourth floor, Kitty's bedroom was long and narrow. Her roommate, Penny, had covered her half of the room in photos and posters, but Kitty's side was sparse, a few items taped to the wall over a navy-blue bedspread. A photo of her and Claire laughing together in front of the river, another photo of her near some palm trees with a man and a woman I assumed were her parents, and a poster for a music festival in a Florida town I had never heard of. Her window looked out onto the road. "Disappointing," she said. "Last year, I got to see the river."

"I have a river view," Claire noted, "which is why we spend most of our time in my room."

"That, and Penny is not a fan of visitors."

"Oh yeah, and Penny is the worst."

"She is not the worst," Kitty protested. "She just likes her space."

"The worst," Claire whispered as we left the room.

In West House, Claire's dorm, the layout and common rooms were almost exactly the same, though the kitchens were painted different colors and the couches were a little shabbier. When Claire signed in, the residential supervisor was slightly nicer to me. But the biggest difference became evident when we got up to Claire's room. She unlocked and opened the door with a grand gesture, and as we stepped in—

"Wow," I breathed.

"I know," she said.

"What I love most about you, Claire, is your humility," Kitty said, but I was too distracted by the room in front of me to laugh at her joke.

Claire had transformed the room completely. It didn't look like a dorm. It didn't look like anything I had ever seen, except maybe pictures in magazines. An enormous number of string lights looped in *Starry Night* whorls up the walls and toward the high ceiling. The ceiling itself had been papered with dark-blue tissue paper and dotted with glow-in-the-dark paint, so it looked like dark clouds with light shining through. She had replaced the gray plastic window blinds with floaty curtains that glittered in the light. I stepped a little closer—gold and silver threads were woven through them here and there, like the sparkles little girls sometimes got in their hair.

There were plenty of personal touches, but they, too, were curated. Claire had pinned photos, postcards, and various other paper goods to the walls between the string lights, all in black and white. A shelf between the two closets was packed full of books and notebooks, sorted by color. School supplies and makeup each had their own color-coordinated shelves on Claire's desk, and her bedspread matched the curtains perfectly.

Her roommate's side of the room was not quite as flawless.

Her desk shelves were much less organized, and her duvet was a brighter blue than Claire's. But her books were clearly blended with Claire's in the color-sorted bookshelf, because I didn't see books anywhere else. And all the photographs on her wall were also in black and white.

"Was this all your doing?" I asked Claire after doing a full rotation.

"Yep. It took the whole summer to plan. And a week to execute once I was here."

"How did you get your roommate to go along with it?"

"She was actually excited," Claire said, smoothing her bedspread. "I pitched it to her before school started this year—I had drawings and fabric samples and everything—and I didn't think she was going to go for it."

"It is *way* over the top," Kitty said. "Claire showed me before she sent the email, and I thought Fiona would reject it for sure."

"This was before we knew Fiona," Claire added. "Kitty had an English class with her sophomore year and that was it."

"But she liked it," said Kitty, shrugging.

"She loved it. She said I could do whatever I wanted. Tell her what I needed from her, and as long as it wasn't expensive, she'd handle it. Fiona is..." Claire paused and looked at the photos on her roommate's wall. All of them were black-and-white snapshots of a thin, pretty girl posing with other thin, pretty girls.

"Fiona is the kind of person who would *like* to do something like this but would never come up with it herself," Kitty finished, and Claire nodded.

"She thinks I'm bohemian," Claire said, waggling her fingers around her head.

I laughed. "Aren't you?"

"I guess," she said, laughing too. "I don't even know what that means. I just like making a space that feels like me. It's home for most of the year, you know? Might as well make it right."

"You have to show us your room at Ms. Nolan's place now," Kitty pointed out.

I looked around again, admiring. I agreed with Claire's approach but had never been able to achieve the same effect. Nor had I ever had a model like this to work from. The twins had shared a room until my parents finally gave up on the guest bedroom last year, and the only décor in their shared space had been their certificates and medals hung up on the wall. Jess's bedroom, meanwhile, was pure chaos, mess exploding from every drawer, with random photos pinned to the walls for a week or a month before being replaced when she grew tired of them.

My room at home had always been somewhere in between. I was tidier than Jess—it was hard not to be—but never quite as organized as the twins. And I had never succeeded at making my space feel like myself. When I hung up photos, they always seemed unbalanced. There was too much plain wall or, in some parts, too little. Now, here at Oma's, I had another opportunity and exactly zero ideas.

I sighed. "You will be disappointed. I did not have a cohesive decorating plan when I moved here. Or a plan of any kind. Not even one single fabric sample."

"Okay, I do want to see your room because I think I can probably help, but is it bad if I admit I mostly want to see where Ms. Nolan lives?" Claire hopped up to sit on her bed, and Kitty followed. I took the desk chair, which rocked perilously as I leaned back.

"It's not that interesting."

"I refuse to believe that. Seeing where teachers live is always interesting."

"Well, I'm sure she'd love to have you. Actually..." I checked my phone. Between our long lunch and our wandering tour, it was past four. "She wanted me to be home for dinner, and I've got a ton of work to do. I'm really behind in Spanish."

"You're not alone," Kitty groaned.

"I told you to switch to French. Mademoiselle Schumaker never even gives us homework. For my final last year, I did a presentation on croissants. Got to eat a ton of 'em."

"But I *like* Spanish. I'm just not good at it."

"Do you know where the croissant originated?"

"France?"

"Wrong. Austria."

"How is that relevant?"

"A question that Mademoiselle Schumaker never asked."

"So I am gonna head home," I interrupted, "but I will make sure she knows you want an invitation to dinner for the future."

"She does not have to invite us to dinner," Kitty said.

"She does," Claire said, "but be cool about it."

Outside, the sun was setting and the air was chilling again, and I wrapped my coat around me tightly as I made my way back to the condo. Partway there, I saw the shadow of a tree on the side of a building, and I almost raised my camera before remembering that I had used up my entire roll of film. I framed the image in my phone instead. It didn't look quite as good through the phone lens, for reasons I could not figure out. But I tapped anyway and sent the picture with a black-and-white filter to Sam, whose number I had received in a flurry of passed-around phones at brunch. **I'm coming for your photography awards**, I said. He responded when I was getting off the elevator on the fifth floor: **my nonexistent trophies will tremble in their nonexistent case.**

I walked in to an excited greeting from Eleanor Roosevelt. Oma was slicing eggplant and listening to classical music.

"How was your day?" she asked.

"Great. Brunch was excellent. And Kitty and Claire gave me a tour of the school."

"I offered to give you a tour," Oma said, sounding slightly indignant.

"Yeah, but you can't really do it from a student's perspective, right?" She rolled her eyes, and I knew it was fine. "How was your day? What did you do?"

"Oh, this and that. A little cleaning and some reading. Took Ellie for a walk. Had lunch with Nadine." Nadine lived on the third floor and was, as far as I could tell, Oma's closest friend. She had come up for dinner one of the nights my family was here, a five-foot-nothing widow with long white hair, and had asked nonstop questions of me, Candace, and Bryan. She was not unkind, but she was loud, and I was glad that Oma had chosen lunch with her instead of inviting her to our meal tonight.

"That sounds nice," I said. I started to go to my room, then doubled back, remembering I was supposed to be polite. "Do you need any help with dinner? It's early for dinner, right?"

"Yes, I'm just getting ahead, and then I'm going to take a bath before putting this in the oven. I might ask you to come cut up vegetables for a salad in a few hours. But I'm fine for now."

I closed the door of my room and sat on my bed, doing Spanish homework. It was a little difficult to spread out my textbooks and worksheets among the blankets. But I was thinking about Claire and the space she had made for herself, and my bed was the only place that really felt like mine. After a week of living here, it finally smelled like my bed at home, and it was pressed right against the windowsill with Rosemary and my books from Jess. I didn't have a lot of photos like Claire, but I did have one, of me and Jess grinning at the camera by the pool last summer, and it comforted me to look at our smiling faces together.

I had only gotten through half my homework when Jess texted me: **call??**

I called her immediately; she picked up on the second ring.

"You're fast," she said, laughing. "Hello, my love." Her voice—the richness, the humor—made me homesick all over again.

"How are you? Are you feeling better since this morning?" I asked.

"Oh, totally. I'm good, thanks to coffee and pancakes. Saw a matinee with Patrick. Now I'm doing homework. You? I assume your day was another dismal experience in the far north?"

"Actually, it was pretty great," I said, stretching my legs and looking out the window, where the sunset glowed pink and orange, bright in the sky and pale in its river reflection. "I ran into this guy, Sam, from my photography class when I was out taking photos—"

"Oh, *Sam*, I see," Jess interrupted with audible delight. "This is the guy you mentioned the other night, right? Leaving Ethan behind so soon?"

"I have told you over and over I have no interest in Ethan."

"Uh-huh. Tell me more about Sam."

"He's a nice guy and a good photographer. He's helping me."

"You're in love with him."

"I am not!"

"You're getting married next month."

"I like him a little," I admitted. "But I don't want to make a big deal about it, okay? There's enough going on. It doesn't matter."

"Sure. Continue?"

"Well, we walked around and took photos for a while, and then we went to brunch with his cousin and her girlfriend. Claire and Kitty. I told you about them a few nights ago when I was talking about Sam? I think we're starting to be friends. The food was incredible. You would have been obsessed with these waffles. And the coffee was so, so good. And then they gave me a tour around the school and showed me their rooms. Claire's room is... I've never seen anything like it." I described the draperies and the metallic accents and the black-and-white photos. "And now I'm at home, and Oma's making dinner."

"Wow," Jess said after a moment. "It seems like you're loving it there."

"Loving is an exaggeration. But today…was nice." I picked at a thread on the blanket.

"I bet your parents are thrilled," Jess said. There was something in her tone I couldn't quite put my finger on, and I didn't like it. "To have you away from me. With better people."

"Jess," I said, trying to sound gentle, though my stomach had dropped with a panicky jolt. "There is no one better than you."

"Okay, but have your new friends ever been almost expelled from school? Because if not, they probably have a leg up on me."

"I don't give a fuck what my parents think. And Claire and Kitty and Sam—" I tried to find the right words. "They're great, yeah, but they're no *you*. Also, I've only known them a few days, and, Jess, I love you more than anyone in the whole world."

"I love you, too," she said quietly after a moment. "I really miss you, you know."

"I miss you, too," I said.

After a few moments of silence, I said, "My parents *are* glad, though. I think more than anything, they're happy to have me out of the house, so they can focus on the twins. I had this awful conversation with them last night…"

"The twins?"

"No, of course not. My parents."

"Okay, good. Because I love the twins, but I'm pretty

confident I could beat them up if you needed me to handle that for you."

I laughed. "Thanks for the offer. They're fine. But my parents just—I'm surprised they spoke to me at all. They so clearly wanted to get off the phone as soon as possible."

"Motherfuckers," Jess muttered. "I thought for sure I was going to break curfew last night, and Mom has sworn for once that she's going to enforce my curfew—"

"An unwelcome change."

"Exactly. And this party was dragging on and on, but I could not get Patrick to leave. This place had a pool table, and it's not like he's *good* at pool, but..." As she talked about Patrick, describing his antics, I could hear the smile coming back into her voice.

Patrick was the first guy Jess had ever dated for more than a month, and like her last boyfriend, I didn't pay much attention to him at first. But when they passed the two-month mark, and Jess told me she'd said *I love you*, I made an effort. I made jokes, asked about his life. I tried to get him to talk to me. I got zero response.

After a few weeks of attempts, I pivoted to just trying to see why Jess liked him so much. At first, I thought it was all aesthetic, because he was undeniably hot—bright green eyes, over six foot, and strong, even though he wasn't on any sports teams. ("That's just how he is naturally," Jess said, smiling and shrugging. I would later learn he spent weekend mornings weightlifting with his older brother.) But as Jess talked to me about him more and more, I understood better. He picked up coffee for her without her asking; he did whatever she wanted to do most weekends; he returned her texts at all hours of the night. But mostly, she said, he listened to her. He didn't try to offer advice or fix her problems; he just listened.

Of all the reasons Jess loved Patrick, most had to do with how he treated her, and very few were about him. I was comforted to know that my initial take on his personality—that it approximated that of an unbaked potato—had been correct. But I told Jess I was glad she had found someone like him.

Even if she'd already had someone like him, because she had me.

"…but of course, Ethan was sober, and he drove us home," she finished. "And I got in right before midnight. Mom was sitting there waiting for me. Like a goddamn movie, sitting in the kitchen in her bathrobe. But I was on time. I was worried she was going to ask me if I was drunk, because I definitely was, but then she went to bed without saying anything. I think *she* was drunk." Jess's voice got quiet. I wished I could hold her hand.

"That seems like it went okay," I said tentatively.

"I guess, yeah. I just feel like we're in this weird standoff where we're both waiting for her to catch me doing something, but also she probably won't notice." There was a short pause, and then Jess laughed sadly. "Do you ever feel like your parents have no idea how to be parents?"

I thought about my mom and dad. About the bouquet of tulips they had gotten for Candace's first voice recital. The late nights they had spent helping Bryan go over his student council speeches and buying construction paper so he could make campaign signs. The basketball hoop they had mounted on our garage and the many evenings of horse they had played with Candace and Bryan, games that even I had joined most nights.

"No," I said. "I think they know exactly how to be parents. They just don't know how to be parents to me."

Silence on the other end of the line. The window in Jess's bedroom faced east. If she was looking outside right now, it would be dark.

"I have homework," I said at last.

"Yeah, me too."

"Do you wanna stay on the phone while we both do homework?"

"Yeah. Definitely."

I put my phone on speaker and set it on the windowsill, right next to the pile of books, and finished my Spanish worksheets with the white noise of Jess highlighting textbook pages on the other end of the line.

In the moment, it was peaceful. If I closed my eyes and stopped breathing—stopped inhaling the soft, dusty smell of the comforter and the scent of Italian spices from the kitchen—it was almost like being at home. *Nothing has changed,* I told myself. *You can do this from afar.*

But then, muffled on the other end of the line, I heard Jess's dad calling for her to come down to dinner. We exchanged goodbyes and I love yous and she was gone, the hum of the phone line conspicuously absent in the air. And all my formless doubts and worries came rushing back in, worse than before.

It seems like you're loving it.

Your new friends.

Better people.

The kitchen timer rang.

"June, dinner," Oma called a minute later.

I emerged from my room to the strong, savory aroma of eggplant parmesan and my grandmother sitting at the dining room table, looking as pleased as punch. In addition to the main dish, she had set out a salad in a wooden bowl, a plate of crusty bread, and a pitcher of ice water.

I pulled out the chair and sat down slowly.

"Are you okay?" she said, her smile fading.

"Yeah," I said. I slipped my napkin into my lap and looked at my plate to avoid her eyes. "Just tired. Thank you for making dinner. This looks great."

"You're very welcome," she said, some of the happiness slipping back into her voice. "I got the bread at the farmers market today. We'll have to go together sometime. I think it'll be nice with this recipe. I enjoy eggplant parmesan so much, and I almost never make it any more. I guess that's because it's best fresh and I never eat all the leftovers. But now I have you to share it with."

I nodded and lifted my fork to my mouth, then set it down. The smell was making me nauseous.

"I'm glad you're finding some friends at school. Especially

Claire and Kitty. They're lovely girls. I remember when they were in my class last year, they—"

I burst into tears.

"Oh my goodness! June!"

I hadn't meant to cry; I hated it, wanted no part of it, but I couldn't stop. The ferocity of my sobbing took me by surprise. My whole body was tight, folded over on itself, utterly out of my control. I dimly heard the clatter of Oma's utensils as she dropped them to run to my side of the table.

"Are you hurt?" she asked as if from far away, and when I shook my head, she exhaled and rubbed my back in circles.

In the back of my head, a tiny voice—the same small angel that always used to be sensible and alert when Jess and I were drunk together—stayed calm. *This is fine*, it said to me. *This feels good, right?*

It did, sort of.

I never would have cried like this at home. If I did, I would've left the house, run down the block or sat in the car where my parents couldn't hear me. They always asked so many questions, and the questions always led to reproach—toward me, or Jess, or the person who had made me feel this way. My parents were people who believed in a single line of causality. They believed in personal responsibility and problem solving. They didn't understand that sometimes I just got sad.

I waited for the same from Oma, my treacherous body having trapped me in this chair, waiting for her interrogation. But she didn't ask me what was wrong. She stayed kneeling beside me for minutes and minutes, until my sobs turned into hiccups. Then, when I was finally quiet, she asked, "Do you want to talk about it?"

I shook my head.

"Can I help?"

I shook my head again.

"Shall I put away dinner? We can have this tomorrow instead."

I paused and then shook my head a third time. "No, let's have dinner."

To my own surprise, I was hungry; it was as if I had cried the nausea out. I blew my nose in an embarrassing snuffle and wiped my eyes, and Oma got up, wincing from the hardness of the floor on her knees.

"I'm sorry," I said.

"You don't need to be sorry, sweetheart," she said as she sat down again. "I just want to make sure you're all right."

I looked at her across the table and saw my mother in her soft face, saw myself. I waited for her to keep talking, but she didn't. I took a bite of eggplant parm.

"This is excellent," I told her. "Really. Thank you."

She grinned. "You're welcome. You know, the secret is the fresh spices. Nadine has one of those grow lights to keep her herb garden going during the winter. There's rosemary and basil in here thanks to her. It's really a pretty neat little setup. Of course we'll have fresh herbs from the school garden once we get into the spring, but for now, I get them from Nadine."

We ate in silence for a few minutes, tearing off pieces of the bread, slowly consuming the salad.

"Oma?" I said finally.

"Yes?"

"I miss home."

It wasn't the whole truth, but it was the core of it. I looked at the wood grain of the table while I waited for her response. I waited for her to say *You made this bed, now lie in it,* or *Your choices led you here.* I waited for her to tell me the truth.

"That's okay," she said at last. "Of course you do."

We ate half the pan of eggplant parm, and Ellie licked our plates clean of red sauce. Then we washed the dishes together without speaking; the sink full of suds, winter rosemary and basil on my tongue, Beethoven playing on the radio.

nine

"Now, for a test strip, we're going to place the film directly onto the photo paper and cover about eighty percent of it. Let me look—a little more than that, Ruby—okay. We're going to click our lights on at exactly the same time, for exactly the same amount of time. Starting with a second. I'll count. Ready? Everyone ready? Okay, three, two, one..."

Click.

"And off again. Move to reveal another twenty percent of the paper. And this time for four seconds, on..."

Click.

All around me, perfect squares of white light pierced the darkness, illuminating the film below, looking like windows to another world.

"Three, two, one..."

Click.

The lights went out, and the darkroom sank into its murky red resting state once again.

I had been surprised by the red light when Erica had first ushered us in two days ago. That day, Tuesday, she had taught us how to develop film, with all of us crowded into the tiny, separate development room. As she showed us how to mix the chemicals and shake the film, the new winter sun had fallen on her shoulders from the floor-to-ceiling windows, and I had almost forgotten about the next step in the process. When she led us into the darkroom at the end of class, I whispered to Sam, "It's so dark in here."

"It literally is called a darkroom," he whispered back. "I'm not sure what you were expecting."

"All right, smart-ass."

Admittedly, I wasn't sure, either. I had seen darkrooms on TV. But I was unprepared for the dense, underwater quality of the air inside, how it made me second-guess what I was seeing with every glance.

"Okay, come bring your strips over here." Erica stood near the counter in the center of the room, which held the large trays of chemicals we would use to develop our prints. "Slip them into this tray—no, not yet—okay, now. We're looking for three minutes here. Maya, can you shake the tray a little? Just enough to agitate the solution." Erica looked up at the rest of the class as Maya moved the tray. "From your reading, can anyone tell me what this is?"

"The developer?" a blond girl said.

"That's right. If you look, you'll start to see the print appear."

Twelve bodies scooted in closer, and twelve heads peered low over the tray.

"Whoa," I breathed. Sam, next to me, nudged me lightly with his shoulder. I could see the smile spread across his face out of the corner of my eye.

In the liquid, clear as water, the strips of photo paper were darkening and changing. Lines of images appeared, starting as blurry shapes and then sharpening. Shades of gray coalesced into clear, precise pictures surrounded by a velvety black and outlined by tiny lines that said 35mm. One end of the test strips was very light, the other very dark. I knew what the test strips were supposed to look like—there were examples in my textbook—but seeing the pictures blossom on the paper was something different.

"It's like magic," I said to Sam under my breath, and then I felt silly. He must have done this hundreds of times. "I know it's how the chemicals react," I added, "but still..."

"No," he whispered. "It's magic."

I looked at him, his face so close to mine, his eyes still on the emerging image, and I felt as if the floor were falling out from under me.

Erica's voice broke the spell. "Now what's happening here is..."

At her instruction, we moved the test strips into the stop bath, then into the fix. The tongs were clumsy in my hands, and each piece of paper felt heavy and thick. I found the whole process pleasantly tactile in a way I had not expected. Before I had realized this was a film photography class, I'd assumed there would be a lot of sitting at a large monitor and fiddling with edit settings. This was nothing like that.

Finally, after the strips had rinsed, we were permitted to take them out of the water bath and inspect them. Erica explained how to use the strip to choose the exposure for our contact sheet, which would show us all our photos and help us decide which negatives we wanted to turn into prints in Tuesday's class. While Erica talked, I inspected my five images, the strip close to my face. It was peculiar to see the pictures for the first time so many days after taking them.

I had chosen a set of negatives near the beginning of my roll of film, photos I had taken right before I got to the graveyard. I felt a vague, unwarranted disappointment that the images weren't exciting, even though I knew I had been pointing the camera aimlessly. It had taken so much work to get to see these little pictures.

Sam had already moved back to his cubby. I went over. "How did your photos turn out?"

"Too early to say." He passed me his test strip. "I think I'm going to do my contact sheet at six seconds. You?"

I examined his strip next to mine. It contained a couple of portraits of a woman I assumed was his mother, then a picture of a mural I didn't recognize, then a few images at the light end that were so overexposed I couldn't tell what they contained.

"Eight seconds," I said.

"Bold. Dark."

"I like my coffee how, et cetera."

"Time for contact sheets!" Erica called out, clapping her hands together once.

As contact sheets came out of the water bath, the group of girls gathered around the drying clotheslines, inspecting the first complete evidence of our weekend assignment.

Looking at the contact sheets of my classmates felt intimate somehow. These were the things that had caught their attention over the last week, arranged in neat rows and dripping water from the line. I felt almost as if I were reading a stranger's diary.

Granted, most of the photos weren't *good*, per se. There were a lot of unremarkable pictures of trees and the river. Underexposed dorm rooms. Blurry, goofy pictures of other students, poorly composed, the depth of field not quite right.

But some I could tell were great, even from the miniature versions on the contact sheets. I saw a portrait of a beaming girl, her hair streaming out behind her as she catapulted toward the camera as if to give it a hug. The next sheet over held a photo of a cat sitting perfectly still in the middle of the beach. Both of them looked like they could hang in a gallery.

My contact sheet was at the end of the line, and I was grateful that not many people were looking at it. I examined the tiny photographs one by one in the deep red light. My favorite was of a grave with the drugstore blurred in the background, the words in the foreground distinct on the stone. And I liked the one I had taken of the courtyard; the light didn't look as I had hoped, but it still had a pleasant, peaceful quality.

"You can leave these to dry or take them with you today, your choice," said Erica. "Your first real assignment is going to be a self-portrait in still lifes, due three weeks from today. I'd like you to make images of items you feel reflect who you are as a person. You'll need to present between three and five final prints, but I'll want to see the whole contact sheet. Shoot at least one roll of film; I'd recommend more. The darkroom is open from noon to eight every day, and we'll spend some time in here during class as well. Any questions?"

Girls were already packing up their bags, securing the black-sheathed bags of photo paper, and clipping their film sheets into sharp new binders.

Erica rolled her eyes. "Okay, lunchtime, I get it. Class dismissed."

Sam and I took our contact sheets with us, even though they weren't quite dry, and walked outside together toward the gazebo. The air was freezing, and the sun dazzled against the river. Kitty and Claire weren't there yet, and I turned to Sam as we walked, half questioning.

"Do you think Claire gave up on her outdoors endeavor?"

"Absolutely not. Never."

"You sure?"

"Yeah. I mean, I'm sure about the strength of her convictions, but also, she texted me. They'll be here soon."

"Got it." We reached the gazebo, and I pulled out my sandwich. "So. Can I see your contact sheet?"

He made a face. "Do you have to?"

"I guess not, but I would like to."

"It wasn't my best roll of film," he said, but he was handing it to me anyway. "If I show you mine…"

"Okay, but if yours isn't your best, you probably won't even recognize mine as photography. It's more like…is there an equivalent of a child's crayon drawing for art photography?"

He rolled his eyes. "You can't get out of this."

"Yeah, yeah." I gave him my sheet, already examining his. There were three sections of photographs: first, portraits of the woman I had seen earlier, then some of two boys I assumed were his friends, then our morning walking around. The pictures of the people were all carefully posed, his mom in front of a low ranch-style house and his friends in the bleachers of an empty football field. The first two-thirds of the sheet appeared to be attempts to get one or two specific pictures right; the last third was looser.

As if reading my mind, he said, "I usually prefer doing very controlled shooting. But I was experimenting on Saturday. I'm not sure if I like how it turned out." He looked down at my sheet. "I like yours."

"You don't have to say that," I told him, handing his sheet back to him.

"I wouldn't say it if I didn't mean it." His eyes briefly flickered up and met mine before he looked down again. "I like your style."

"I don't have a style."

"You do. You're doing some things with light and shadow. And it feels spontaneous. That's cool. That's the opposite of what I do." He gave me back my sheet with a rueful smile. "Ugh. I did it again. I'm sorry. I shouldn't explain your own photos to you. That's a dick move. I'm just saying, don't sell yourself short."

Claire's voice pierced the air before I could respond. "Look how enthusiastic you two are about my outdoors initiative!" she shrieked. I turned to see her and Kitty strolling down the hill, Kitty rolling her eyes, Claire beaming. Kitty held two travel mugs, and when they reached the gazebo, she handed one to me.

"Sorry we're late. I needed more coffee. I thought you might as well."

"God bless you and keep you," I said fervently, sipping it immediately. It was exactly the right strength and temperature. As always, the taste of good coffee made me miss Jess, which made me realize that she hadn't texted me since our normal morning conversation. But then Kitty started telling us about some recent drama in her dorm hall, and I set the thought aside.

Between a lively lunch and the rest of my classes, I didn't get to send any messages to Jess until I was walking home. **what objects best represent me?** I asked her, to no response. I checked and rechecked my phone until I got to Oma's door, and there was still nothing, even though I knew she was out of school. Only two weeks here and already I felt like she was responding more and more slowly.

I was probably imagining it. *You're absurdly insecure*, she used to tell me when I would look too long at my body in the mirror or say something self-deprecating about a grade I had received. *Why can't you understand that you're fucking perfect?*

Her tone was always scathing, angrier than made sense, and the compliments were painful. But for days afterward, they ached like a sunburn—I was always poking at them, reminding myself of the radiant light that had hurt me.

Oma wasn't home yet, so I let myself into the condo, went to my room, and started spreading out my homework on my bed, as had become my routine. I got through my math homework and half a chapter in my history textbook before I gave up. Jess still had not texted me back. ??? I texted her. I looked at my last message: **what objects best represent me?**

To my own surprise, my photography homework was the only assignment I wanted to do.

The problem was doing it. I looked around my room, at the sparse walls and the lonely windowsill. There were barely any objects at all, let alone objects that represented me. My personality was nowhere, if—as I was now beginning to question—I had a personality at all. I raised the camera to my eye, then set it down.

My phone buzzed. I snatched it up. Jess: **I JUST HAD THE WILDEST AFTERNOON I NEED TO TELL YOU ALL ABOUT IT BUT I CANT IM GOING TO A MOVIE WITH PATRICK**

!!!!! I responded. I paused for a moment, not sure what to say next, and she responded with six hearts and the message **ok previews starting love you bye!**

I stared at the message. There was no follow-up.

I flopped back on my bed and put a pillow over my face.

I lay there glumly for a few minutes, but it got stuffy, and my legs felt restless, and I still had tons of homework. So I gathered up all my things and moved to the kitchen table. Eleanor Roosevelt curled up by my feet, and I did my best to focus on Spanish. It was there that Oma found me when she arrived home.

"She emerges," Oma said. She unraveled her scarf and hung it up. "I thought you only did homework in your room."

I shrugged.

"What are you working on?"

"I'm supposed to translate this poem from Spanish to English."

"I assume from your expression it's not going well." Having removed all her winter gear, Oma stretched and went into the kitchen. I heard the sound of the sink running. "Do you want a glass of water?"

"Yes, please." She brought it to me, and I took a sip. "It's only that my vocabulary is behind."

Oma disappeared into the kitchen and reappeared with her own glass of water and an apple on a cutting board. She sat down across from me and started to slice the apple into crisp eighths. "You're not behind on everything, right?"

"No. I have no idea how to do photography, but I don't really know how that's graded."

Oma slid a napkin across the table, half the apple in neat slices. "I've talked to Erica. It's fifty percent homework, twenty percent quizzes, and thirty percent final project."

"No, I know that, I just mean—" A thought occurred to me. "Wait, why did you talk to Erica about the grading for my photography class?"

"Your mother wanted to know."

Of course. I clenched my jaw.

Oma bit into an apple slice, swallowed. "But I was curious, too."

"Mom could've asked me. I would've told her."

Oma gave me a look.

"Anyway," I said, annoyed, "what I meant was I don't know how she grades each assignment. In terms of the quality."

"Give me an example. And eat your apple. You look like you have low blood sugar."

My mom was always talking about low blood sugar. If the twins or I were sluggish or grumpy, that was what she blamed it on. It was infuriating, but eating something did usually help me feel better, so it was hard to be too mad about it. Now I knew where she got it from.

I ate an apple slice, then answered. "Like this homework assignment. We have to create a self-portrait in objects. Things that represent who we are. But I just..." I gestured to the empty air around me. "First of all, I don't have any things here. And second, I don't know what I'd take a photo of if I did. Much less how I'd make it interesting."

"Do you want to brainstorm?"

"No."

She gave me that same look again and changed the subject. "You keep looking at your phone. Expecting a call?"

"No." I deflated a little as I picked up another apple slice. I hadn't realized I was checking it more than usual. I guess I was hoping that Jess would text me even though the movie had started. When we used to go to movies together, we would sit in the back row, and she would respond to Patrick's texts no matter what. But maybe she had changed.

"Okay." Oma kept eying my phone. I did not want her to ask again. I was finding it difficult to lie to her, and the last thing I wanted was to explain all my stupid insecurities about my best friend, especially when I knew my parents had warned her about Jess.

"Let's brainstorm," I said. "I changed my mind."

Oma grinned, as though she'd won a point in a game. "Great. You start."

"That's not brainstorming," I protested. "That's just turning it around on me."

"We're only a two-person team. One person has to start. It might as well be the person doing the assignment."

I sighed. "Okay. Fine." I thought about my bedroom here. "I think Rosemary is a good representation of myself."

Oma furrowed her brow. "Well, that's a start. I guess I could get some fresh from Nadine if you—"

"Rosemary is the name of my cactus," I corrected her.

"Oh. Okay. Well then."

"Your turn."

She looked thoughtfully at the river for a moment, then turned back to me. "You could get your parents to send you something from home and take a picture of it here."

I tried to think about what object I would use if I were at

home. Then I imagined the conversation with my parents: *Well, is it small enough to put into an envelope? No? It's not cheap to send a box. Can it wait until the next time we're up there? I don't know if we have time to get to the post office this week. Candace's rehearsal schedule...*

"I don't think that'll work," I said.

Oma shrugged. "Okay. Your turn."

"It's impossible. The only things I have here are my clothes and the stuff on the windowsill in my room."

"Then you've got it."

"What do you mean?"

"You have a bunch of clothes. And there are at least ten or twelve books on that windowsill. You only need three photos, right?"

"Three to five. And those things aren't photogenic."

Oma got up from the table, picking up the knife and empty cutting board. "Well, sometimes the best representations of ourselves aren't the most aesthetically pleasing."

"Is that..." I screwed up my face. "An insult? Are you trying to say something about how I look?"

Oma laughed. She disappeared into the kitchen for a moment and reappeared, hands empty, before coming over and lightly stroking the side of my face. I looked up, only somewhat unwilling. Her eyes were kind and wrinkled.

"You're beautiful, my summer girl," she said. "But you don't have to be beautiful all the time."

The next morning, I woke up early. Sam had said the light

was soft in the morning, and it turned out he was right. I took a photo of Rosemary with the sun brushing up against her spines. And then, in case that image didn't work out, I took five or six more, positioning her in different places on the windowsill. For the last one, I used the camera's timer to snap a photo of her cradled in my hands, taking as much care as I could to touch only the ceramic pot.

As the sun slowly rose outside the window, I sat on the floor and looked at the room. Bed, table, lamp, none of it mine. The only things that I could call my own were the clothes in the closet and the things I had stacked on the windowsill. I pulled a book down at random and opened it.

It was a poetry anthology, the cover blue with gold accents. On the first inside page, Jess had scrawled a message in her hurried handwriting: *June—think you'll love this one. Try pg 29, 85, 116, 163, & esp. 77.*

My breath hitched. I hadn't known she had written messages in the books like this.

I laid the book carefully on the floor and framed her message in my camera. I turned the focus ring until all you could read was my name, *June*, in her handwriting and took the picture.

I put the book back on the sill beside Rosemary without reading any more. It didn't matter much what she had picked out. It was enough, more than enough, to know that she had looked at a poem and thought of me.

ten

"Would you let me put up a *few* photos? Or some posters?"

"I don't really need them. I like the walls as they are. And see, there's a photo of us."

"Yeah, one photo. It's *clinical.*"

"It's neat. And clean."

"It's *killing* me."

Kitty grinned as Claire fell back into her lap with an exaggerated moan. She ruffled Claire's hair affectionately. "Really, I wouldn't mind you decorating, but this is way more fun."

It was finally February, it was finally Friday, and I had gotten an A on my self-portrait assignment, which had consisted of—as Oma suggested—only three prints. (For the third, in an act of pure desperation, I had photographed my coffee mug on the balcony. The steam looked nice, at least.) Claire, Kitty, and I were celebrating all these things with a sleepover in Kitty's room. We had just finished watching an old movie on Claire's laptop.

"This would have been way better if we'd done it in my room," Claire grumped. "It's ideal for activities."

"Well, Penny is home for the weekend and Fiona is not, so I'm gonna stick with my place being the better option."

Claire hopped down from the bed to sort through the tray of cookies we had nabbed from the cafeteria earlier, selecting an oatmeal raisin. She gave me a chocolate chip before climbing back into the bed and snuggling into Kitty's side. Kitty unwrapped a piece of candy from the bag next to her, and the three of us sat there, looking at one another and eating contentedly.

"This is really nice," I said.

"Glad we could arrange it," Kitty replied, rolling her eyes and smiling.

The eye roll was deserved. I'd never had to spend so much time coordinating a sleepover. At home, Jess and I were at each other's houses practically every weekend. Here, because I wasn't a boarding student, having me stay in a dorm room overnight required consent forms from Kitty, her roommate, and both of their parents, plus a short interview with Rebecca, the dour residential supervisor. The list of rules for overnight guests was three pages long, covering both the standard rules for residents (no candles, no boys, obviously no alcohol) and a special set of rules for visitors (no staying more than one night, no sleeping in common spaces, and no borrowing keys).

And all that was nothing next to the conversation with Oma.

She had been so supportive of my friendship with Claire and Kitty that I hadn't expected any pushback, but when I'd asked her about the sleepover over dinner, she'd just looked at me skeptically. We sat there for a long minute as it became clear she was not going to give me an answer without more information.

"It's only Kitty's dorm room," I said, hearing how defensive I sounded. "You wouldn't believe how many rules there are."

"I would," she said. "I helped write them."

"Then you should know there's no way I'm going to get into trouble."

"I *don't* know," she muttered. "Girls manage."

"I'm not going to try anything."

"You'd be out from under my roof for an entire night." Her expression was both concerned and annoyed. "I promised your parents I'd take care of you, you know. If you fuck up, they'll blame me."

It was the first time I'd heard Oma curse, and it pleased me. I didn't mind this kind of back-and-forth. I was used to negotiations. "I won't mess up," I told her.

"Well, June," she said, "you don't have a great track record."

All my arguments fell away, and I looked down at my empty plate.

It was a colossally unfair thing to say. I had done nothing wrong since I got here, nothing. I hadn't had even one sip of alcohol, had never stayed out past my absurdly early sunset curfew. Apart from spending a few evenings in the library with Kitty and Claire—which Oma allowed only because her friend

Deirdre, the librarian, would keep track of me—I hadn't gone out at night at all. No drugs, no trouble with teachers, no boys except Sam, who was only a friend. No nothing. And still.

What did I have to do to prove I was good?

Oma sighed. "I'm sorry," she said.

I looked up.

"You're seventeen," she said evenly, "and no matter what you did to get here, you deserve a new start. So yes, you can go. But if I hear about any kind of trouble—anything—the rest of your semester will be rather unpleasant."

Later, when I was telling Jess all this, I described Oma's look at that moment as *petrifying*. But that was an understatement. I hadn't been lying to her: all I wanted from the sleepover was to talk and listen to music and get sick on candy. If I had been planning some kind of mischief, though, that look would've knocked it right out of me.

Now, in Kitty's room, it felt like all the hassle had been worth it. I was happier than I had been in ages. Even if we were out of things to do at 11:00 p.m.

"We could watch another movie," Kitty proposed.

"Not enough time. I have to leave in an hour," Claire reminded her.

I stayed quiet. Generally at this point in my and Jess's sleepovers, we would be drunk or getting there, but that was not an option. Even if I'd had some way of getting booze or felt I could break Oma's trust—which I didn't—I doubted these two girls would be interested. For the entire month I'd known them, neither of them had ever talked about drinking, and every time I brought it up, they changed the subject.

"Maybe cards?" Kitty asked hopefully. I had gathered that a lot of the girls here played rummy 500 or poker in the evenings, and Kitty was supposedly quite good.

"I don't want to play cards," Claire said—Kitty's shoulders drooped in disappointment—"but we should play a game."

"What kind of game?" I asked.

"Truth or dare."

"Really?" Kitty rolled her eyes.

"I'll do that," I said. I settled back onto the bed. Before Kitty could say anything, I said, "Kitty, truth or dare?"

She looked exasperated. "This is the stupidest game. It's such a cliché."

"It's not cliché, it's classic," Claire said, grinning. "But I won't make you go first. June, truth or dare?"

I wasn't about to admit it, but I had never played truth or dare. My friends in middle school had been really into board games, so that was all we did when we had sleepovers—endless games of Scrabble, Monopoly, and Ticket to Ride. And with Jess, the game had been unnecessary. Every conversation we had was truth. Everything we did was dare. When she wanted to do something foolhardy, she did it, and she never had to ask me to join her. I followed, without question, every time.

I opened my mouth to say "dare," then closed it again. Claire and Kitty were not rule breakers. Claire would probably dare me to do something silly like send an unintelligible text to Sam or eat all the rest of the cookies. But there was a small chance she'd give me something that would constitute a real risk. And after that, there was a small chance I'd be caught. Oma's severe face appeared in my head, followed shortly by my parents' and the residential director's. I didn't want to go through all those meetings again, like I had after the dance. I couldn't.

"Truth," I said.

Claire wrinkled her nose in concentration. "Huh. I don't have any questions ready."

"That is the whole point of the game," Kitty said.

"Let me think."

"I have one," Kitty said, her eyes fixed on me. "If you'll allow me to jump in."

"Yeah, go for it."

"That time at the dance, was that the first time you ever drank?"

I laughed; I couldn't help it. The question was so ludicrous. "No, absolutely not. We drank all the time."

"Okay, follow-up."

I looked at Claire. "Is this allowed?"

She shrugged.

"Indulge me," Kitty pressed. "That wasn't my real question, anyway. My real question is, why did you used to drink so much?"

I could feel her gaze hold on me, waiting for my answer.

"It was fun," I said. My eyes slipped away from hers.

"Okay," she said.

I glanced at Claire, who shifted next to Kitty, looking both uncomfortable and intensely curious.

"You don't have to answer if you don't want to," Claire said.

Kitty's eyes still held that challenge, though, and I sat back, trying to figure out if I wanted to answer with the truth.

The truth was, I drank because Jess did, and she drank because she was—we were—bored. Because it was explicitly forbidden and therefore it felt to her—to us—exciting. Because her parents were at least tipsy half the nights of the week anyway, and because it was convenient: her mother's wine, her father's whiskey, Patrick's inexplicable ability to show up to a party with *something*. Because she and Patrick and most everyone around us were doing it, and if you had asked me that old cliché—*would you jump off a bridge if*—my answer would have been yes, of course I would, if she were holding my hand.

But all of that was why Jess drank, not why I did, not exactly, and I closed my eyes. It didn't make sense, but I wanted to answer Kitty's question right. It felt like a test.

"I liked the feeling of being drunk," I said slowly, opening my eyes and staring at my hands.

"Alone?" Kitty asked. Her voice changed slightly, getting more guarded. "Wait, are you still drinking here?"

The questions behind the question, of course, were, *Are you drunk now? Are you going to get us into trouble?* I should have known better—they would never dare me to break a rule. I would be shocked if Kitty had ever even been called to the principal's office.

"No. Oma doesn't drink, so logistically…" I shook my head. "It doesn't matter. No, there's no point by myself. I liked it with Jess specifically. When we were drunk together and no one else was around, it was like…"

I remembered the bathroom stall. The giddy giggles bursting from our chests.

"It was like we were the same person. We were so close."

In every way. Holding hands, touching hips, her warm, sour breath on my neck.

"We were always focused on each other. Like…like our edges were bleeding into one another."

I exhaled and finally looked back up at my friends just soon enough to catch them exchanging a glance. "I'm sorry. I know that doesn't make any sense."

"It does," Kitty said, and I couldn't read her tone.

"Anyway, Kitty, truth or dare?" I asked with some relief.

"Dare," she answered.

"Okay, I dare you to text someone from your middle school at least a hundred characters of gibberish."

"*Great* dare," Claire complimented me as Kitty scrolled through her phone.

Over the next forty-five minutes, we talked and laughed and finished all the cookies on the plate. I asked Kitty who her first kiss was. (Grayson Meadows, sixth grade, at the school dance he asked her to.) Kitty asked Claire if she would rather have to play the piano for five hours a day or never play the piano again. (Five hours a day, easy, but—"Forever? I'd never have time for anything else," Claire moaned.) I asked both of them if either of their roommates had ever walked in on them hooking up, and dissolving in laughter, they told me yes.

"I think it was the first time Penny saw my boobs," Kitty said, her face buried in her blanket in mortification. "Which was a blessing for *her*, obviously, but not what I intended for that Tuesday."

"She shrieked like she had seen a spider," Claire said, shaking her head and grinning.

Every time it got to me, I chose dare. I had to attempt a handstand, allow Claire to draw a temporary tattoo on my ankle in permanent marker, and sing a minute of improvised karaoke from the country radio station. They were all unmitigated disasters, but I didn't mind. I liked making them laugh, even at the cost of getting an enormous, poorly rendered drawing of a bird imprinted on my calf.

And it was better than thinking about that question or others like it.

Finally, fifteen minutes before the Friday midnight curfew, Claire reluctantly said, "I should go."

I left the room to brush my teeth and lingered in the bathroom for a while, absentmindedly imagining myself living here, showering in these small communal stalls, washing my face at the long row of white sinks. I knew, though neither Claire nor Kitty had said it, that by being here, I was taking up time they could have spent alone in a bed together. I didn't feel guilty; they had invited me, and besides, boarding school had to give them plenty of opportunities for privacy. But I wanted to at least let them say good night.

When I came back, Claire had left, and Kitty went to the bathroom to get ready for bed. I cleaned up candy wrappers and cookie crumbs, changed into my sleep clothes. I felt suddenly self-conscious. This was the first sleepover I had attended without Jess since middle school.

I climbed up into Penny's bed and checked my phone, which was serenely empty of texts or notifications. Jess had a mild cold and had gone to bed early. I both wanted to talk to her and was grateful that I wouldn't have to do so. I plugged in the phone and was stretching out when Kitty returned to the room and jumped into her own bed. She switched off the light.

"I'm not tired yet," she said after a moment. "I just hate those fluorescents."

"Me too," I said. "I like the streetlamps." The velvet gold of them spilled through the window blinds and onto the floor.

"Me too."

I looked at her across the room, both of us horizontal. Her hair fell into her face, and in the half-light, my vision wouldn't stop adjusting: she was lost in the darkness one moment, illuminated clearly the next. I wanted to find my camera in my bag and capture her like this, but we were holding something precious between us in the silence, and it would crack if I stirred.

"Thanks again for having me," I said softly. "Sometimes I feel awkward about being a third wheel with you and Claire, so..."

"You shouldn't. Honestly, things have been better with her this last month since you've been around."

I recognized the shift in tone, the turn toward the confessional. "Were they bad before?"

"Not bad, exactly. We weren't on the verge of breaking up. But we've been together for a year and a half now, and before you came, we only had each other. So whenever one of us was in a bad mood or we had a fight, there was no one else to go to."

"But Claire has Sam."

Kitty sighed. "That's true. And Sam is really great. But he's not around all the time. And it used to be less. You know that he's been hanging out with us a lot more since you got here?" Kitty looked at me for a reaction, and I tried not to show one, though I felt something—a shiver, a warmth. "Besides, I love Sam, but he's her friend first. I don't have anyone to talk to if things get weird between me and Claire. Or I didn't."

"No friends at home?"

"Not really. I have an older sister, but we're not close. My friend group from Montessori kind of drifted apart. Here, I have my Spanish study group, and I've gotten dinner with some of the girls in this hall a few times. Everyone's *nice*. They're just not my friends."

I stayed quiet for a minute while she stared at the ceiling. "I'm sorry," I said finally, and she turned back to face me, smiling.

"Don't be," she said. "Because you're my friend now, and I'm happy for that."

"I am, too."

Quiet. She shifted in her bed, rustling the sheets. Somewhere down the hall, a girl laughed, a door slammed, and then silence again.

"So," she said, "how are things with you and Jess?"

I glanced instinctively at my phone, dark and still, on the dresser beside me.

"I miss her. A lot. We text a bunch, and we talk four or five times a week. But it's not the same."

The truth was, I felt further and further away from her. When I first got here, the only people she talked about were Patrick and Ethan, with Patrick's other friends and their girlfriends orbiting in and out of her sphere. But recently she mentioned hanging out with Ashleigh King, lunches at school and going to parties together. Sometimes without Patrick and Ethan at all. Ashleigh had been new at our school last semester and fell in with a small group of girls who wore black and stage-managed the school plays. I knew nothing about her except that she was exceptionally pretty and she was now, apparently, Jess's friend.

Kitty was lying there, waiting for me to say more. "We were inseparable," I said at last.

She was quiet, looking at the ceiling, and even as I appreciated the grace she was giving me, I could feel the question hanging in the air. The thing that had been coming since she asked about drinking.

She delivered it as a statement. "Maybe I'm way out of my lane here, but the way you talk about Jess, it's not just as a friend."

There.

No one had ever said it to me out loud before, and I weighed the words in the air, how they could be so tentative and yet so clear. I wasn't wholly surprised. I had a measure of self-awareness, after all. I heard myself say her name and I knew how it sounded, heavy with love. How many times had I looked at her and thought—what if?

But. "I don't think I'm gay," I said to Kitty, and this time, I *was* surprised at how quiet and scared I sounded. I had never talked to anyone about this before, ever. But it was cold outside and warm in here, and everyone around us was asleep, and she was a new friend, so why not start off new myself? "I've had crushes on guys before. I had a boyfriend one summer. I didn't like him all that much, but still."

Kitty rustled the bedcovers again and turned to face me. "Bisexual people exist," she said. "Claire is bisexual. I am not, but I thought for a while I might be. In fact, I assume that everyone is bisexual until proven otherwise."

I smiled. "Valid approach."

I turned and stared at the ceiling tiles, counting the squares. And I did what I had never, despite everything, allowed myself to do. I imagined kissing Jess.

Back in the bathroom stall before everything fell apart. I'd lean against her like I did, but this time, in this universe, the lock on the door would hold. Instead of straightening, I'd turn my head and pull back the tiniest bit, and her face would be there, and her lips would be so close to my lips, and—

"It's not platonic," I said slowly to the ceiling. "So I guess maybe I am bisexual."

Across the room, Kitty said nothing.

"But with Jess, it's also not… She's my best friend. She's my favorite, favorite person. But I don't think—okay, freshman year, I was obsessed with this guy Lucas in my history class, and every time I saw him, all I could think about was sex. I've never even *had* sex, and I couldn't look at him without thinking about it. That's not how I feel about her."

Kitty laughed a little. "I think every relationship is different, personally. I think you can like somebody without constantly thinking about hooking up with them."

"Yeah, but what if it's not a difference between platonic or not platonic? What if it's something in between?"

I turned back to look at her. She looked happy and sad.

"Then I guess you need to figure out what you want from her," she said.

She kept looking at me, but I didn't know what to say, didn't know even where to begin, and I stayed quiet. Eventually, she closed her eyes, and I turned over onto my side, facing the cinder-block wall. Minutes passed. Her breathing evened out into a light, intermittent snore. I reached out to touch the wall. It was cold, the white paint thick.

The question was impossible to answer. As much as I tried, I couldn't imagine being with Jess the way Kitty was with Claire: holding hands all the time, light kisses in quiet moments, the particular way they got irritated with one another. I couldn't really imagine anything more physical with her, either. Setting aside that the furthest I'd ever gone was second base, the idea of being naked with her was foreign, unreal. I thought about calling her my girlfriend and envisioned the word stuck in my throat like a seed, not entirely wrong but not quite right.

It was possible that all that was what I wanted, and I just didn't know it yet.

More likely, there was nothing going on in my subconscious, and our friendship was exactly as it should be. I looked at Kitty asleep across the room, her face tight in concentration on some dream, and I thought, *you're wrong*.

Try as I might, though, I couldn't fall asleep.

Because the question was impossible, but it was easy, too. I wanted more. More time in her car, the music so loud it swelled like an ocean around us. More of her jokes, more of her laughing at mine. More drunk sleepovers, just the two of us, and McDonald's hangover mornings. More pollen-soaked picnics in spring, more turquoise-bright pool days in summer, more costume parties in autumn, more popcorn and movies in winter. More teasing. More secrets. Of her, I always, always wanted more.

eleven

When I awoke in Kitty's room, the blinds were up and the sun was bright in my eyes. I squeezed them shut, my neck hurting from the unfamiliar pillows, disoriented from more than the new bed.

"Good morning, friend," Kitty said cheerfully from the other end of the room. I peeked at her: she was dressed, face washed, eyes alert. "It's a new day."

We picked up Claire from her dorm and went to a late brunch at Harold's. It was equally as good this time as it had been that first week, and I had four or five refills of perfect coffee. After brunch, Claire and Kitty returned to school, Claire off to practice the piano and Kitty citing homework. I stayed in town to photograph.

Having completed self-portraits, our next photography assignment was landscapes. Erica had encouraged us to "redefine the landscape," whatever that meant. More concretely, she had told us we couldn't take more than one picture of the river, no matter how beautiful it was. Given that, I'd gotten my one permissible river shot from the condo's balcony at sunset a few nights ago, the bridge arcing over the water and meeting its own blurry silhouette at the edges. It was nice, but too easy. If photography was art, and art was work—which Erica and Sam had started to convince me it was—landscapes were an appropriately difficult assignment.

When Oma heard about it, she offered to drive me to one of the nearby Civil War battlefields. But the gleam in her eye made me wary of being stuck with her, a lifelong history teacher, on a multihour trip to a historical monument. I declined, saying I wanted to keep photographing the town.

In the moment, this was an excuse, but when I thought about it later, it was true. I was starting to see ordinary things and places differently, using the camera lens as a window to the more beautiful, interesting world hidden inside the mundane. On weekends all through the last month, I had walked around town with my camera when I had nothing to do. Sometimes Oma and Ellie joined me, but mostly, I went out alone. It was one of my favorite parts of the week. I felt my mind clear in the cold. I liked the quiet in the morning and the surprises I stumbled upon: the church sign that had a different religious pun every Saturday, the garden gnome outside the gas station buried, several inches into the ground, upside down. Moving here, I had been so worried about being alone, but these walks, more than anything else, were why I looked forward to the weekends.

Now, I wandered west. I passed the toy store and the insurance office and paused at the Catholic elementary school, which had a small playground and a child-size soccer field. A few jerseys were draped over the fence, and a deflated soccer ball sat in the back of the goal. I backed up across the street, lined up the lens to center on the goal, adjusted the settings, and snapped.

Then, for good measure, I moved to a few different angles with minor changes in settings and took the picture a few more times. That first roll of film, Erica had told me that a lot of my pictures might have been strong but for one or two minor issues. I could correct this pattern, she told me, by taking the same photo more than once. "Give yourself more chances," she told me. I was trying.

I kept walking for an hour, maybe more. I tried not to check my phone for the time. It was easier than usual, because I wasn't getting any texts. Jess hadn't sent me anything today. Normally, I would've reached out, but I felt divided from her, as if we'd had a fight, even though nothing of the sort had happened. I couldn't talk to her until I had sorted through my thoughts, colorful and knotted like a mess of yarn. So I kept my phone in my bag, reaching in only to get another roll of film. The sun would tell me when it was time to go home.

I had gotten to downtown—such as it was, a short row of restaurants and trinket shops—and the sun was dipping lower in the sky when three boys turned the corner toward me. I grinned instinctively and raised my hand in greeting when I saw the one in the middle. Sam was already laughing at something his friend had said, but his smile got wider when he spotted me.

"June!" He gave me a hug. "Having a good Saturday?"

"It started out with Harold's pancakes, so I'm great."

Sam groaned in jealousy.

I waved to his two friends. "Hi, I'm June. I go to school with Claire."

"Alex," said the taller one.

"Justin," said the other, adjusting his glasses.

"Nice to meet you," I said, and done with our formalities, we stood in a loose square, a little awkward, the boys still chuckling from whatever they'd been joking about earlier.

"So what're you up to?" Sam asked me. "Landscapes?"

I nodded. "Trying to reimagine them. As one does."

"I've been doing the same. Not sure how successfully."

"Oh, you're Sam's photography friend," Justin said, looking between us. "Now this makes sense. We've heard a ton about you."

"They have not," Sam protested.

"Well, now I'm insulted."

"We've heard exactly the right amount about you," Alex said with an eye roll and a smile. "It's nice to meet you."

"Likewise!" I had heard about them, too. Sam and I didn't talk much when we weren't actually in the same place, but during and after class and on the weekends with Claire and Kitty, he mentioned his friends often. Unsurprisingly, they were also frequent photo subjects. They had featured in the first roll of film Sam took for class, and I'd seen a few other photos when he had let me look through his binder of prints.

"What're y'all up to?"

"Oh, Justin works here on weekends." Sam gestured to the Italian restaurant to our right. "And we've just been inside my house playing video games all day, so Alex and I figured we'd walk him to work."

"Very gentlemanly," Justin said. "And speaking of…" He checked the time. "I gotta go. Bye!" He waved as he headed into the restaurant and added, "Nice to meet you, June!"

"You too!" I called.

He had barely opened the door when Alex said cheerfully, "Well, it has been an excellent day, and I'm gonna head home."

"So soon?" Sam looked surprised. "It's not that cold out. We could walk around some more."

Alex glanced at me for the barest flicker of a second, then shrugged at Sam. "I should help my mom with dinner. Have a good night, you two."

And then it was just me and Sam. *You two.* I looked at him, focusing somewhere around his shirt collar, suddenly self-conscious. Apart from that one afternoon the week I'd arrived, we hadn't spent much time alone.

"I was about to head back to my grandmother's, actually," I said, nodding in the general direction of the condos. "Sunset is my curfew."

"How quaint," he replied, smiling. I let my eyes flicker up to meet his, warm and dark. "I'll walk you home?"

I appreciated that it was a question. "Yeah, sure."

We set off that way, quiet at first. Around us, the town was about as lively as I'd seen it, restaurants opening up and people streaming in from nearby parking lots to window-shop or eat dinner. Bundled in coats and scarves, everyone seemed comfortable despite the cold.

"This is nice," I said, gesturing around me, and at the exact same time, Sam started to say something.

"Huh?" we said at the same time, and he looked bashful.

"You first," I said.

"No, you."

"Mine was nothing. I insist."

"I was saying, I heard Ms. Nolan let you out of the house last night."

"Oh." I laughed. "Yes. My first sleepover. It's like I'm back in fourth grade."

"How were the dorms?" There was genuine curiosity in his voice. "I've never seen them," he explained. "There is no way to sneak a boy in there. Claire's showed me pictures of her room, but that's all."

"Her place is pretty amazing," I admitted. "But the dorms in general are only okay. It was nice to hang out with them past curfew, though. How was your Friday?"

He shrugged. "Good. Fine. Dinner with my parents, went to bed early. Not to brag, but I'm kind of a thrill seeker."

"So I've noticed."

We ambled through the golden hour as the cold slowly deepened. I stopped to take a picture a few times. The sidewalk was narrow, and we walked close together. His hands were thrust into his pockets, and mine were tucked into my armpits, my arms tightly folded, but I let myself imagine a warmer day, when our hands swung next to us and brushed. In class sometimes, I looked at his hands, slim and strong and nimble.

Then an image of Jess forced itself into my mind, a memory of her doubled over in laughter as we cut across the soccer field on our way to get coffee after school. The green of the grass behind her and her hair flying everywhere, her eyes like sunlight on water.

What did her hands look like? For the life of me, I couldn't remember. All I could think of were her fingernails. She bit them if she wasn't careful, so they were always too short and covered in colorful, chipping polish, the cuticles peeling away like dried paint.

I edged a little closer to the grass, away from Sam. If he noticed, he didn't say anything. I wanted to talk to him about it, Jess and the conversation with Kitty last night, but he was a part of it, too, my thoughts about him and his hands. I wished I could call Jess and tell her everything. I wished I felt nothing at all.

But we were still a mile from home, and I couldn't think of much else.

I was grateful when Sam broke the silence: "I hear Italian Night at the cafeteria is next Friday."

"Yeah, Kitty's getting me a guest pass. Are you coming? The meatballs are supposed to be amazing."

He chuckled. "No, my family usually does Friday night dinner all together. Also, I can't eat meatballs."

"Are you allergic to Italian spices? Or delicious things?"

"No," he sighed. "It is something of an embarrassing story."

"Well, now you have to tell me."

"If you insist." He grinned at me. "It's not that interesting. Just, when my parents sprang the sex talk on me, it was at dinner. Spaghetti and meatballs. And they gave me the lecture about— you know—what to do in the event of, whether the whole thing was with a girl or if it was with a boy. It was *extremely* detailed. I'm glad my parents have a 'you love who you love' approach to all this. I just don't love the fact that they gave me an in-depth tutorial on safe sex practices at a formative age while I had a plate full of meatballs in front of me."

I laughed. He was beet-red but smiling.

"So you can't eat meatballs," I teased, "but has the spaghetti curse worn off?"

"I strongly prefer penne." He nudged me very lightly with his shoulder. And even through the shirts and sweaters and coats between us, I still felt a spark, small and effervescent as a firefly. I tried to hold it in my hands, but it flickered away.

We crested a hill and came into view of the river, glittering in the sunset. I looked at Sam next to me. Strong jawline, hair all over the place, ears big enough that someone probably made fun of him in elementary school.

He caught my eye, and I looked away and then I looked back. I thought about telling him: *Kitty thinks I'm bisexual. Maybe I am.* It wouldn't be that big a deal. He wouldn't think about me any differently.

But I couldn't say it. The words felt foreign in my throat, and even though I knew it was fine, I stayed quiet. I needed more time.

We came to a stop in front of the gates of the condo. Sam turned so he was facing me.

"It was nice to walk with you," he said softly. "Have a good rest of your evening."

"Thanks." I looked down at my camera, fiddling with the strap. "I hope you get the hang of landscapes."

"You too," he said.

He stood there, shifting from side to side, and I said, "Well, see you soon," and hugged him. I held on tightly for a long moment, breathing in the scent of wool and shampoo that lingered around his neck. How good it would be—how perfect—if we could just stand like this, warming each other against the cold of the world, for minutes or hours, and when we separated, not ascribe it any meaning. If we could take comfort in each other without taking anything else.

But that was not how the world worked. There was a column for *boyfriend* or *girlfriend* that meant someone who would hold you for as long as you needed to be held. And there was another column for *friend*, which didn't allow for hugs longer than a few good seconds. Never the two shall meet, I guess. I released him and stepped back.

"Bye," he said.

I raised a hand in farewell and stepped through the gate. Walking across the courtyard, I looked up at the windows of all the condos, little squares of yellow light or gray shadow in the near-dark air. Oma's was in the upper right, and as I glanced up, I saw her standing there, leaning over the railing and looking at the river. She looked down as if expecting me and waved. I waved back.

twelve

_____

February and March brought routine. After the four tentative weeks of January, I had settled in. I left home at the same time every morning, my not-quite-right cup of French press in hand, and shivered my way to school. I ate lunch with Claire and Kitty, loyally spending the requisite time outside while Claire crowed and Kitty complained. On photography days, Sam joined us, with his quiet jokes and big smile. My classes got harder; I did my homework.

At night, Oma made dinner or got food delivered, and we ate at the table or sometimes in the living room watching TV. I did the chores I was supposed to, which were a lot easier with two people than they had been at home with five. I talked to Jess on the phone every other day and texted her...well, almost as much as I always had. On Wednesdays and Sundays, I video chatted with my family, and on weekends, I slept in and did homework and hung out in Claire's and Kitty's dorm rooms, gossiping and arguing and laughing.

Bedtime each night was eleven, given how early I had to get up. But I could never sleep. I worried. I got sad. I lay in bed staring at the ceiling, thinking about Jess and my parents and the twins and Sam and guilt and love and my next photography assignment until at last, worn out by thinking, I fell asleep.

One day in February, it snowed. Class was canceled, and the whole school had a snowball fight on the riverbank, girls shrieking and laughing in the powder. I saw the whole thing starting from Oma's balcony and tossed on my coat and scarf, running up to the school just in time to throw a snowball at Kitty as she was taking her first steps out of her dorm.

My favorite part of my routine was my afternoons in the art building. I liked developing film, and I loved making prints in the darkroom. A lot of the other girls in the class tried to fit most of their printmaking into our Thursday darkroom classes. I didn't fault them; at the beginning of the semester, I had expected to be one of them. But I adored printmaking, the tuning and experimentation needed to make a picture not fine but great, and I wanted to see as many of my photos blown up as possible.

As a result, I frequently found myself alone. While I was working, the only thing to do was handle each step one by one, and they all required waiting. I had to make a test strip before I could make a contact sheet before I could make a print. Each of those things took time. And I had to be deliberate. Not only could I lose half an hour on a bad print, but the paper was precious. I had paid blanket lab fees that covered some film and photo paper, but if I went over my allotment, I'd have to buy my own.

With the eerie red light and the white noise from the running water in the rinse tray, the darkroom was a meditative space. I got to focus and be productive but still think in the background. And if my thoughts became too much for me, well, I could concentrate harder. It helped that I couldn't use my phone. No one could find me or talk to me. In the darkroom, I was in a world entirely my own.

Which was why I started with surprise on the Thursday before spring break when the rotating door opened and my grandmother emerged, blinking to adjust to the darkness. Fortunately, I had just dropped a print into the development bath, and my small jump served only to agitate the solution more.

"There you are," Oma said. "I've been texting you."

"Sorry, my phone's in the classroom. I can't use it in here. Is everything okay?"

"Oh, yes. Your mother was asking what time we're planning on meeting her tomorrow."

"Was it that urgent that you had to come find me?" I glanced at the clock and picked up the print with the tongs, shaking off the excess developer and moving it to the stop bath.

"I didn't *have* to," Oma replied with the tiny edge in her voice that I had come to recognize as a warning: *Calm down. I'm not the enemy.* "I figured you'd be here, and I wanted to come see the darkroom. I haven't been up here in years."

She walked around the room slowly, peering at the enlargers.

"I was thinking we could leave at six tomorrow, if that's okay with you," I said after a minute. "Miss most of the Friday night traffic."

"And meet your mother around eight. Yes, that's what I was thinking. She was talking about maybe doing all this on Saturday morning, but I told her I had plans."

"Do you?" I moved the print to the fix.

"Yes, I'll be taking Ellie for a walk with Nadine and going to the farmers market," Oma said, serene, and smiled at me from across the room.

"Thanks," I said. I smiled back, but I was having a hard time not gritting my teeth, thinking about Mom trying to postpone my homecoming for spring break. Of course she was. We had made the plans weeks ago: Oma and I would leave on Friday and meet Mom in a little town in Virginia halfway between St. Anne's and home. Minimal driving for everyone involved, and I would be back in my old bed well before midnight, ready for Jess to pick me up for our first day back together on Saturday morning.

Until my family phone call last night, however, I had forgotten to tell my parents that Jess and I were spending the day together. And despite the fact that Mom and Dad had no plans for Saturday, as soon as I mentioned Jess, they were full of ideas and excuses. After an hour of protests, I had worn them down to just dinner and game night with the twins, keeping most of the day for myself.

But now here came Mom, trying to take more of my time with my best friend.

I transferred the print into the rinse, where it could roll around in the water indefinitely, and returned to my enlarger. I took a couple of deep breaths. There was no reason to get angry. I had won, after all. And thankfully, Greenmont's spring break lined up with mine, so Jess and I would have the whole week together.

"Wow!" Oma's exclamation interrupted my thoughts. I turned to see her holding the wet print by the edges, examining it under the brightest of the red lights. "This is really something, June. You took this photo?"

"Yeah." I walked over to look at it with her. It was for our third assignment, abstracts. After this, we would launch into our final project, although Erica hadn't told us anything about it yet. I really, really hoped it was not more abstracts.

Oma turned it vertical, then horizontal again. "Is it supposed to go this way?"

I grimaced and took it from her, turning it upside down again. "This way."

"Ah." She looked at it closely. "Is that my glass paperweight?"

"Yeah. On the red carpet with all of Ellie's dog hairs underneath it."

"Oh, that's what those are. I thought they were…mitochondria or something like that."

"Well, you're not supposed to be able to tell what it is."

"What does it mean?"

"It means we should vacuum sometime," I sighed, and Oma raised her eyebrows. Vacuuming was supposed to be my job.

"We?"

"Okay," I said defensively, and Oma laughed.

"So what do you have left to do here?" she asked.

"Not much. If I like the look of this one after I see it in the light, that'll be it. If not, I'll have to do another version. But that shouldn't take me long."

She wandered back over to my enlarger, where my things— photo paper, binder, camera—were scattered all around. "So let's see it," she finally said.

"See what?"

"How to make a print. Can you teach me?"

"Um…" I glanced at the clock. The darkroom would still be open for another few hours, long enough to redo my abstract if I needed to. "Yeah. Sure. What do you want to make a print of?"

She thought for a moment. "A few weeks ago, you took a picture of me and Ellie on the couch. Could we do that one?"

"I think it's kind of dark, but sure." I flipped through the binder until I found the right set of film, sliding the negatives out of their plastic protector. I showed her how to fit it into the enlarger, set the paper into the correct position, and took a guess on the right exposure. Listening to myself answer Oma's questions, I could almost believe I knew what I was doing.

I let Oma slip the paper into the developer. We watched as the image burst to life. "Oh," Oma said with a soft gasp of delight. This was my favorite part.

I remembered taking the photograph. It had been when I was working on landscapes, and I'd needed to use up the end of a roll of film. A Monday, and Oma had come home earlier than usual. She claimed a headache, but I saw her grab the book she'd had her nose in all weekend. I had been doing homework at the kitchen table, and Eleanor Roosevelt jumped up on the couch beside Oma and put her nose on top of the book. "Hold right there," I'd said as I picked up my camera. Oma had looked up and smiled automatically. "No, no, just look back down at your book like you were." She obliged me. It was right before sunset, the light was rich and gold, and I knew before I lifted the camera to my eye that it wouldn't be enough. The photo would be dark. Still, I snapped.

I hadn't looked at the image beyond glancing at it on my contact sheet. As I'd suspected, it was much darker than the rest of the film, so I couldn't tell if there was any value in it. But now, it looked like I had chosen the right exposure for the print, because right before my eyes, the details were filling in: Eleanor Roosevelt's fur and the rough texture of the paper of Oma's book, the pattern of the blanket in which she had curled. It was still too dark, the composition unremarkable. But it was a nice photo. I congratulated myself silently for getting the focus right.

"Time to move it along." I nudged Oma to pick up the tongs. We kept watching it circulate in the stop bath, not saying anything.

"Thank you," she said tenderly after a while. "I think I'll get it framed."

"It's not that great," I said, a little embarrassed. "It's not good art or anything."

"It doesn't have to be *good art*. It makes me happy. You should be proud of that."

I wasn't sure what to say to that, so I didn't say anything.

"I always wanted to learn how to develop film," Oma said, leaving me to finish the print as she started to walk around the darkroom again. "Never managed to get to a class. But I used to carry a camera around everywhere."

"Really?" Oma never even took pictures with her phone.

"Oh yes. All the time. I must have thousands of photos of your mom. She was hard to get a picture of. Always running around all over the place. And as a teenager, she *hated* having her picture taken." Oma laughed. "Or maybe she just didn't like me taking her picture, I don't know. We fought a lot. It's hard to say exactly what about."

"I'm sorry that she was horrible to you," I muttered.

"I didn't say she was."

I didn't say anything.

"She wanted to live her life on her own terms," Oma continued. "But I disagreed with some of the choices she wanted to make, and I won, because she was a teenager and I was her mom. Thus the fighting."

"But if that's how she felt when she was my age," I burst out, "then why is she so awful to me?"

"In what way is she awful?" Oma asked calmly.

"She…she…" I moved the photo to the water bath, my

hands shaking around the tongs. The emotion had risen in me suddenly, and I wanted to put it away again, to make the darkroom go back to a quiet, isolated space. But Oma was waiting for an answer, and I knew it wouldn't be possible. The waters had already been disturbed.

"She acts like she doesn't trust me to do anything," I said finally. "When I do something *bad* or whatever, it's like that's what she expected all along. And when I do something good, she doesn't pay any attention. You know I have not gotten a single B on a high school report card? Ever? But she never makes a big deal out of my grades. She brags about the twins to anyone who'll listen, but she only cares about me when I'm in trouble."

Oma stood there, looking at me. She was in a shadow; I couldn't read her expression.

"And—" I didn't mean to keep going, but I couldn't stop. "Jess. She *hates* Jess. My best friend, who loves me more than anyone. Mom hates her. That's why she wants to meet us on Saturday instead of Friday, you know that? Because if I don't leave until Saturday, she'll take her time on the way home, and then I'll miss a whole day with Jess. That's what she wants."

I turned away from Oma to hang the print on the line to dry. Up close, I could see its flaws. There was a speck of dust in the corner of the lens.

"Your mother wants the best for you," Oma said after a long moment. "Like I wanted the best for her."

I picked up a clothespin that had fallen on the table and clipped it back onto the line.

"It's hard to see your daughter make mistakes," she said.

"Jess isn't a mistake," I said fiercely.

"Of course not," Oma said. "No one *is* a mistake. That's not how it works."

I stayed quiet. She came up beside me to look at the two prints on the line, my weird abstract and the one of her and Ellie.

"Thanks for taking this," she said. She plucked it down. The water droplets still clutching its surface dripped onto her shoes. "And for teaching me. This is fun, and you're good at it."

"Thanks."

"I mean it." She put a hand on my shoulder, and I turned a little, unwillingly, to face her. "I really am going to hang this up."

"Cool." I fidgeted under her touch. "Maybe we could put it on that wall in the living room above the bookshelf."

"That sounds like a perfect place." I could hear the smile in her voice. She hugged me, then stepped away. "Will you be back soon for dinner?"

"Yeah. I want to make sure this abstract print is okay. Then I'll be done."

"Okay." She paused by the door. "Don't come back too late."

"What are you making for dinner?"

"Leftover pasta from yesterday."

"Nice."

"Love you, June."

"Love you too, Oma."

I let her footsteps fade away, down the hall and down the stairs, before I plucked my abstract print from the line and went outside the darkroom to inspect it in the dying sunlight. It was fine. It was an adequate print of an adequate photograph, the best of the shots I had. I couldn't figure out a way to make it better. The other finished photos in my abstract set were more interesting, so if I turned this in, I would probably still get an A. I could hang it back up to continue drying, clean up my space, and go home for dinner.

Instead, I grabbed my textbook and turned to the section on experimental prints. We hadn't talked about this section in class, but I had flipped through it while looking for something else, and it had caught my eye: double exposures, distressing the negatives, and other oddities. Some of these techniques would ruin the negative for any future prints, but what did it matter if the picture wasn't that great in the first place?

By the time I left forty minutes later, I had several new versions of my abstract print, each more abstract than the last. On one, I had exposed the paper to light in one-second increments, turning it a little each time so the image swirled and darkened like a shadowy kaleidoscope. On another, I had unevenly waved a piece of paper back and forth across the whole image during exposure, so some parts were darker than others. For the last one, I had scratched the negative in stripes with a paper clip. That one was my favorite. It looked injured, offended.

I hung them on the drying line, where I would pick them up tomorrow, and left the art building, setting out across campus toward home. It was still busy, girls drifting to and from the cafeteria and standing in clusters chatting after sports practices or rehearsals. No one could say it was warm, but it wasn't so cold anymore: it was March, and spring was coming, if slowly. After spring break, the Garden Club would have its first meeting of the semester. The streetlights lining the sidewalks flickered on as I walked.

I checked my phone. Sam, who almost never texted, had sent me a message saying **I'm dreading turning in this abstract assignment tomorrow, how are you feeling about it?** I sent pictures of my last few prints with the caption **BAD**. He responded quickly: **wow, those are...abstract!**

I grinned as I walked and was about to respond when a message from Jess popped up: **TWO MORE DAYS.**

I tripped over an uneven edge in the sidewalk and received a severe glance from a teacher walking by. It was dark enough now that the contrast with my phone screen was making it hard to see, so I pressed Call and held it up to my ear, waiting for Jess's voice to explode in excitement. She had missed our normal call this week, and I figured since she was texting me now, she was free.

But the phone rang once, twice, six times, and went to her voicemail: "Hi, you've reached Jess, leave a message," in a cheerful tone that sounded nothing like her. I hung up. Almost immediately, she texted me: **sorrrryyyyy can't talk having dinner with patrick and ethan and ash!**

I bit my lip.

I texted back, **no worries SEE YOU SOON**

She responded with a bunch of hearts, and I put my phone

back in my bag. I imagined her sitting at a McDonald's booth, curled into Patrick's chest, eating fries and giggling at an inside joke with Ashleigh. *Ash.* Maybe Ash was dating Ethan now. He and I hadn't talked lately. I felt a tiny twinge of jealousy, even though I had never wanted to be more than Ethan's friend.

I took out my phone, then put it back in my bag again. I wished I had sent Jess the pictures of my prints. Maybe if she saw them, she would get it. The scratches and the shades of gray. The four different ways of looking at the same thing, which barely looked like anything, trying to make sense of something that didn't have a whole lot of sense to begin with. Or maybe she would just ask which side was up.

thirteen

The rosé shimmered on my tongue as I took the last sip from the bottle. I met Jess's eyes as I swallowed and watched the smile spread across her face. She fell back against Patrick's chest and clapped. I drank in the sight of her: her hair, messy and short, fell in her face; the red strap of her tank top slid down her shoulder.

"More," she cried. "More for my girl!"

Patrick, trapped beneath her, shrugged and looked at Ethan beside me. Ethan groaned and got up, disappearing down the stairs to the kitchen, where presumably he would find another bottle. I never understood where the alcohol came from. Until I went away, I never questioned it, but now I couldn't stop wondering, though I didn't want to ask. It was boys, always boys, who provided.

Jess arched her eyebrows, and I shook my head.

"Your tolerance is shot," she said, tossing a balled-up napkin at me. It hit me in the shoulder and bounced off.

"I'm a cheap date," I retorted.

She wavered in my vision, as if she were standing in a parking lot in the summer.

I picked up my camera from where it sat beside me, held it to my eye, and clicked. I knew the settings were right for the room; I had checked earlier. She didn't see until it was already done, and she rolled her eyes.

"No photos! You've had that thing with you all week."

"I can't help it," I said. "You're too gorgeous."

It was Tuesday, and we were in Ethan's bedroom. We were ostensibly playing the board game Sorry, but mostly, we were drinking and laughing at each other. Outside, it was raining hard, and with the sound of the raindrops and the shadows from the window, it could have been any time of day or night. The actual time was two in the afternoon. Ethan returned with a six-pack of beer and sat down next to me.

"No more wine," he informed the group. "Beer only."

"I'll live," I said.

"I'll die," Jess said.

"Whose turn is it?" Patrick asked.

Jess flipped over a card and knocked one of Patrick's players back to his starting line. "Sorry," she said, face mocking. It had been my turn, but I stayed quiet. I plucked an Oreo from the open box between us and ate it slowly as Ethan considered his play.

When Mom had picked me up on Friday, I'd been prepared to fight. Oma and I listened to a true crime podcast all the way down to the halfway point, a Panera Bread near the Virginia border, and I couldn't stop thinking about all the things Mom might bring up on the long ride home. But as soon as I opened the car door, she gave me a big, long hug, squashing my face into her shoulder. She smelled like clean laundry and rose water, a scent unique to her, and I missed her more right then than I had for the last two months combined.

On the way home, she asked me about all the things I wanted to talk about, my friends and my classes and Oma and photography, and it seemed like she listened. She barely even complained about the hours of driving to pick me up. Of course, she also asked about my grades and spent a little too long discussing the twins' accomplishments, but I didn't mind that much. A two-hour car ride with my mother was *nice*. As I texted Kitty later that night: **What?**

Now, in Ethan's house, Jess won the game. Ethan had never cared about it in the first place, and I was too drunk to make sense of the board; Patrick did care, but Jess had made it her mission to beat him, and beat him she did. She pushed the board to the side after crowing her victory and then reached across the carpet to grab my hands.

"What do you want to *do*, June? My homecoming queen?"

"I'm happy with anything." My voice sounded distant to me, and in the back of my head, I tried to figure out how many drinks I'd had. How many drinks was half a bottle of wine? Or had it been three-quarters? No, more. There had been more than one bottle when we started. Where had they gotten all that wine? And wait, there had been vodka, too.

I tried to focus. "We could play another game."

"No more games." Jess shook her head hard. How much had she had? More than me, I was sure.

"We could watch a movie."

"I'll fall asleep."

"It's rainy. It's the right kind of day for a movie." The idea felt good to me, cozying up on a couch with the storm shutting us in. Sometimes Jess and I cuddled together under a blanket, and that sounded good too, her warm, soft legs tangled with mine—

I caught the thought and swept it away. "We can make popcorn," I proposed.

Jess's eyes widened. "Popcorn! God! Ethan, do you have popcorn?"

"I have popcorn," he said solemnly. "I will make the popcorn."

"I need to drink some water," Patrick announced. He rose and staggered down the stairs.

Ethan followed him, and Jess and I looked at each other across the discarded game. Her face split open in a grin, and she crawled to me, the board crunching under her knees. She slung a clumsy arm around my neck. I laughed and let her tug me to the floor. I lay beside her, looking up at the ceiling fan's slow rotations.

"I missed you, baby," Jess said. Her voice sounded slurred and distant. "I'm so glad you're back."

"I missed you more," I said.

"I mean it."

"I mean it, too. Jess—"

I turned toward her, her arm still tucked under my neck, and she turned to face me, and that was when I realized my face was very close to hers.

"Hi," she said. She giggled.

"You're so beautiful," I whispered. I knew I shouldn't have said it, but I couldn't help it, because her eyes shone like planets beneath the dark arches of her eyebrows; her lips were full and pink and shining. To not say it would have felt like lying.

She smiled. "You're so nice to me," she said. "I love you."

I know how she meant it; I knew how she meant it. She had only ever said those words in one specific language. But there was the wine. The liquor. She was so close.

The back of my head pleaded, *No, don't, you can't, no, you'll ruin*—

I closed the distance between us and kissed her.

Her lips were as soft as they looked. Softer. All of her was soft, her hair, her nose, her arm under my neck, her other hand resting carelessly on my waist. She kissed me back. She tasted like I tasted, like Oreos and pinot noir. I felt simultaneously outside my body and wholly under its command. Something treacherous inside me was shrieking in need.

I took a breath, and she pulled away.

Dread rolled over me like a thundercloud.

She sat up and touched her lips and started laughing.

"Oh shit," she said. "That was weird. Do you think that counts as cheating?"

I was speechless.

"Jess, June, come on," Patrick called up the stairs. "Movie's starting."

Jess stood up, almost falling as she did so. "Shh," she stage-whispered, putting a finger to her lips. Still laughing, she made her way downstairs, clutching the handrail. "Coming, baby," she said to Patrick.

I lay there, staring at the ceiling.

"June?" Patrick called after a minute.

I found my voice. "Coming," I called back.

I bit my lip. The room around me felt unreal, too crowded.

I walked unsteadily down the stairs. Jess and Patrick were curled in one corner of the couch, Ethan in the middle. The beginning of a superhero movie was rolling on the TV, and Patrick absently kissed Jess's neck, stroked his hand over her arm.

I went to the bathroom and vomited.

When I came out, I sat on the other end of the couch, next to Ethan, with whom I split the bowl of popcorn. I drank glass after glass of water while Jess and Patrick worked their way through the six-pack of beer. I felt adrift, dizzy and floating. I wished I had some coffee. I wished I could go home. But I needed to be sober first.

Abruptly, Jess stood up. "We're going to run an errand," she announced.

"What?" I looked up at her. "What errand?"

"Just an errand." Next to her, Patrick was getting up, yawning.

I paused the movie. "You guys can't drive." I glanced at Ethan for support, but he avoided my eyes. "Right? Aren't you drunk?"

"We'll walk."

"It's still storming so hard. And the drugstore is, like, a mile away." As if to emphasize my point, thunder cracked outside the window.

"We're just running an errand. It's fine, June, okay?" Now Jess sounded annoyed. I didn't want her to be mad at me. I looked up at her, pleading with my eyes for her to explain. She met my eyes, sighed, and looked meaningfully at Patrick.

I wasn't sure what I was supposed to understand from this, but I was afraid of speaking up again. Without saying anything else—without Patrick ever having said anything at all—she put on her shoes and walked out the front door, still clutching a half-full beer, Patrick at her heels. The sound of the rainwater hitting the front steps got louder as they opened the door, and then they closed it, running out of sight, and the house was entirely quiet.

"They can't drive," I said pathetically into the silence.

Ethan set the empty popcorn bowl on the coffee table and leaned back again, pulling out his phone. "They're gonna go hook up in his car."

"What?"

"You know he got that minivan from his grandparents?"

"Yeah, Jess told me."

"Yeah, well, it's like their own personal rolling bedroom. They do this"—he exhaled—"pretty regularly."

"Oh."

I squeezed my eyes closed tight, hoping that when I opened them, Jess and Patrick would be back on the couch. But I peeked and saw only Ethan, playing a game on his phone. He glanced up at me, something like pity in his eyes.

"It's pretty shitty that she's not spending more time with you on your one week home," he said. "I've seen you almost as much as she has, and I don't even miss you."

"You miss me." I threw a pillow at him, which he dropped his phone to catch. He grinned.

"I do. But my point stands."

"No, it doesn't. She's spent a ton of time with me."

It wasn't a complete lie. On Saturday morning, she had picked me up at home, and it was like it used to be, the two of us alone, everything I'd remembered and longed for in Virginia. We got McDonald's drive-through coffee at the corner by school and sat in her car in the parking lot, tilting the seats so we could lie back and face each other and talk. We caught up, speaking over each other and laughing until we gasped. We spent the whole day like that. When Dad picked me up later that night to go out to dinner, I was so overwhelmed with happiness that I could hardly explain what we had done that day. He pressed me for details, but I was telling the truth. What we had done was be together again. That was all.

I'd spent the next day with my family before the twins went back to school. On Monday, yesterday, I got in the car, expecting another day like Saturday. But Patrick was in the back seat already. He greeted me with the same enthusiasm I felt.

"We're picking up Ethan next," Jess said as she pulled away in the rain. She was chatty and affectionate and funny, but not quite as much as she was when we were alone. I tried not to be bothered. We went to her house and got drunk and did a puzzle.

Yesterday and today, at least, she had spent the whole day with me—if not with *just* me. Now, though, tipsy and alone with Ethan on his couch, I knew it wasn't enough. She had only been gone five minutes, but I would have given anything, anything, to have her beside me.

"She loves me," I murmured, almost to myself. "She said so."

"Seems like she loves Patrick more," Ethan commented as he turned the movie back on. I felt another wave of nausea and pressed my lips closed. He paused again a few seconds later and looked at me with an expression of awkward apology. "I'm sorry. I didn't mean that."

"You're fine."

"I really did miss you. Ashleigh is way less interesting."

I swallowed hard at how clearly, apparently, Ashleigh was slotting into the space I had left. I tried to sound casual. "If she's been hanging out with y'all that much, shouldn't she be here now?"

"She's in Colorado. Visiting her grandpa. It's his eightieth birthday."

"Oh." I said a small, selfish thank-you to the universe for Grandpa King's longevity.

"Yeah. And she's fine, really. She's not a terrible person or anything. I just don't have that many good friends with you gone."

"But you do have other friends, right? Guy friends?"

"Yes. Every single one of them is terrible."

I smiled. "Even Patrick?"

"Especially Patrick. Jesus, we've been friends since we were five and I still can't stand him. Never liked the guy."

I made myself laugh; Ethan started the movie again. I closed my eyes. *All this*, I told myself, *is fine.*

I opened my eyes at the sound of the door slamming and Jess yelling something incoherent. I must have dozed off, because the movie was almost over. I blinked and looked toward the door, where she and Patrick were giggling and shaking the rain from their bodies.

"It is very fucking wet outside," Patrick said breathlessly.

"We nearly drowned," Jess added. Neither she nor Patrick was carrying anything—no shopping bags, no candy bars. Everyone had been in on the errand joke except me.

Patrick said, "I'm gonna shower," and headed upstairs to Ethan's bathroom, and Jess sat down between me and Ethan.

"What've you two been doing in here?" she said, a tease in her voice.

"Sleeping," I said truthfully.

"Watching a movie," Ethan said, still playing his phone game.

"Uh-huh," she said, but then she snuggled under my arm and said, "Ooh, this is my favorite part."

I disentangled myself from her, and she pouted. "Another

glass of water," I said, gesturing to my empty cup. She shrugged and looked at the screen, and when I came back to the couch, I sat closer to Ethan than her. But I couldn't stop looking over at her, trying to unbraid all my emotions. Even as I got more clear-headed with each glass of water, the alcohol still fogged up my brain, softening all my sharp edges.

The knowledge that she and Patrick had just—*just*—had sex, an hour after I had kissed her, made it hard to think about anything else.

I went into the guest bathroom, clean and the color of a peach, with an unlit lavender candle sitting in the corner of the counter. I leaned in close to the mirror and stared at myself. Tipsy, I could only focus on one part of my face at a time. It made me feel like a collection of puzzle pieces that someone had thrown on the floor. Here, an edge piece with frizzy hair; there, an eye, brown and serious. A thin nose, a slice of jawline plagued by acne, a pair of lips a little chapped.

I stepped back, washed my hands, and splashed water on my face. "Chill," I said aloud at my reflection.

When I returned to the couch, the credits were rolling, Patrick had returned, and Jess was yawning and stretching. I checked the clock. Five fifteen. I didn't really have to leave until five forty or so, but...

"I should go," I said. Three heads turned toward me.

"Not yet," Jess said, alarmed. "You don't have to leave until six, right?"

"I have to be home at six. And my parents are being really

picky about it. Especially since I was almost late yesterday." This part was true: I had walked in the door at precisely six o'clock, and Mom had given me a very heavy sigh.

"Well." Jess looked at each of us in turn, apparently bewildered by the time. "I certainly can't drive you home."

I stared at her. Mom and Dad had both asked me, multiple times, if I was sure that Jess could take me home today. They had made it very clear that they were available. But I had insisted. Partly out of stubbornness and partly because I wanted every possible minute with her, I had told them she would drive me. And now...

"You're still drunk?" My voice came out louder than I intended.

"You aren't?"

"No!" I was, of course—only a little—but I couldn't bring myself to say it. Besides, my mouth was dry and my head hurt, and that meant I would be sober soon.

Jess looked at me skeptically. "Okay. But we split that wine upstairs."

"And then you had almost that whole six-pack to yourself!"

Her face broke into a dreamy smile, and she laughed. "I did, didn't I?"

"You did," Patrick stage-whispered to her, ignoring me.

"I'll take you," Ethan interjected. "I haven't had anything all day."

I rewound the day in my head. It was true—I remembered him bringing in drinks and snacks for the rest of us but never taking a sip himself, always and only drinking from his water bottle.

"Are you sure?"

"Yeah. Come on." He grabbed his car keys and wallet from the counter. By the couch, Jess and Patrick were giggling at some private joke. I inserted myself between them to hug Jess.

"See you tomorrow," I said.

"See you tomorrow, baby," she said. I breathed in, trying to reach the familiar scent of her hair, but it smelled like rain and dust and not like her. I stepped back, and she kissed me on the cheek. "Love you."

"Love you, too."

In the car, Ethan didn't put on any music. It was still raining so hard that the road was difficult to see. I watched the raindrops chase each other across the passenger-side window and imagined Jess and Patrick alone at Ethan's house, doing God knows what. I steeled myself for dinner and board games with my family. Maybe I could shower first. Maybe the hot water would help. I still felt scattered.

"What Jess said," Ethan spoke up, and I started—I had been so lost in thought I forgot that he was there. "About what we were doing when she and Patrick were out."

"Yeah?" We were at a stoplight, and he was staring straight ahead. My headache started to pound a warning.

He took a deep breath. "I have something I've been wanting to talk to you about. I'm not sure how you feel about…us… but…"

Oh no. Not now. He was going to say he liked me, and I was going to have to tell him I didn't like him back. But I couldn't hurt Ethan, not when he was so nice, driving me home, not when we still had half of spring break left.

"I don't like you in that way," he finished.

I simultaneously laughed and exhaled in relief. This produced an odd, cough-like sound that Ethan must have interpreted as distress, because he continued quickly, "I'm sorry. I know that Jess and Patrick want us to get together, and you're amazing, but I just—"

"Ethan, I don't like you that way, either," I said, grinning. The light turned green. "You don't have to apologize."

"Oh," he said. There was a long pause. I couldn't stop smiling.

"Did you think I liked you?" I asked playfully.

"Oh my God. This is mortifying."

"I'm serious!"

"So am I. I would love nothing more than for an asteroid to strike my car right now."

"Listen, I was worried *you* liked *me*."

"I tried," he said, finally laughing with me. "For, like, three weeks when Jess and Patrick first got together. I thought it would be nice if we could date, so I gave it a shot, but it didn't..."

"Fit," I finished. "Exactly. I did the same thing. It was nothing about you—"

"No, God, that's not what I meant—"

"You're great, it's just—"

"Right, *you're* great, but—"

"Very handsome, honestly—"

"Great…hair."

We were both giggling.

At the next stoplight, he shot me a thankful look over the center console. "I'm glad we're friends."

"Me too. Thanks for driving me home."

"Yeah, of course."

He pulled up on the street in front of my house. I was twenty minutes early for my curfew, and it was still pouring. I wanted to stay in Ethan's car, where a new closeness had grown between us, the air purified by our mutual honesty. We could sit in the rain, and I could tell him everything, Jess and the word *bisexual* buzzing in my head like a trapped wasp.

But he was looking at me expectantly, and why shouldn't he? He had to go deal with our drunk friends before his parents got home.

"See you tomorrow?" I asked before I got out, and he nodded.

"See you."

I got out, my camera on its strap around my neck and my purse slung over my shoulder, and shut the door. The rain instantly soaked me, but a thought occurred to me, and I turned around, tapping on the window. Ethan rolled it down.

"You okay?"

"Yeah. Can I take a picture of you?" I had to speak loudly to be heard over the rain.

He gave me a look, but he nodded. "What do you want me to do?"

"Nothing. Just look at me."

To his credit, he didn't make a face. I took the picture, framing him in the window, then straightened up and waved. "Thanks," I called.

"Anytime."

Ethan drove away, and I went up the walk slowly. The rain was cold and hard, a blessing. I let it wash away the afternoon, the game, the wine, the kiss, Jess's eyes, Jess's lips, Jess and Patrick in the car, me alone. I let myself believe that Jess would think it had been an accident. A joke. No big deal. *"Oh shit."* I made myself believe it. I unlocked and opened the door.

fourteen

As it turned out, I shouldn't have worried.

When Jess arrived to pick me up the next morning, forty-five minutes late, she was in a wonderful mood despite the ongoing rain. "Good morning, June," she sang as I climbed into the car. "I slept for twelve hours last night and I feel amazing."

"I'm so glad," I said. I had slept for approximately three hours and felt terrible. I checked the back seat—no one there.

"Ethan's already at Patrick's house," she said. "Patrick's brother's friend got us some tequila for today."

"That's awesome," I said, though the idea of tequila was nothing short of horrifying.

She reached over and squeezed my thigh, smiling. "I'm so glad you're back," she said. She pulled out into the road.

I took a deep breath. During the hours I'd spent not sleeping, I had prepared a speech, carefully calibrated to deflect any suspicions

Jess might have held about how I felt about her. I would apologize. I would make it clear it had been an embarrassing mistake, a drunken, meaningless impulse, maybe some kind of a joke.

For about two terrifying minutes, I had considered telling her the whole truth. But only two minutes.

"About yesterday," I began. "I know it was really inappropriate and out of line, and I just wanted to say—"

She shot me a bemused look that stopped me in my tracks. "What?" she said.

The thought occurred to me that she had been so drunk that she might not even remember. But if that was the case, it would've been even more wrong not to say something.

"The...um..." I tried again. "The kiss."

"Oh!" She looked startled, and then she burst into laughter. I wasn't sure what reaction I had expected, but this wasn't it. "Oh my God, I had totally forgotten about that. How funny. But I mean, it happens, right?" She smiled, shrugged. "I've kissed Ashleigh, too. It's no big deal."

"Sorry, what?"

"Not, like, frequently. But a couple of times at parties, sure. Patrick dared us to, so we did."

I stared at her. She glanced at me and laughed again, a little more self-conscious this time. "Jesus, June, it doesn't mean anything. It's not like we *hooked up*. It was just one kiss a few times. I mean, you're drunk, someone's there, it's human nature to kiss them, right? I'm still straight. So is she. And Patrick doesn't mind, if that's what you're worried about."

"That is not what I was worried about," I said.

"Then what's the big deal?"

"Nothing. It's not—it's nothing." I wished it weren't raining so I could roll down the window and get some fresh air. "I just felt bad about it, yesterday."

"Oh, well, don't feel bad. I really don't care."

It knocked the breath out of me. I knew it would've been better to stop talking, but I couldn't. "I can't believe you didn't tell me about Ashleigh."

She sighed impatiently. "Well, June, I knew you'd judge me, and I didn't want that."

"I'm not judging you."

"Yes, you are. I can tell. And it sucks, okay? I haven't done anything wrong."

"I know. I'm sorry."

She drove in silence the rest of the way to Patrick's house, and with the rain rolling down the windows, I congratulated myself. I had gotten what I wanted. She didn't think it was a big deal. She wasn't going to ask any more questions.

It felt awful.

We got to Patrick's house, and he let us in the side door, wrapping a possessive arm around Jess's waist as she leaned in to kiss him. "Where's the tequila?" she asked as soon as she came up for air. It was eleven thirty in the morning.

Ethan played bartender that day, and when I asked him quietly for seltzer with lime, he didn't ask any questions. Jess and Patrick disappeared into his room around one, and Ethan and I listened to music and played chess with Patrick's parents' beautiful, rarely used marble chess set. It was one of those two-person tables with drawers for the pieces and the board in the top, and sitting there by the window, playing chess in silence on a gloomy gray day, I felt pleasantly adult. The pieces were smooth and cool under my fingers. As we put them away, I found an extra queen rolling around in the drawer, her crown simple and rounded like a beret. I slipped her into my purse.

———

"You are bad at this game."

Candace laid down her last card and smiled. Bryan cursed, which sounded kind of funny in his twelve-year-old voice.

"I am bad at all games," I told her. Apparently, since I'd left, my family's traditional movie nights had been replaced by game nights. Over the course of the last week, Candace and Bryan had patiently taught me their three standard board games, all of which were complex, three- to four-player odysseys with opaque rule sets. Now, it was Saturday night, my last night at home, and I had begged them for relief. They relented. We were playing Uno. Which I was bad at, but at least I understood the rules.

"I don't understand how this happened," Bryan said as he gathered up the cards and expertly shuffled them. "We're both so good at games."

"In all things, I am the exception to this family," I said wearily.

"We love you." Candace reached across the table to give me half a hug.

"Yeah, things are a lot more boring with you gone," Bryan said. He started dealing the next hand, sliding the cards across the smooth tabletop.

"When do you leave again?" Candace asked.

"Tomorrow after lunch."

"Couldn't you stay later? Mom said we could go out for ice cream if we can get all our homework done."

"I have to get settled in at Oma's. Thanks, though."

Candace sighed as she picked up her cards, and on the table beside me, my phone buzzed. There were a few messages on my group text with Sam, Kitty, and Claire about their last-night-of-break plans—mostly nice dinners with family, so they were comparing restaurant menus. And one from Jess: **are you SURE you can't come out tonight???**

positive, I replied.

ok but are you sure, came the response. **because it's gonna be at Ash's house and you know how she lives way out in the woods? it's v spooky but in a fun way.**

I hesitated. Before December, I would've said yes. It wouldn't be that hard. My bedroom window opened onto the roof, and years ago, I had learned how to shimmy down onto the edge of the first-floor porch swing, dropping from there onto the ground. Getting back up was harder but not impossible, especially with a boost from Jess. My parents had discovered me gone once, but that was over a year ago now, and I doubted they'd check on me in the middle of the night this evening.

But then I pictured Jess and Ashleigh kissing in a crowded basement, and I didn't even want to try.

"June, come on," Bryan said, nudging me. "It's your turn."

I picked up my hand. It was hard to tell with this game, but I was pretty sure I had terrible cards. I picked up a two and immediately played it, which seemed to be a legal move. Then I peered at my phone screen again.

"Come on. Don't look at your phone," Candace protested. "You said you'd play with us."

"I have shitty cards," I retorted.

"We all have shitty cards," Bryan said, which made me smile. Cursing was new to the twins this year, and I found it delightful, the practiced, deliberate carelessness with which they pronounced the words. "That doesn't mean we can't pay attention."

"You're right. I'm sorry." I texted Jess a quick **I honestly can't I'm so so so so sorry.** She responded immediately with several sad faces, and I put my phone facedown, switching it on silent. But as we played, her texts still nagged at me. I wanted to pick up my phone and say something. I just didn't know what.

Bryan yelped in excitement, holding up his last remaining card. I still had four cards in my hand.

"Fuck," Candace swore, then quickly glanced at me to see my reaction. I couldn't help but smile as Dad walked into the kitchen.

"Candace!" he said, but he didn't look that shocked.

"Sorry, Dad."

"Time to clean up for dinner. Your mom ordered pizza."

"Yes," the twins muttered in unison. Bryan played his last card and won. I glanced at my phone.

Ethan: gonna miss you tonight, it was good to see you this week

Kitty: actually looks like the cafeteria is closed tomorrow for dinner but we could get dessert at harold's at 8 if you and your grandma are having dinner early? or we could just go ahead and do dinner, ms nolan could come

Claire, in our group text: Y'ALL YOU WON'T EVEN BELIEVE IT BUT THIS RESTAURANT HAS OFF-MENU RISOTTO BALLS

Jess: ugh

After dinner, the twins disappeared to play video games, and I was left at the table with my parents, half a veggie pizza between us. All three of us were still eating—the twins had finished dinner fast, excited by the promise of whatever level they were about to attack—but the mood was different with my siblings gone.

Earlier in the week, all of us had been eating chicken enchiladas at this table when my dad had said, too casually, "So, June, do you know if there are any interesting summer session classes available at St. Anne's?"

I had put down my fork. "You can't be serious." I might've still been the slightest bit tipsy, though ever since the day of the kiss, I had been drinking a lot less.

"Wait." Bryan looked back and forth between me and our parents. "June is staying in Virginia over the summer?"

"You can't," Candace said. "Right, Dad? Mom? Why are you asking that?"

"I am not," I said deliberately, "staying in Virginia over the summer." I looked hard into Dad's eyes. He shrugged.

"I was just wondering," Dad said.

"I am not staying in Virginia over the summer," I repeated.

Mom said, "Honey, we know," and Bryan, anxious to break the tension, started talking about the upcoming student council vote to change one of the theme days in Spirit Week.

I had not been alone with my parents since. Now, I swallowed my bite of pizza and took a sip of water and waited.

"So," Mom started, which was about what I had expected. I never knew the exact words she was going to use to tell me she was disappointed in me, but they usually started with *so*. "It's been really great having you home this week," she continued.

"We miss you very much," Dad added quietly. "You know, if you ever want to come back just for a weekend, we can absolutely arrange that."

"It's okay," I said. With AP exams and the SAT coming up, it was going to be a busy few months. "But I miss you, too. And the twins."

"They've been thrilled to have you here," Dad said, smiling. "They asked if they could have the whole week off school to spend time with you."

"The week after spring break?" I laughed.

"Yeah, we told them there was no chance." Mom smiled, too, and it felt for a moment as if we were all on the same side. But then she glanced at Dad, trying to communicate something silently, and I knew the other shoe was going to drop. I kept my breathing calm and tried to prepare myself to hear them tell me to stay in Virginia over the summer. Since that dinner, I had prepared a defense.

"We wanted to talk to you about this summer. Your father and I have discussed it, and we really think—"

"I'll get a job here," I burst out. "I've already looked online, and it's a little early to send out applications, but I was thinking I could be a barista. Or I can try waitressing or hosting. I could find a place that wasn't too far from your work, so you could drive me, or if it's in the evenings, I could borrow a car maybe. Or I can learn the bus system." I took a breath and continued. "It'll help me put away some money for college. I could spend more time with the twins. And just, overall, I love Oma. We get along a lot better than I thought, and school is okay. Sometimes it's really good, actually!" I was going off script, babbling. I paused for a moment and got myself on track. "But I miss home a lot. I miss the twins and Jess. I really, really want to come home for the summer."

I folded my hands in front of me and exhaled.

They blinked.

"Well," Dad said, adjusting his glasses. "This is a surprise."

"I know you want me to stay in Virginia, but I really want to be here," I said. It sounded like pleading, and I was reminded of my conversations with my parents before they sent me to St. Anne's in the first place. I pushed away those memories. "I miss home. Can you get that? No matter how nice things are in Virginia, I miss home. And this summer and next summer are the only times I'm going to get to be here for months at a time ever again."

"June," Mom said gently. Amusement and sadness battled on her face. "We miss you, too. We were going to suggest you get a summer job here. At home."

"Oh."

My dad looked like he was struggling not to laugh. "You made the case quite convincingly."

"Wait," I said, still trying to internalize this shift. "The other night at dinner—"

"I was just saying it was an option," Dad said, putting his hands up. "Truth be told, your mom and I are looking forward to having you home for the summer, so we didn't love the idea, either. We just thought, since your Oma says things are going well up there, we'd talk about it. But clearly, it's not something you want."

"Getting a job here sounds great," Mom said. "I can help you with applications in a month or two."

"Oh, okay. Thanks." All my built-up anxiety dissipated, and I laughed a little in relief. "Well, cool. Thank you."

My parents both started laughing, too.

Candace poked her head around the corner. "What's funny?" she asked suspiciously.

"I'm coming home for the summer," I said.

"Well, yeah, I knew that. That's not funny."

"No," Mom sighed between giggles. "It's not."

"The boss we're fighting is too hard," Bryan announced as his head appeared next to Candace's. "Will you guys come and play that new game with us? The one with the giraffes? June, we've been playing it with four people, but it's way better with five."

As Candace and Bryan walked me through the new game, I flipped circles from green to red and back again, moved my little clay giraffes into and out of the nine segments on the board, and tried to stay focused. The rules were complex and confusing; no matter how I tried, I always did the wrong thing. But I didn't mind. Somewhere in the woods, in Ashleigh's house, Jess was dancing and flirting and drinking, and I was here at home, losing at a game I didn't understand. I should have been sad. Instead, I could only feel grateful.

fifteen

I hadn't wanted to admit that I missed Virginia. Wanting to go back to Oma and school felt like a betrayal to Jess, to the twins and the trappings of home. But as Dad pulled up in front of the condo and Oma waved at me from her balcony, the river glittering beneath her, something inside me split open, a stone piercing the surface of still water. I wanted to be here. It wasn't home, not exactly, but it was right.

I took a picture of the school from the passenger seat and texted Claire, Kitty, and Sam, **I'm back!!!!!!** Their responses were immediate.

"What are you smiling at?" Dad asked as he parked.

I looked up from my phone. "Just my friends. They're happy I'm back."

"I'd love to meet them."

I looked at my father carefully, trying to figure out if he was skeptical. But he seemed genuine. Just like Mom a week earlier, he had been entirely pleasant on the drive, not raising the issue of the summer even once.

"Maybe at the end of the year," I said.

Dad helped me start a load of laundry and chatted with Oma before leaving. After he left, the only noise in the condo was Eleanor Roosevelt's snoring. Oma sat down at the kitchen table and looked at me across the room.

"How was your spring break?" I asked her.

"Boring. Nice. I did a lot of prep for the Garden Club meeting tomorrow; I think we're going to plant cauliflower. How about you?"

"Same, kind of. Minus the cauliflower."

"I notice that you're not as depressed to return as you were when you got here in January."

I looked out at the river and the redbrick buildings of St. Anne's. Girls were moving around on the lawn, with one intrepid group having laid out a picnic blanket in a vain attempt to sunbathe. The sun sent pale warmth through the window.

"I'm not going to say I missed it here, but..."

Oma smiled, and I remembered a question that I had nearly forgotten in the wake of last night's discussion with my parents. "Hey, before I left, you said if I didn't get in trouble over spring break, I could have a nine o'clock curfew on weekends. You weren't just saying that, right? Because I didn't get in trouble this week."

I did not mention that I had, in fact, been drunk half the days

I was gone. I held my breath as she paused for a moment and then nodded.

"Yes, I think that's fine. I still want you back by sunset on weeknights, though, unless you're studying in the library."

"Thank you," I said in a rush. Sunset was getting later and later anyway. "And for the purposes of the extended curfew, does weekend mean Friday through Sunday, or Friday and Saturday, or Saturday and Sunday, or…"

Oma rolled her eyes. "Friday through Sunday. But do not abuse this, June, I'm warning you. And you still have to tell me where you are."

"I never go anywhere interesting."

"June."

"I promise." I hesitated before continuing. "Does that mean I can go to Harold's with Kitty and Claire for dinner tonight? An early dinner. Like five o'clock?"

Oma laughed. "Back for an hour and already leaving again. Fine, but you'll have to let me walk with you. I slept in, and Ellie didn't get a walk this morning."

Seeing Kitty and Claire walk up to Harold's hand in hand, I couldn't stop grinning; they looked so happy. When they spotted me, Kitty waved and Claire threw open her arms. It was comforting to know that even if things had changed at home in some indefinable way, this here, these two, were the same as they had been when I left them. Granted, it had been a week rather than two and a half months, but still.

Over pancakes, we caught up on one another's spring breaks.

They had both gone home and spent most of their time sleeping, reading, and hanging out with their parents. Kitty had a lot of pictures of her toes in the sand with the ocean in the background. Claire and I groaned in envy.

"What did you do, June?" Kitty asked, spearing a blueberry with her fork.

"Hung out with Jess and some of our old friends and my family. I learned a lot of board games. It was pretty boring. But nice." I wasn't exactly unwilling to tell them the entire truth—Kitty, especially, I wanted to talk to more. I just didn't want to do it there, in Harold's, under the cheerful yellow light with breakfast for dinner spread out in front of us. "What's Sam up to tonight?" I asked, trying to change the subject. After we had settled on this time after lots of discussion in our text thread, he hadn't said anything, and I hadn't been sure if he was coming or not.

"It's Justin's birthday tonight," Claire said. "I think they're doing a dinner with his family. Sam sends his regards."

Kitty gave me a look, and I couldn't tell what she meant by it. I stared fixedly at my plate. *What right do you have to ask about Sam when you can't stop thinking about Jess?* I imagined her saying. But when I looked up, she hadn't looked away, and what I saw in her eyes was mostly pity.

Even if I set aside all thoughts of romance, I was still looking forward to seeing Sam. I caught his eye when he walked into photography on Tuesday, but he was late, and Erica started talking almost as soon as he sat down.

"Did everyone take some great photos during spring break?" she asked the class enthusiastically. She received mostly unenthused nods, but mine was genuine. I had spent Monday afternoon developing the three rolls of film from last week, but I hadn't had time to print contact sheets yet. I couldn't wait to see the pictures. I wanted to send them back to Jess and Ethan, show them what I was trying to do every time I raised my camera to my eye.

"Good to hear. So! We've bounced around a lot, but we're going to devote the whole second half of the semester to portraiture. In the classroom, we'll be studying some of the great portrait photographers, and you'll have an essay next month that will be part of your final project grade. In the darkroom, your project will be a collection of portraits—of people who are important to you. These portraits should tell the viewer something about who this person is and what they mean to you."

As she talked, she was passing out sheets of paper. I scanned the rules for the assignment when she handed them to me—no fewer than six prints and no more than ten, use up at least eight rolls of film, hand in contact sheets along with final images. The due date was just a few days before the end of the semester. And...

"We'll also be presenting them in a show on the last day of school," Erica announced. Everyone perked up. "This is the first time we've had this opportunity. The school has decided to move the paintings in the hallway downstairs to the alumni building, so your photographs will hang in that hallway through the summer and all next semester. Given the timing, I'm hoping some of your families will be able to join us for the opening reception."

The room swelled with the sound of girls talking to each other and flipping over the assignment sheet to read the back. Sam looked excited and more than a little nervous, which was almost laughable; he was an incredible photographer, and everyone was going to love his work. Mine, on the other hand...

"For a whole semester!" he said. "I know it's just the arts hallway, but a lot of people walk through there." He scanned the assignment sheet himself, lips moving a little as he read.

He was right. The arts hallway got a lot of traffic. It encompassed the big windowed room at the entry of the building and the long, broad path that ran down the middle of it. I could just imagine my family walking along, admiring my classmates' photographs, then getting to mine and going silent. "So this is what you spent your semester on?" I heard my mom saying after a long, doubtful pause. "Will this help you get into college?"

At the same time, I was making a list in my head: Who would I photograph? How would I do it? Was there supposed to be a theme? I was even more glad that I had taken so many pictures on spring break, because there were people at home I wanted to include. Maybe I had captured an incredible portrait without even knowing it. Probably not, but maybe.

Erica let the class talk for a minute and then shushed us,

starting a lecture on the elements of a great portrait. I tried to stop thinking about the assignment or my parents' potential disappointment and just take notes.

When class dismissed for lunch, though, Sam and I left the building in a chorus of girls talking about their plans for the project.

"This is going to be great," Sam said.

We burst forth into the sun. Today, for the first time all year, it was warm, not hot yet, but bright and mild. I had dared to wear a T-shirt under my jean jacket instead of a sweater. For once, I thought we might spend our whole lunch hour outside.

"Do you know who you're going to photograph?" I asked as we walked toward the gazebo.

"Mom, Dad, Claire, Alex, Justin, Kitty," he recited. He glanced sideways at me; I saw it in my peripheral vision. "You, if you'll let me."

I felt warmth on my face and hoped it was the sun. "I'll let you if you let me."

"Deal. How about you?"

"Oma, Claire, and Kitty for sure. You, I guess." I caught his eye and he smiled. "I'd really like to include Jess and my friend Ethan, and the twins and my parents. But I don't think they're visiting, so we'll see if I got good pictures of them when I was at home."

"I never asked. How was your spring break?"

"Good. Weird."

"Weird how?"

I shrugged. We had reached the gazebo before Claire and Kitty, and I sat down on the sunny side, Sam dropping down only a few inches away.

"I never wanted to come here." The curve of the gazebo bench placed him at an angle to me, and I saw something cross his face that made me want to take back my words. "Not that I'm unhappy here," I rushed to say. "Actually, I love living away from my parents. Oma is great. And Kitty and Claire and you…"

He looked directly at me, waiting.

"I've never had friends like this before," I said, realizing the truth of it as I said it. "You know, a cohesive *group*. At home, it was always just Jess. And then her boyfriend and our friend Ethan, I guess, but it was mostly just her. And here I have y'all, and it's really good.

"But leading up to last week, I still missed home. My parents a little and my siblings a lot. And Jess a *lot*. So maybe I built it up in my head too much, I don't know. But it ended up being weird."

"Yeah, but weird how?" he pressed.

I glanced up the hill. Claire and Kitty were walking down toward us, laughing at something, Claire's hair drifting around her in the breeze.

"Everything is almost the same as when I left, but not quite," I answered. "The things that are different, I don't recognize. And the things that are the same, I don't want to be part of anymore."

Sam looked down at our feet, stretched out onto the floor of the gazebo. He was wearing black-and-white sneakers; I was wearing my boots. He tapped the toe of my right foot with the toe of his left.

"That sounds hard," he said quietly. "I'm sorry."

Kitty and Claire reached us and set down their bags. Kitty glanced between us and looked like she was about to say something, but Claire spoke up first.

"At last, my plan to spend time outside has paid off," she crowed. "Aren't you glad we've been preparing for this all semester?"

"As I told you walking down here, our preparation wouldn't matter today, because it is actually an acceptable temperature," Kitty told her. She passed me a thermos of coffee from her backpack, and I mouthed *thank you*. "In Florida, this is as cold as it ever gets."

"Claire, I'm going to wait until the next really cold night and make you pose in a T-shirt and shorts to take my portrait of you," Sam said, laughing.

"Why are you taking a portrait of me?" Claire tied up her hair and unwrapped her sandwich. We told them about our photo assignment, and Claire actually clapped her hands. "So you're telling me that not only one but two pictures of me are going to be hanging in the art hallway for six months? That is *great*."

"It's something," Kitty said, looking a little uneasy. "You have your work cut out for yourself with me."

"You are the most beautiful girl I've ever met," Claire said, kissing her on the cheek.

"Do you not like having your picture taken?" I asked.

Kitty made a face. "I don't hate it. I just don't like most photos of myself. I don't think I have a good face for cameras."

"She's lying," Claire said. "And I say this as someone who *absolutely* has a good face for cameras, so I would know."

"I'm just saying," Kitty protested, "don't go for gritty realism, okay? If people are going to stare at me while they wait for drama class to start, I want to look good."

"You will look great," I promised, and Sam nodded.

———

It was easy—easier than I had expected—to fall back into my routine in Virginia, made easier by the fact that we had switched to daylight savings time and the weather was finally getting warmer. Every day, the sun shimmered on the river for a little longer, woke me up through my window a little earlier. When I called home twice a week, I asked for the twins first, then talked to my parents for a few minutes.

I talked to Jess less than I used to, justifying it by telling myself that we were both busy. I didn't let myself think too hard about my feelings for her, except after we talked. I missed her so much after we hung up that I had to lie on my bed and focus on the ceiling for a half hour after our conversations finished. But that was fine. It was okay.

Especially because I was legitimately busy. My classes weren't getting any easier, my Monday SAT prep class had expanded to fill my Wednesday study hall, and my photography assignment took up all the mental energy I had left at the end of the day. In addition to planning the four pictures of Oma, Kitty, Claire, and Sam, I needed to figure out how to include my friends and family at home. I hadn't gotten any good photos of my parents or Jess; I had taken pictures of the twins and Ethan that I thought might work, but I wasn't sure. Erica had patiently sat with me while I pored over the contact sheets, and she had agreed there were some good images, but they weren't perfect; I would need to look at cropping, brightening, or darkening them, which was a lot harder in the darkroom than it was on the computer.

Plus, I wanted to spend time with my friends. Now that it was warmer and my curfew was later, suddenly there was always something to do. There was coffee at Harold's or a dorm dinner I was invited to join; there were blankets on the lawn and study sessions in the gazebo and movie nights on Kitty's laptop. They came over to Oma's and we made dinner for her, burning the garlic bread and overcooking the pasta so it fell apart on our tongues, but the tomato sauce was so good—thanks for the herbs, Nadine!—that it didn't matter. Sam joined us for a trip to one of the local antique stores, and we laughed at magazine covers and haunted dolls. Sam was around more than he used to be; sometimes Justin and Alex joined us, too, and I grew to like them both, Justin for his quick wit and Alex for his earnest need to argue about books.

On days when I wasn't spending time with them, I still wanted to be outside. I joined Oma on her walks with Eleanor Roosevelt, ambling around the neighborhood while Ellie sniffed at rocks and tried to eat the crab apples that fell from the trees. It was on one of these walks that I took my photograph of Oma. We were slowly making our way down the beach, the river lapping at the sand to our left and the school rising up on our right.

When I had thought about Oma's portrait, I had considered capturing her at the dining room table, symbolizing the quiet evenings we spent together while I did homework and she graded papers. Or cutting peppers in the kitchen, to reference the long conversations we sometimes had while she cooked and I cleaned. I hadn't intended to take the picture—or as Erica said, *make the portrait*—on the beach. I just had my camera with me because I always did.

But there, as she and Ellie walked ahead of me, she paused and looked out toward the horizon, and I felt the moment slip into place: a key catching in a lock. I held my breath and raised the camera to my eye. The frame saw her in profile, the setting sun draping itself over her features; to her left, the river flashed and flickered, and to her right, the bank was grassy and still. I adjusted some settings quickly, quietly, then clicked and exhaled.

She looked back at me and smiled. "Sneaky with that thing, aren't you?"

"You looked really beautiful, Oma." I picked my way over the rocks and sand to catch up to her.

"So was that it?"

I had told her about the portrait assignment. We had even brainstormed her photo together. She said she could find a pedestal to stand on if I wanted to portray her as my life's greatest hero.

"That was it."

"What is it going to say about me?"

I parted my lips to make a joke. But then a rogue wave splashed up onto the rocks, soaking both of our shoes, and we laughed in unison, and I said, "That I love you very much, and I'm very grateful that you've let me into your home."

She stopped and hugged me until Ellie pulled us forward.

"I love you, too," she said, and then we talked about homework.

sixteen

If you had asked me that spring about my plans for college, my answer would've been pretty vague. I had thought about it, of course, but only in broad and abstract terms. I knew that I was expected to go, that I wanted to go, and that I wanted somewhere far away—or at least far away enough that I'd have a few hours' head start if my parents decided to visit. I knew that I wanted to go someplace good, though I had enough self-awareness to understand that I was not Ivy material. I knew that my parents could pay for some of it and that I would need to pay for the rest in some combination of scholarships and loans.

The woman in front of me, however, was more serious about college than anyone I had ever met. She looked at me severely through large glasses before opening the folder in front of her.

"June," she said.

"Yes?"

She was shuffling through the papers in the file. There weren't many, but given that I hadn't even known I *had* a file until a few minutes ago, even a small number of papers was concerning. I waited while she skimmed before, finally, she sat back in the chair with a sigh.

"I apologize," she said. "I'm meeting with a lot of students today, and I haven't had a chance to review everyone's file in advance."

"That's okay."

"Did you find the presentation useful?"

Earlier today, the entire eleventh grade had come together in the assembly hall so that this woman—I think her name was Mrs. Wagner, or maybe Weber—could tell us what it took to get into college. Oma had told me to expect a presentation about the different kinds of colleges out there, with tips about how many schools to apply to and how to write a strong application. Similar speakers had come to visit in the past, she said, and they had been well received. But the message Mrs. Wagner-or-Weber had delivered was that we, all of us, were teetering on the edge of failure, and the slightest misstep could tip us into the chasm.

"Your future success rests upon your ability to choose, apply to, and be admitted to the right university," she had told us with the solemnity of a prophet predicting a death. "It is not the time for games."

Now, I was sitting in front of her in the guidance counselor's office, at the individual appointment I had been required to attend after school. To her question, I nodded. Yes, I had found the presentation useful.

"Good," she said, businesslike, sitting up straight again. "So.

Academically, you're doing well. It's nice to see the number of AP classes you've taken. If you keep getting these kinds of grades, you'll be in a good place there." She glanced down. "I see you're in the SAT prep class. How are your practice tests?"

"Good."

She sat expectantly, waiting.

"I don't remember the number, I'm sorry." I did, but I didn't want to tell her.

"Well, as long as you're scoring high. How's your writing? For your personal statements and essays?"

"Pretty good, I think. I get good grades on my essays."

She nodded and turned a page. There was a long silence as her eyes moved down the sheet of paper, the font too small for me to read across the desk. "I see that you're new to the school this semester. It's unusual to switch schools midyear; can you tell me any more about that?"

I looked at her carefully, trying to judge whether my file said exactly why I had been sent away from Greenmont. The file was slim, and since I had technically left of my own accord, there was no reason for the school to know what had happened at the dance. When I talked to an administrator at St. Anne's before arriving in January, I had done what my parents told me to do: obliquely reference a difficult social situation, say I needed to be more challenged in class. But these things, I knew, had a way of getting around.

Mrs. W stared right back at me with the exhausted rigidity of a woman with a task to complete and too little time.

"I needed a change," I said finally, to which she nodded. I was waiting for her to ask more questions—it was not a good answer—but clearly, she'd just had a box to check. I sat back in relief.

"Well, that just leaves extracurriculars," she continued. "It's problematic that you're not involved in any clubs. The ideal applicant has interests outside school."

"I do photography," I said weakly.

"Lean into that. Submit a supplemental art portfolio if you can. A lot of schools don't weight them heavily, but it can't hurt. Now, I don't know if you've thought about budget and where exactly you'll be applying, but..."

She started pulling brochures out of her bag. The next twenty minutes passed in a haze of glossy photographs, tuition costs, and application deadlines. I almost believed she was paid by the number of pamphlets she handed out. I didn't get a chance to tell her that I didn't want anywhere too cold or ask whether I got in-state tuition in Virginia or North Carolina or both. By the time I staggered out of the office, bag bulging with brochures, I was pretty sure the best path would be to melt into the earth and never go to college. That, or apply to thirty schools. There didn't seem to be any in-between.

Thankfully, Claire was waiting outside when I emerged, having taken the appointment before mine. She hopped up when she saw me.

"How was it?"

I made a face, which she mirrored back.

"Yeah," she said. "Mine was bad, too."

"You didn't have to wait for me," I told her, but she shook her head.

"I figured if I went back to my room, I'd just fidget around and make things look worse."

"You don't have to clean up for the portrait, you know. It's just supposed to be a picture of you in your room."

"I know! I want it to look good."

"But it is *amazing.*"

"Yeah, I know."

We set off across the lawn toward her dorm, the fresh air a welcome change from the stuffy office. At the edge of campus, I could just barely see Kitty jogging along the sidewalk on her daily afternoon run.

I didn't usually spend time with Claire alone, and as a result, I was finding it hard to start up our normally easy conversation. We had decided on her room as the setting for her portrait a few days ago, and at the time, I thought it was perfect. The room was practically a portrait of her in and of itself, and it represented the ways she had welcomed my friendship; after all, when your only private space is half a dorm room, inviting someone into that space is an intimate gesture. I had thought she'd be happy with the setting, too. She was proud of her room, and she had been openly excited about being framed in our new art gallery. But now...

"Don't be nervous," I told her. "It's nothing, really."

She laughed and looked at me, smiling in a way that instantly put me at ease. "I'm not nervous. I've seen your stuff. You're incredible."

"I'm not."

"I think that college counseling session just really freaked me out," she continued.

"Oh my God, me too," I said in relief, and the dam broke, both of us bubbling over with indignant questions and complaints.

"She told me that if I didn't get an A in precalculus this year, I might as well not even apply to any out-of-state schools."

"She wouldn't even say if I could try for Virginia tuition."

"I asked what she'd recommend doing to prep for essays, and she literally said just to *do my English homework*, as if I'm not doing that already."

"I'm pretty sure now I'm not going to get into college at all."

"Same!"

I gave her a grateful look. As she swiped open the door to her dorm, I asked, "For real, though, do you know where you're going to apply?"

"Yeah." We started up the stairs side by side. "UVA, Virginia Tech, and Hollins here in Virginia, Penn State to have an option near home, and then a few safeties I haven't figured out yet. Oh, and MIT as my stretch school, but I won't get in there."

"Don't you want to go somewhere with a good music program?"

"Nah. It would be a nice bonus, because that would probably mean good practice rooms that aren't on the far edge of campus, but I'm not gonna be a music major. It's too much practicing. I want to do physics. Or maybe straight-up math, I don't know." We had reached her room. "What about you?" she asked as she unlocked it.

"I'm not sure," I said, trying to sound more nonchalant than I was. I felt a headache coming on, as if the pressure of the looming decision and all its attendant anxieties—SATs, grades, my near expulsion from Greenmont—were literally expanding inside my head, threatening to burst.

Thankfully, Claire didn't ask any more, preoccupied with straightening her room and suggesting spots for the portrait, though I had told her a hundred times she didn't need to give me any direction. Ever since we'd decided on her room, I'd had the idea of photographing her from below as she stood on her desk, so her head floated close to the starry-night ceiling. I knew a lot of girls were planning on photographing their friends in their rooms, so I'd have to make my image stand out. I could see it in my head, the flickering lights around her hair, her looking out into the distance as if she really was standing beneath a midnight sky.

Reality, however, did not match my imagination. As soon as she got up on the desk, I sensed it was wrong. The frame caught too much of the walls and not enough of the ceiling. The severe angle was not flattering; it caught the bottom of her nose and the acne on her chin in a way I knew she'd hate. Most of all, the desk was not built to hold a girl standing on its back corner. Every time she shifted her weight, it shook perilously, and she kept glancing down. She didn't say anything, but I really, really didn't want to be the reason her desk collapsed into pieces.

I shot half a roll of film trying to make it work. But when she took a small step and we heard a crack, I said, "Okay, this isn't working. Let's try something else."

She came down off the desk visibly relieved. "Can we try one of my ideas now?"

"I…" The words were on the tip of my tongue: *I told you, this is my project. It's not about you.* But it was about her—why she was my friend, why she was important. I owed her a try. "Yeah, okay."

"All right, here's what I was thinking…" She busied herself moving around the pillows on her bed and pulling over a chair. "I'll lie on my bed like this, and you stand on the chair like this, and then you'll shoot down at me, okay?"

I looked at her doubtfully, but I had said I'd give it a shot. "Okay."

I held the camera to my eye and pointed it where she directed, but the angle of the bed distorted her limbs, and the frame caught something awkward no matter where I focused. I shook my head. "No good."

"Just try it," she protested.

I took a few shots, knowing they wouldn't work, as the tension built in the room. This was supposed to be fun, but it was serious, too. What Erica had taught us about the rule of thirds, the fundamentals of good portraiture, collided in my head with Claire posing on her bedspread. I let my camera fall on its strap against my chest and took a picture with my phone. I held it out to her as I climbed down off the chair. It wasn't exactly what I saw through the viewfinder of my camera, but it was close enough. "See?"

She glanced at it and wrinkled her nose. "Is that what I look like?"

"Not normally," I admitted. "Normally, I'm just looking at you straight on like this."

"Okay, so take a picture like that."

"I can't. It's not right."

"Oh my God, you are taking this way too seriously," she said, laughing and breaking a little of the tension. "It's just a photo."

"But it's going to hang up for ages."

She made a face at me. I made a face at her.

Then she made a more exaggerated face, twisting her eyebrows and sticking out her tongue.

"Photograph me like this," she said. "It's how I want to leave my impact on the world."

"You're not funny," I grumped. She made an even more ludicrous face, and she kept making faces at me until I broke. We were giggling together, she was still making faces at me, and I raised my camera and took photo after photo. I wouldn't get a good grade, but at least I had a good friend. I snapped and snapped and—

Suddenly, I knew it was right, this unposed here and now. She was laughing, looking at me just above the camera, her eyes shining and her hair falling around her cheeks, with the magnificent art of her room dancing unfocused behind her. I yelled in delight.

"That was it! I got it!"

"You got it!" she yelled back, raising her hand for a high five. "Did you get it when my cheeks were puffed out?"

"God, I hope not."

"I hope you did."

———

Sometimes at night, after Oma went to bed, I couldn't focus on anything. I would sit in my room staring at my homework, reading the same page from my textbook over and over, or watch mediocre TV on my laptop until my eyes hurt. It made no sense to me. I should have just gone to bed. But alone in the little blue room, I felt an inexplicable melancholy draw over me, and I was afraid that if I turned out the lights and closed my eyes, it would possess me completely.

After the bizarre college counseling meeting and near-failed photo session with Claire, I was having one of those nights. I had been on the same section of my math worksheet for half an hour. I texted Jess, asking if she could talk, even though we didn't usually talk on Mondays, but she didn't respond. The clock read 11:53, which meant I had to get up in seven hours and seven minutes. I kept looking at my phone. It kept not lighting up.

Until it did. I grabbed it and peered at the text. Not Jess. Sam.

first of all, sorry to bother you so late. second, can you remind me what chapters we're getting quizzed on in photography tomorrow? I was an idiot and I can't find it in my notes.

I felt myself smiling, just a little. This was an odd text to receive, given that I had been sitting beside him in class when he jotted down the quiz info last Tuesday.

chapters 8 and 9, I replied. **how are your portraits going?**

thanks! ok I think—haven't developed any film yet, he said. **looking forward to yours tomorrow, I have some ideas I think might work well.**

same! I justified this response by telling myself that it was only partially a lie. We'd made plans to meet up and photograph each other after school tomorrow, and I *was* excited. But I absolutely did not have any ideas. I was hoping I would be struck by inspiration, which was, I recognized, not my best-ever strategy.

My phone was quiet, and I scrolled back through our text history, which consisted mostly of us coordinating where and when we'd be meeting our other friends. He wasn't going to say anything else. He was going to do his photography reading and go to bed. The same thing I should have been doing.

I texted him, **I know it's late, but could I call you?**

He called me a few seconds later. I picked up on the first ring.

"Hi," I said.

"Hey, are you okay?"

"Yeah, I'm totally fine. I just can't sleep."

"Oh." He laughed. "Well, I'm never asleep at this time, so you're in good company."

His voice on the phone was deeper than it was in person. It made me feel simultaneously more relaxed and more awake.

I drew looping figure eights on the back of my math

homework while I tried to figure out an excuse for calling him so late at night on a Monday. I could say I had a question about development techniques. Or tell him that Claire wanted to plan a picnic this weekend. I could—

"Claire told me y'all had a college counseling meeting today," he said. "She said it was bad."

I sat back against my pillows. "It was."

"I don't envy you."

"You don't have college counseling?"

"Nothing formal like that. I like my advisor, so I've talked with her about it. But I have no idea where I want to apply, so I guess she hasn't helped much."

A wave of relief swept through me. "I don't know, either."

"Really?" He sounded surprised. "But you're so smart."

I laughed. "You're smart, too."

"Thanks, I agree. I just would've assumed you had this all figured out ages ago."

"Smart doesn't mean I'm good at planning. And remember my plans got screwed up when I got kicked out of school."

"Asked to leave, right?"

"Yeah. Asked to leave." I outlined the figure eight over and over again. I had told him the story of the dance more than once, opening it up a little more each time, giving him more details, more memories. I didn't mean to, but it was where all my stories from home and some of my stories from here inevitably led. Before and after, my parents and Oma, the reason for my curfew, why I always followed the rules in Virginia. Jess, Jess, Jess.

"Do you ever regret it?" he asked quietly.

I stopped drawing. On my bedside table, my lamp glowed, and outside my window, the night was soft and dark. It felt like everything should be dark. My phone sandwiched between my shoulder and cheek, I stacked my homework and set it gently on the floor, and on the other end of the line, Sam waited in silence. I turned off the light and sat back against the headboard, my eyes adjusting.

"I can't regret that one night without regretting all of it," I answered finally. "Of course I regret getting drunk that one particular night. I wish we hadn't. But I also wish that Jess and I had stood in separate stalls. Or that Mary Elizabeth hadn't walked in when she did. Obviously, we were going to drink; we always did for dances. It was tradition. So to regret that…" I struggled to explain.

"I get it," he said.

"Do you?"

"I think so."

"It feels inevitable," I said. "It all feels inevitable."

I snuggled under my blanket, pulling the covers up to my chin and turning to face the wall. It had to be past midnight now. Tomorrow already.

"What are your greatest regrets?" I asked him. I had meant to say it like a joke, to lighten the tone of the conversation and make him laugh—not to really ask him. But it came out soft and tentative, and I couldn't take it back.

"I don't have anything like that," he said. "Nothing that's ever gone really wrong for me."

"Something less serious, then," which is what I had been going for in the first place.

He sighed, but when he spoke, I could hear the smile in his voice. "This is embarrassing on a number of levels."

"You don't have to tell me."

"No, I should. But you have to promise not to tell Kitty and Claire." He sighed again. "Well, Claire already knows. And actually, Kitty probably does, too. But promise not to talk about it with them."

"Cross my heart."

"So I got into photography in middle school, right? Not film at first, just digital. My uncle—Claire's dad, actually—gave me a DSLR for my bar mitzvah. I spent all my free time photographing everything and everyone around me. I was incredibly annoying, I'm sure."

"Were any of them good photos?"

"Absolutely not." He laughed a little. "But I didn't know it at the time. In fact, the summer before ninth grade, I convinced myself that they were good enough to sell. So I spent all my savings getting my favorite ones printed and framed, and then I went around to every restaurant and art gallery in town, asking them if they would hang my photos."

I winced. "Oh no."

"Oh yes. I had no shame. And it paid off, because finally this café called Latte Love agreed to hang them. Mostly around the bathrooms, some in the seating area."

"Oh *no*."

"Unfortunately, yes."

"They were just displaying them?"

"Not just displaying. Selling. In theory."

"Sam."

"I priced them at two hundred fifty dollars apiece."

"*Sam.*"

"You'll be shocked to learn that not a single one sold."

I was shaking with giggles, trying to keep them out of my voice. "So if I show up at Latte Love, can I still see them?"

"You cannot, because Latte Love went bankrupt four months later."

"Wait. Let me get this straight." I took a deep breath to still my laughter. "Your art was so bad that it put a coffee shop out of business?"

"I like to tell myself that it wasn't a hundred percent my fault. Turns out they hadn't been making a profit in months. I can't imagine my photos were the straw that broke the camel's back. But still."

"So where are they now? Hidden in the garage? Or are some of them hanging up in your house?" I had never been to his house, and all of a sudden, I was intensely curious about what it was like. I had seen Kitty's and Claire's homes, at least the ones they had here. What *was* hanging on his walls?

"Oh, I never got them back."

I made an incoherent sound of indignation, both for him and for myself. I wanted to see these pictures.

"I showed up one day, and someone had put a padlock on the

door. I could see them inside, but I couldn't get to them. I tried calling the owner about thirty times. He never picked up. And then a few weeks later, I was walking by, and the whole place was cleaned out." He sighed again. "So, June, that is my greatest regret."

"Which part?"

"Pretty much every part. Except not getting the photos back. I lost hundreds of dollars, but that's a small price to pay for no one ever having to see them again. They were bad art."

"I mean, what is good art?"

"Definitely not those."

We stayed on the phone in companionable silence for a long minute. It had been ages since I'd talked on the phone like this— late, in the dark, with an easy intimacy borne of that lateness and darkness. I used to talk to Jess like this all the time. When had we stopped?

"Anyway," Sam said, "I should go to bed."

"You mean read your photo chapters."

"Oh, right. Yeah. Those."

I ran my fingertip along the cool windowsill. "Thanks for calling, Sam."

"Thanks for talking, June."

"Good night."

"Good night."

I hung up first. Outside, a car drove across the bridge, cutting a lonely path of light above the water, hurtling toward some late-night adventure, or else coming home.

seventeen

The next day, I stood outside the arts building after school, fidgeting with my camera strap while telling myself that there was nothing to be nervous about. Last night's conversation felt dreamy and indistinct, blurry at the edges, and I had woken up thinking I might have imagined it. But at lunch, Sam had greeted Claire by announcing, "I told June my greatest secret."

Claire clapped her hands over her mouth. "The Latte Love story?"

"Correct."

"Wait, what's the Latte Love story?" Kitty looked bemused.

Sam rounded on Claire. "You didn't tell her? I thought you told her everything!"

"It was your *greatest secret*! Of course I didn't tell her! What kind of cousin do you think I am?"

So then he'd had to tell the whole story again, and I knew that I hadn't made it up.

Now, though, Sam was walking across the grass to meet me so we could photograph each other, and I still had no ideas for his portrait. I badly wanted to impress him, even as I knew it was unnecessary. He liked my work already—he had told me a hundred times. As he got closer, I resolved to relax. I would come up with something.

Sam hugged me lightly when he reached me, both of us taking care not to crush our cameras between our bodies.

"Good to see you," he said. His smile was big and genuine.

"You too."

"Do you wanna do me first?"

I arched my eyebrows, and he flushed. "Okay, that's not what I—"

I laughed, his discomfort making me feel more at ease. "You take your picture of me first. You said you had ideas, right?"

"Yeah, I narrowed it down." We set off across the grass, him leading me toward Oma's condo.

"So, tell me more about these Latte Love photos," I said. He winced. "We've been over the story, but I want the aesthetic details."

"Do I have to?"

"Paint me a word picture."

"Oh God. Okay. There was this one photo where I had taken a picture of my dad mowing the backyard just as it had started raining, and I used this free editing app to make it so that the

226

lawnmower was the only thing in color and everything else was black and white, so—"

"Why would you do that?"

"Well, because I thought it looked cool and also because it was like the mower was cutting down life—you know, the grass—while the water was *giving* life, so the mower being red symbolized hell…"

He entertained me all the way to the condo with stories of his middle school photos. I expected us to cut into town, but instead, he stopped in the parking lot. I stood two steps behind him, looking around. It was not a photogenic place. The lot was half full of cars, the walls surrounding the courtyard were tall but plain, and the condo building itself, while impressive in scale, was not architecturally interesting. Which could only mean he wanted to take the picture inside.

"I didn't tell Oma you were coming over," I said. "Want me to text her?"

He shook his head. "I want to do the portrait out here."

"Out where?"

"Stand over there, by the entrance. But leave your stuff here."

"You sure? There are lots of prettier places."

"Yes."

"Okay, as long as you don't give me the lawnmower treatment."

After piling my backpack and camera on the ground beside him, I walked over to the gates, conscious of his eyes on me. When I reached the closed gates, I turned around and called, "What now?"

He yelled something back, but it was windy, and I couldn't hear him. I shook my head and pointed to my ears, and he jogged over, camera bouncing against his chest.

"Center yourself," he said.

"Like in meditation?"

"No, like—" He reached out to touch my shoulders, then paused. "May I?"

I nodded. He took both my shoulders in his hands and moved me gently a few steps to the right so my back was against the place where the two halves of the gate met. He rotated me a few degrees to the left, then stepped back, stepped closer, rotated me again.

"Turn your face toward me," he murmured. We were very near to each other. If he had taken one more half step forward, if I had tilted my chin up, if he had angled his head down—

"Okay," he said. "Like that. You can relax into it. You don't have to stay so tense." He turned to jog back to where he had been standing, and I exhaled. I had been holding my breath.

Back in place, he raised his camera to his eye, gave me a thumbs-up, and—I assume—took several photographs. I saw him turn the camera to take a vertically oriented shot, so there were at least two. I looked away from the camera, then back at it. While I watched him shoot, the idea for my picture of him coalesced into being.

When he put down his camera and gave me a second thumbs-up, he started walking toward me, and I yelled, "Stop!" I jogged over before he could get much farther.

"Stay right there," I said breathlessly when I got within speaking distance. Lord, my cardio was bad. I really needed to take Kitty up on her offer to go running sometime. "Stand just like you were, with your camera up to your face."

He considered for a moment, then nodded. "Okay."

I grabbed my things from the ground and ran back to my place by the gates. As I had requested, he put his camera up to his eye.

When I looked through the viewfinder, it was as I had hoped. Sam was the only person in the scene, standing in the middle of the road with the hill toward town rising up behind him. His camera obscured his face, as it had for so much of the time I had known him. He looked like a gatekeeper or a guide, a sphinx to which you had to give your face in a photo. Your soul, if you believed the saying. But unlike the creatures from myths, he did not look malevolent. With his curly hair falling over his forehead, he just looked like a boy with a camera.

"Was that your idea the whole time?" he asked me when I had gotten back to him.

"Alas, no. I'm happy with it, though."

"Well, congratulations on completing another part of this enormous project," he said. "Celebratory hug?"

I smiled. "Yes, please."

This time, he slung his camera around his back before opening his arms, and I did the same before I stepped into them. Seconds passed as he held me. I treasured the feeling of his T-shirt against my cheek. So close, again. If I looked up, and if he looked down. Another second, two. Surely this was longer than a hug between friends was supposed to last. I pulled back a fraction of an inch and—

He let me go, stepped back. He cleared his throat, pulled his camera back around so it rested on his chest where I had a moment before.

I found my voice. "I told Oma I'd help with dinner," I said.

"Yeah, I'm gonna go develop this film."

"See you tomorrow?"

"Yeah. See you." He smiled again before turning and leaving, and the whole way through the courtyard and up the stairs to Oma's, I wondered if I had imagined the eagerness in that smile, or whether it had really been there for me.

———

"I will have the biscuits and gravy, please," Kitty said.

"And I'll get the grilled cheese and tomato soup," I said, passing both our menus back to the waiter.

Kitty leaned back in the booth across from me, smiling blissfully as he walked away. Outside Harold's, the sky was just starting to deepen into a sunset shade of blue. "God, I love this place."

"Why do you always get breakfast food? They have so much other good stuff."

She shrugged. "Best meal of the day. No reason to mess with something perfect. And besides, I always get something different off the breakfast menu."

She looked out the window at something, her mouth turned

up a little at the edges, and I quickly raised my camera and snapped a photo. She turned back to me and gave me an exaggerated frown.

"There was a very good dog walking by," she said severely. "You can't take advantage of my seeing a good dog."

"You said I could take pictures tonight," I protested, and she sighed.

"You're sure this is the right place? You couldn't take a photo of…I don't know…me running? From a distance?"

"This is the right place." She rolled her eyes, but she smiled, too, and I took another quick photo. Harold's was the first place we'd spent time together outside school, and though Claire and Sam loved this place just as much as she did, I associated it the most with Kitty. Her enthusiasm about their coffee and her deep love of breakfast didn't hurt. Still, as much as she adored Harold's, she did not adore having her picture taken, and I was glad she had let me invite her out.

"Are you sure it's okay that you're missing the seder at Sam's?" I asked.

"Oh yeah." Kitty took a sip of water. "Passover is obviously important to Sam and his core family, but for Claire, it's not as big a deal. She wasn't really raised religious. I know she feels awkward about going to religious events with Sam's family sometimes. So I think my being there might be more weird than good for her."

"Got it," I said, though I didn't, not really. Claire had never talked to me about the way her family practiced—or didn't practice—Judaism, and coming from a family of only-on-Christmas Episcopalians, I didn't have a lot of experience with religion myself.

"Also," Kitty added, "she didn't invite me until this morning."

"Okay, that tracks."

Our food arrived, and Kitty and I shuffled containers of ketchup and glasses of water to make way for our enormous plates. My so-called cup of tomato soup was at least a bowl and possibly a tureen.

Kitty looked down at her plate with a tenderness that might have been sweet if it hadn't been directed at a plate of biscuits. I very slowly raised my camera. At the sound of the shutter, she looked up at me sharply.

"You are not taking photos of me eating," she said. "There, I draw the line."

"That was the last one, I promise." I pulled off my camera strap and tucked the whole thing into my bag at my feet, raising my hands in surrender. "See?"

"Okay," she said, mollified. "As long as I can eat in peace."

"Wouldn't dream of stopping you."

We ate. As always, the food was perfect. My grilled cheese was crisp and buttery, and the tomato soup was wonderfully rich, thickened with more cream and butter than I cared to imagine. I passed Kitty a bite of my sandwich and snagged a forkful of gravy-drenched biscuit. Outside, the sky slowly darkened; inside, yellow walls met red tables, and fake sunflowers perched cheerfully in mason jars next to the salt and pepper shakers. The tables around us buzzed in conversation, but while we ate, we were quiet.

After several minutes, it still looked as if we hadn't made a dent in our plates. Kitty sighed and sat back in her chair, hand on her belly like a cartoon of satisfaction.

"This is such good food," she said. I nodded, my mouth too full of soup to answer properly. "You ready for AP tests?"

I sat back, too, and grimaced. "I don't have to be ready yet. We still have ten days."

"Spoken like a girl who's not ready."

"I'm ready, I guess. Oma made me write a study plan a week ago. There's nothing in particular I'm worried about. But I have four APs this year, and last year, I only had three. Plus, switching schools, I don't know if anything got lost in transition." I took a bite of my sandwich. "What about you?"

"Yeah, I feel okay. I only have three, thank God, and they're all subjects I'm good at. I have a lot of brushing up to do in history, but that's just memorization. It's just so much pressure, you know? Especially since we have to take the SATs at the same time."

"The worst fucking timing," I said gloomily.

Kitty nodded. "The worst."

"Maybe college admissions boards will take that into account?"

Kitty made a noise that was half cough, half laugh. "Sure. Yeah. Let's dream that."

Between the mandatory counseling sessions and our

looming tests, every conversation this month inevitably turned to college—not just between me and Kitty or Claire but among all the junior girls at St. Anne's. Kitty hadn't told me much about her counseling session, only that it hadn't been helpful. When I'd asked her where she thought she would apply, she told me she wasn't sure. She'd quickly asked me the same questions back and listened when I'd admitted my confusions and fears. Overall, though, it didn't seem to be her favorite subject, so I was trying to figure out a way to pivot to a new topic when she spoke up.

"I wish we could just stay here," she said. She played with the silver bracelet she always wore, circling it around her wrist.

"Harold's won't kick us out," I said. I craned my neck to look at our waiter, who was occupied on the other side of the room. "They like to move tables fast, but we still have food in front of us."

She smiled at her hands. "I don't mean *here*. I mean, broadly, the here and now. School, spring, junior year. It feels like... everything is in its right place, you know?"

"Yes." And I did, even if I didn't feel exactly the same way all the time. For me, it wasn't so easy. Even on my happiest days in Virginia—and I was happy, sometimes overwhelmingly so—home tugged at me, making it hard to be completely present. Almost every night, I was on the phone with someone. The twins were doing great without me. My parents still acted suspicious when I said I was doing well. And there was Jess. Some days, I thought of her barely at all, or with platonic fondness, and felt silly for thinking I loved her any other way. Other days, I woke up aching, having dreamed of her, a blur of laughter and soft skin and kisses in the pink flannel sheets of her bed. Those days made me honest with myself: I couldn't possibly be straight, nor could I continue being happy as only her friend.

But I knew what Kitty was saying, too. There were moments in the gazebo, with her and Claire and Sam, when we were all giggling at stupid jokes and drinking coffee—iced coffee, now that it was warm! And she'd be leaning against Claire, Claire's hair curling in the wind, and Sam and I would be sitting close together, and he would look at me as if he thought no one else saw how he looked at me, as if I were something to look at. Our cameras were forgotten in our bags. And even Jess was forgotten, and my parents, and our books lay forgotten on the ground. And I would squint out at the river, the sun shining down on it and all of us, and the whole world would glitter.

In those moments, I wanted to stay in the here and now and never leave.

I snapped back to myself, to Kitty sitting across from me, looking sad despite talking about happiness. "Aren't you excited, though?"

"About what?"

"About..." I shrugged. "College. I know the counseling was bullshit, but you have great grades. You'll definitely get in somewhere good. You'll probably get scholarships. Aren't you looking forward to not having the school set your curfew anymore? Not having to sign out every time you leave campus? And more interesting classes that you actually get to choose?"

She rolled her eyes. "Sure. That all sounds great."

I was taken aback by her cynicism. "I'm sorry," I said, not knowing entirely what I was apologizing for. "I didn't mean…"

"No, I'm sorry. That does sound great. It's just…" She spread her hands on the table in front of us. "I don't know what's gonna happen with me and Claire."

Her words hung in the air, surrounded by the hum of conversations in Harold's—other people's words, other people's problems and victories and mundane lives. I got the sense that she had been waiting to say those words for a long time.

"Oh," I said.

"I know it's stupid," she said in a rush. "I know you're not supposed to take things like that into consideration when you're thinking about your future. But Claire is my first girlfriend. I love her so much. Like—*so much*. Even though she drives me up the wall sometimes. I don't know where I'd be without her. I don't talk to that many people, you know? I don't make friends easily. She makes it easy for me. She takes care of me." Kitty looked at me across the table intently, as if trying to make me understand.

"I know," I said. I searched for adequate words and came up empty. "It's not stupid. It's really hard. I'm sorry."

"It's fine," she said quietly. She took her hands off the table and folded them in her lap. "Who knows? Maybe we'll end up at the same place."

"Or close together."

"Yeah."

"And if not, there's always long distance."

I was trying to be helpful, but it was clear that had not been the right thing to say.

"I hate talking on the phone," Kitty said. "I don't think that would work."

"You could get better," I said.

Her face softened. "Yeah. I guess if the only way to stay with her is to talk on the phone more, I could do that." She picked up her fork again and ate a few more bites of biscuit. I nibbled at my grilled cheese, just to have something to do with my hands.

I looked across at Kitty carefully, trying to judge if she had more to say. I wanted to talk to her about something else, and I hadn't wanted to bring it up via text or with the others around. She caught my eye and smiled.

"You don't have to worry. I'm fine," she said. "It's just what comes up for me whenever I think about the future. What about you? How are you? What's going on?"

"I think you were right," I said.

"Not surprised. About what?"

"I think I'm definitely bisexual," I said. It was the first time I had said it aloud, as something *I* thought, and it felt strange on my tongue, like a food I had never eaten.

"Cool," Kitty said. "Welcome to not being straight."

"Thanks, I guess?"

"You're welcome." She smiled, really big this time, and I laughed in relief. I took a deep breath and released it, feeling a little less tightness around my chest.

"Have you told Jess?" she asked me, and immediately, there it was back again, that familiar constriction.

I shook my head. "No. But I kissed her." I swallowed hard at the memory.

Kitty sat up straight. "Oh wow." She looked at my face, which must have been dismal. "Oh no. It went badly?"

"We were drunk," I said. A flicker of judgment crossed Kitty's face, but she didn't say anything. "I played it off the next day. So in a way, I did the exact opposite of telling her. Oh, and she confirmed that she was straight, by the way, because it turns out she's also kissed this other friend of hers."

Kitty furrowed her brow. "So she's kissed multiple girls, and that means she's straight?"

"It doesn't mean anything. That's what she said."

Kitty shook her head. "Well, okay, I guess we can set that aside. But she's still definitely the reason you're realizing this?"

"Arguably, you're the reason I'm realizing this," I said as I took a spoon of soup, and when I looked up, I saw alarm in her eyes that nearly made me spit out my food. "No, God, not what I meant. I just mean you're the first person who talked to me about it."

"Oh," she said, her shoulders slumping. "Thank goodness. I don't know what I would've done if you were trying to involve me in a love triangle. Probably just thrown myself into the river headfirst."

"No, to answer your original question," I said, wiping my face to make sure no stray soup had found its way onto my cheeks, "Jess is the reason. But also…"

Kitty arched her eyebrows. "Yes?"

I lost all the bravery I had summoned for this conversation. I didn't even know what I wanted out of it, anyway. "Never mind. It's nothing."

"Were you going to tell me you're into Sam?"

I looked at her, feeling a guilt I wasn't sure I'd earned, and she laughed.

"It is obvious," she said. "It is in fact the most obvious thing I have ever seen. Closely followed by how obvious it was that you were into Jess when I first met you. You are not a closed book, June."

"I don't—I just—*ugh*," I finished. I tried again. "I don't want to be a cliché."

"It's no different than if you were straight and into two guys." Kitty shrugged. "Except maybe some assholes will look at you differently. But you don't want to hear from them anyway. And besides, I don't think you're planning on trying to date both of them at once, right? It'd be fine if all three of you were into it, but..."

I shuddered at the thought. If anything could make this whole situation more confusing, it would be that. "No. Also, I'm currently not dating either of them. Jess both has a boyfriend and is straight as far as I know, and Sam..."

"Sam what?"

"Don't you think Claire would be mad?" It had been weighing on me for weeks. Sam was her cousin, her family, her best friend in the world—as close to a brother as she had. I was pretty sure it was a friendship rule that you weren't supposed to date your friends' brothers.

Kitty looked like she was trying very hard not to laugh. "Are you kidding me? Absolutely not. She'd probably throw a parade."

I shifted in my seat. "Are you sure?"

"Yes. One hundred percent. She's seen the way you two are together."

"Have you talked about it?"

"No," Kitty admitted, "but she's not blind. I promise you, she'd be fine with it."

I nodded. I felt a little better. But… "I shouldn't just be with him because he's here and single and Jess isn't. That's not right."

At that, Kitty nodded. "No. That's not fair."

I looked down at my plate, feeling nothing short of miserable. Kitty's hand reached through the maze of plates and cups and came into my field of view. I grabbed it briefly and squeezed. Across the table from me, her eyes were gentle.

"You're doing fine. You know that? You're doing great."

"*We're* doing fine," I corrected. "We're both doing great. You and Claire will figure it out." A shadow passed over her face again. "And if you don't, you'll still be okay."

She sighed and withdrew her hand. "You're right," she said. "But it can still suck, right?"

"Yes. It can still suck."

We ordered lemon meringue pie to split for dessert, and when it came, the lemon portion was as thick as my forearm, the meringue as tall as my head. Kitty played hide-and-seek behind it, ducking her head out from behind the mountain of meringue, and she granted me an exception to take one more picture of her eyes peeking over the top of the pie.

We ate it all, every flake of crust and sticky glob of Day-Glo lemon. In the end, the only thing left separating us was the clean and shining dish.

eighteen

The first two weeks of May passed in a haze of standardized testing. The first Saturday was the SAT, which was held at the public school where Sam went; Oma dropped me off with Claire and Kitty in the morning and took us all to lunch after. I had Sunday to study for my AP Spanish exam on Monday, and then a few days until AP U.S. History. The following week was AP English, which by that time felt like a nice break in the action, and then finally AP Econ. When I closed my eyes, I saw empty ovals of questions waiting to be answered.

The world narrowed: study, sleep, eat, take test, discuss test, repeat. My AP teachers offered early-morning study sessions with coffee-and-donut bribes, and girls showed up in their pajamas, yawning and hauling backpacks full of notes. My non-AP teachers relaxed their homework demands. Oma upped her cooking game and made bracing dinners each night: chicken piccata, sweet potato chili, steak and potatoes. Fortunately, with each test, another class period opened up to become a study hall. By the time the tests were done, my only remaining classes would be precalc, physics, and photography.

Despite the grueling schedule, I felt pretty good. The entire eleventh grade was singularly focused on the same tests, and that helped, along with the consistent routine Oma made sure I kept. My conversations with my siblings were a welcome break as well—Candace's musical had been the night of the SAT, so I hadn't been able to go, but she showed me about a hundred videos, all of which I watched and rewatched when I was stressed. But there was one other thing that made it bearable, easier, that propelled me forward through each study period and multihour test. The weekend after my tests were complete, Jess would visit me.

When I got the text, I yelped so loudly that Oma and Ellie both ran into my room. As Oma asked if I was all right, I showed her the phone, wordless. **COMING YOUR WAY MAY 18 BABYYYY**, read the message from Jess, to which I had already responded with a billion exclamation points.

I had never expected a visit. Jess had her license and her own car, but her parents never would've allowed her to take such a road trip by herself. But her mom was going to DC for a weekend conference, and Jess had convinced her to drop her off with me on the way.

She had not, of course, cleared this with Oma. That was up to me. It took most of a day—cajoling, pleading, promising, calling my parents and passing the phone back and forth between me and Oma—for us to finally settle on a plan. Jess would be allowed to visit. She would sleep on the pullout couch in the living room. We would not leave the condo after she arrived on Friday night, and on Saturday, if we went out, we would be back by nine. We would not be loud or rude or cause any kind of trouble. We would not sneak out. We would not drink.

It was easy to agree to these rules; they were obvious and straightforward. Besides, it wasn't like we would have myriad opportunities to misbehave. In Virginia, I had never been invited to a party like the ones Jess and I went to back home. (I'm sure they existed somewhere, but I didn't know who hosted them or where they would be.) There was no alcohol in Oma's house, and Sam, Kitty, and Claire weren't exactly delinquents.

When I called Jess to tell her yes, I could hear her beaming over the phone. "I never doubted you, my love," she said. I felt sunbeams shining in my rib cage, threatening to split me apart with their light.

———

My last test was on Thursday. On Friday, I spent most of the day lounging on the lawn with Claire and Kitty, ostensibly finishing my math and physics homework.

"Jess will probably want to sleep in on Saturday," I said as I scribbled an answer to a word problem, "so I don't think we should meet at Harold's until 12:30. That's still okay with y'all?"

"For the hundredth time, yes," Kitty said, not unkindly.

"I'm just making sure." I took a deep breath. "And then we can walk around town a little, maybe?"

"Still sounds good to me," Claire said.

"Okay. Cool. And then we can play it by ear until dinner. I just have to find some time in there to take Jess's portrait—"

"Too much uncertainty for me, sorry," Kitty chimed in.

"Really? Because I could plan something more structured, I just thought…" I trailed off when I saw her grinning.

"I am *kidding*, June. It's just a weekend. Relax."

"I just want to make the most of it, that's all," I said. I looked at the worksheet in front of me and shook my head, shoving it back into my backpack. I lay back instead, looking up at the crisp blue sky, white clouds bursting like flowers. "I wasn't expecting her to visit. I want to make sure she has a good time."

"It's just a weekend," Kitty repeated.

"I'm excited to meet her," Claire said. She set aside her physics book and lay down beside me, settling in the grass. "I've heard so much about her, I feel like I know her already."

"She's excited to meet you, too," I said, though I was not entirely sure if this was true. I talked to Jess about my friends all the time, but she rarely asked about them. And when I tried to line them up next to each other, it was hard to find similarities. They shared some qualities: smart, funny, prone to quick excitement. But Jess's humor had a bitter edge to it, and she scorned rules in a way I knew my friends here did not understand. These differences were the real reason I was anxious—all the planning in the world wouldn't help if Jess hated my friends or if they hated her.

And then, of course, there was the fact that I couldn't stop thinking about kissing her.

"You have to chill," Kitty said, joining me and Claire on the grass.

"Yeah," Claire said. "She's your best friend. It's going to be great."

I sat up enough to take another gulp of my coffee, watered down with melted ice cubes. She was my best friend. That made it harder.

"Overthinking never helped anyone," Kitty said.

It's going to be great. It's just a weekend. You have to chill.

I repeated their words to myself as I watched Jess's mom's car pull into the parking lot a few hours later. Jess was in the passenger seat, waving wildly.

She jumped out of the car before her mom had turned it off. "We made it!" she shrieked. "God, what a drive."

"Welcome to Virginia!" I ran over, threw my arms around her. I breathed her in, her familiar smell, and while part of me stayed just as nervous as before—maybe more so—the rest of me calmed down. This was not some strange and unknowable goddess. This was Jess, my Jess, only Jess.

Her mom got out of the car on the other side and stretched as we separated. I helped Jess grab her multiple weekend bags from the back seat, and her mom and Oma greeted each other with a businesslike handshake. They were just starting to make small talk when Jess interrupted.

"Have a good time in DC, Mom," she said, giving her mother a one-armed hug, a duffel bag slung around her other shoulder.

"It's not going to be fun. It's work," Mrs. Finn said. She looked back at Oma. "It's our annual conference, and I've been helping organize—"

"Okay, well, I want to go set down my stuff, so I'll see you Sunday," Jess interrupted again.

"See you. Be safe. Love you." Mrs. Finn raised a hand but didn't really look at Jess, and as she resumed talking to Oma, I led Jess toward the gates. Oma caught my eye with a look that said *she'd better not interrupt me that way*, and I made an expression that I hope said *she won't*, and then Jess and I were through the gates and traipsing across the courtyard, and she was sighing happily.

"This is cool," she said, looking around the courtyard and up at the balconies. "Is it all old people or what?"

"Mostly. I think there are one or two families with kids. No one my age. But school is right back there."

Jess stopped in her tracks and turned around. From this angle, we could only see the edge of campus. No one was out, but a few girls had their window shades open to show us glimpses of their dorm rooms.

"Wow," she said reverently. "Like college. I'm jealous."

"Well, I live here, with the old people," I said, feeling like I had to defend myself, though I didn't know from what. Jess started walking toward the doors again. "And the dorms have pretty strict rules. I practically had to write a petition to go to a sleepover."

Over her shoulder, Jess tossed me a look, an irreverent, biting glance I knew well. It said, *Fuck the rules. We're beyond the rules.* It was sexy and familiar and impossibly cool and completely unnecessary. I didn't know how to tell her that things worked differently here.

In Oma's condo, Jess dropped her things beside my bed and looked around my room as I stood in the doorway, picking at the hem of my shirt and waiting for her reaction. Her gaze traveled past the books she had lent me, only half of which I had read, to my pictures. As I had done more work in the darkroom, I had started to hang up discarded prints here, ones that were too dark or too bright or crooked on the page. There was a copy of the picture of Oma and Ellie I had printed before spring break, a few snapshots of my friends, a poorly composed image of the twins, and a blurry picture of Jess from that day at Ethan's house. She didn't acknowledge them.

"This is nice," she said finally. "Smaller than your old room, but nice."

"Thanks," I said. "I like it."

In the living room, she stepped onto the balcony and looked out at the river, resplendent in the sun.

"Wow," she breathed.

Her hands curled around the wrought-iron railing, her chest leaned over it a little, her hair floated around her face, her lips parted, and she looked like a sparrow, ready to burst forth into the air. Like she was meant for nothing less than flight.

———

Oma made pesto pasta and chicken for dinner while Jess and I sat on the balcony, our legs between the bars, dangling off the edge into the emptiness below. We talked for an hour, until Oma called, "Girls, dinner!"

I was expecting some conflict. When Jess was present for meals with my family, there was a tacit agreement that we would all focus on the twins; Jess and my parents barely spoke. But the twins weren't here. I could feel the tension vibrating off me as we sat down, me and Jess on one side, Oma on the other.

Oma served herself some salad from the bowl in the middle. "So, Jess," she said pleasantly, "how did the SAT go for you?"

"Good," she said. "At least I think. There was a math question that really threw me off. It was the word problem about the laundromat…"

"I had trouble with that one, too!" I had specifically called it out to Oma, and I looked at her to see if she remembered; she nodded.

"Must've been a doozy," she said. "How about APs, Jess? When was your last one?"

I'd had more than enough test talk over the last three weeks, but I didn't mind one last conversation if it would get us through dinner. Maybe it would even show Oma that Jess was serious about school, and Oma could tell my parents.

We sat at the table for longer than I would have expected. After we had said all you could say about standardized tests, we discussed the classes Jess was taking this year and the ones Oma was teaching. Jess asked thoughtful questions. If she was a little more stiff and polite than usual, Oma probably couldn't tell. I was so relieved by the time we had finished eating that I offered to do the dishes without Oma having to remind me.

"I'm assuming you don't want to watch TV with me tonight?" Oma asked as I picked up her plate.

"Nah, if it's okay with you, I think Jess and I are just gonna hang out in my room."

"As long as you don't mind if I watch the next episode without you."

"Yeah, I'll catch up later."

"Okay. I'll make up Jess's bed."

Oma made her way into the living room and turned on *Murder at the Manor*, and I heard the creak of the futon opening up. I started rinsing plates and loading the dishwasher. Jess joined me in the kitchen, hopping up on the counter next to the sink. She kicked her heels against the cabinets like a little kid.

"Jesus, I thought that dinner would never end," she said under her breath.

I looked up at her, startled. "What?" The water and the dishes in the sink, the genteel British tones filtering in from the living room—I must have misunderstood her.

"I said dinner took forever," she said, a little louder, and I let a handful of forks drop and clang, hoping against hope that Oma hadn't heard her.

"I thought it was fine," I said.

"Yeah, it was *fine*. That's just way more conversation than I expected to have to have with your grandma."

I focused on scrubbing a stubborn piece of pasta off a plate. I liked dinner with Oma. I liked talking to her. But I didn't want to argue with Jess.

"Anyway," she continued, unbothered, "when are we going out? Does your grandma go to bed early?"

My hands stilled in the sink. The water was so hot it burned. "Jess, I told you, we can't go out."

"Then what are we going to do?" She sounded impatient, but I had told her this already. I didn't know why she was acting surprised.

"I thought we would just talk. And watch TV or whatever. At home, it's not like we were going out every night. This isn't that different?" The questioning tone came up unbidden. I didn't mean to ask her approval.

As she stayed silent, I felt my resolve weakening; a rusty part of my brain started spinning, figuring out how we could sneak out and back in. If we waited until very late, and if we took off our shoes to be soft on the wooden floor, and if we took the stairs instead of the elevator...

But it would be so much more difficult than it was back home. The condo was not large, and Oma slept with her bedroom door cracked open. Plus, she knew everyone in the building. If anyone saw us, they would tell her. And on top of all that, as I'd told Jess, there really was nowhere to go. I opened my mouth to say these things, but she spoke before I could begin, the displeasure heavy in her voice.

"Fine. We'll just stay in."

I kept washing dishes, the water scalding my hands. I didn't know what to say.

After a few minutes, she jumped down from the counter-top and started drying the things that were too large for the dishwasher. "It'll be nice to just catch up," she said quietly, and I turned the water to cool.

It was—nice, I mean. Oma went to bed early, and we sat out on the balcony again in the warm night air, sipping cold mint tea and watching the reflection of the streetlights on the water. I wasn't surprised when Jess pulled out a flask and offered it to me. But I shook my head, and she, too, didn't seem surprised at my refusal.

"Suit yourself," she said, tipping it into her tea. Vodka, maybe, or gin. I didn't try to stop her. Technically, I wasn't breaking the rule I'd agreed to with Oma. I thought it was sort of a silly rule, because we wouldn't hurt anyone by getting a little drunk at a sleepover. But unlike my parents, Oma actually trusted me. I didn't want to disappoint her.

Jess and I talked for hours. Mostly, she talked. She told me about problems with Patrick—he showed up to things late, she'd seen him flirting with another girl—and a little about Ethan, things I already knew from texting with him. She told me about adventures with Ashleigh that had her giggling as she explained them but didn't sound that funny to me. She named people on the periphery whom I didn't know. She didn't bring up the things we used to talk about, big questions about our futures or books we had both read or complaints about our parents. I got caught up on all the things I didn't need to know.

She started getting tipsier and cozier, tilting her head on my shoulder and leaving her hand on my knee. But it wasn't right. I shied away from her even as I wanted to lean in.

It was late, almost midnight, when she laughed and said, "Oh my God, and then this one time at Ashleigh's house, her older sister and her girlfriend were home from college for the weekend, and they brought this rum—"

"Wait, Laura has a girlfriend?" I remembered Laura King, Ashleigh's older sister. She was two years older than us and had been well-known at Greenmont, a lacrosse star with supernaturally gorgeous hair. I felt the conversation open up to me. A possibility. A way in.

"Yeah. They've been together for, like, six months."

"That's cool."

"Anyway—"

"Do you know if she's out to her family?"

"Um…" Jess tipped her head up to the sky. My heart was racing. "Yeah, I guess. Yeah. Because she brought the girl home. She was cool. I think she was the one who got the rum. Why? Did you know Laura?"

"No. Just wondering, I guess."

"Okay." She shrugged. I could feel the moment slipping away. "Anyway—"

"Actually—"

Jess stopped. She turned her body toward me and let out a heavy sigh. "What is it?"

"I think I…um. I think Laura and I have that in common."

"What?" She was drunk, impatient.

I took a deep breath. I said, "I think I'm bisexual. It turns out."

Jess stared at me. Then she chuckled, bit her lip. "Huh," she said.

Instantly, I regretted it. I watched her face, hoping against hope that she would not connect this with the kiss in Ethan's bedroom. I wondered if the condominium board would be able to trace it back to me if I vomited over the balcony. I waited for her to speak again.

"Well," she said finally, "that's cool."

"The way you're saying that doesn't sound like it's cool," I managed.

"No, it is. It's cool. I'm glad you told me." She sighed, leaned back on her elbows, and looked at me with affection. She reached up and tousled my hair, something she only did when she was drunk. I relaxed the tiniest bit. "I just think it's funny that you move up here and make these new friends who are queer, and suddenly you realize you are, too. I just feel like, you know. You're a new woman up here."

"It has nothing to do with Kitty and Claire," I said, even though I wasn't entirely sure if that was true. I could hear the edge of panic in my voice. I took a deep, long breath. The air was warming but still crisp this time of year.

"What does it have to do with, then? Do you like someone here? I thought you were into that guy Sam, but is there a girl?"

I looked at her, stretched out there on Oma's balcony, her hair falling on her shoulders, her shirt riding up to expose a soft line of bare skin. I remembered how her lips had felt on mine, her tongue in my mouth. How our bodies fit together—that night at the dance in the stall and so many other nights, asleep in the same bed, sharing the same space. I wanted to dissolve myself inside her. To have her surround me so completely that I could feel nothing else.

"No," I said finally. "It was just something I figured out, I guess."

"Well," she said. She sat up again and squeezed my hand, smiled. "It doesn't change anything, as far as I'm concerned. You're still my best friend. You just have a larger dating pool. I mean, I'm jealous."

"Yeah." I tried to return her smile. She hadn't brought up the kiss.

She took a long sip from her teacup. "But yeah," she said, "so Laura's girlfriend had bought this rum, and we were all at Patrick's house, and his parents were out with friends..."

We talked for a while longer, and I let her voice wash over me without listening. I had told her. Part of it, at least. I should have been relieved, but relief didn't come. Instead, I just felt sad. I wished I was not so committed to following Oma's rules. I could've used some vodka.

After she finished yet another long, rambling story about her and Ashleigh, I rose, grateful for the steadiness of my feet underneath me. "I'm gonna go to bed," I said.

"Oh." Jess looked up at me, her pupils wide and dark. "Are you sure?"

"Yeah, it's just been a tiring week."

"Okay. I think I'll stay up a little bit."

"I'll wake you in the morning for brunch. We need to leave around eleven."

"Okay."

I turned to go inside, leaving her with her legs swinging off the balcony into the night. As I was about to slide the door closed, she spoke up. "I love you," she said.

I paused, looking at her, the curves of her waist and her smooth sloping shoulders and her hair brushing against her neck. The cup next to her was almost empty. "I love you, too," I said and closed the door.

nineteen

I had made the walk downtown many, many times. I never ceased to love it: quiet and still, with the streets laid out in a rough grid, I could take any number of paths to the same destination, depending on how much time I wanted to spend walking. There was the way that went by the cemetery, or the route that intersected with the wholesale bakery that sometimes gave out free samples, or the one that led past the shade tree with a bench that was good for reading.

I felt more like myself, walking alone on these narrow, familiar streets, than anywhere else. The only other times I could remember feeling so completely in my element were the long hours I used to spend with Jess at home, in the park or in our rooms, just the two of us. I assumed that bringing these things together would result in a combination as perfect as each experience was apart.

This was not the case.

"God, there is actually nothing to do in this town, is there?" Jess yawned.

"It's not like home is a thriving metropolis," I said. I was trying hard not to be annoyed. I adjusted my camera strap around my neck. The thin strap that had been comfortable over sweaters was less ideal on bare skin; I had to ask Sam where he had bought his, which was nicer, made of embroidered canvas.

"Yeah, but there's a movie theater," Jess said. "And a mall and bookstores. And you can drive everywhere. You don't have to walk."

"We have a used bookstore," I pointed out. "And there's a movie theater if you drive fifteen or twenty minutes north. But I like walking. At home, we never get to walk anywhere."

She tipped her enormous sunglasses down at me, skeptical. "But it takes so much longer."

"But it's nicer. It's…contemplative."

"Okay, well, I can be contemplative when I'm not hungover."

I bit my lip and didn't tell her that she shouldn't have been drinking in the first place. We passed the cemetery in silence. It was the kind of thing I thought she would like, but she was in such a mood, and I felt peculiarly protective of the graves.

As we turned the last corner, I saw Sam and Claire and Kitty had beat us to Harold's. The sight of them leaning against the bright blue wall, usually so wonderful, made my stomach turn. This wasn't right. This wasn't the Jess I wanted them to meet. But I couldn't turn back. They had seen us. Claire started waving.

I exchanged hugs with everyone as Jess hung back a little, and then I said, "Jess, this is Claire, Kitty, and Sam," pointing to each of them in turn. "Y'all, this is Jess!"

Blessedly, she took off her sunglasses and smiled. "Nice to meet you guys," she said. "June has told me so much about you, I feel like I know you already."

"Same here," Kitty said.

Claire was the first to step forward for a hug. The others followed, and as they did, I started to breathe a little easier. It was understandable that Jess had woken up in a bad mood. It was a little too warm out, she was a little hungover, she'd had a long car ride yesterday.

"Table for five?" Leah called from the door. I introduced her to Jess, and Leah greeted her so warmly that by the time we were all tucked into a booth, Jess and I opposite Kitty and Claire with Sam in a chair at the end, I really did feel fine.

Jess opened her menu. "So, what's good here?"

The table exploded with suggestions.

After we ordered, Claire asked how Jess and Patrick had met, and Jess smiled and told her. She asked how Claire and Kitty had met; they told their story, and Jess cooed and laughed at the right places. I asked how Claire's practice was going for her end-of-year piano recital in a few weeks. Jess and Kitty talked about a book they had both read recently, and though they disagreed—Jess had liked it, Kitty hadn't—at least it was a shared experience. We talked again about standardized tests.

There were times, of course, where Claire, Kitty, Sam, and

I were giggling over something and Jess didn't know enough context to join us. And other times, when Jess was telling a story about a party where she and Ashleigh had been wasted— moments when she brushed aside the fact that she couldn't *quite* remember what had happened—when I was aware of Kitty's eyes flicking to Claire's, laughter coming forced if it came at all.

As the others spoke, I kept sneaking glances at Jess, trying to read her expression. Last night, I had thought she was enjoying dinner, when she had apparently been bored. Was she bored now? Did she like my friends? Did she approve? She looked at her phone a lot, and I knew the others noticed. But then she smiled with a genuine joy, and I hoped the others noticed that, too.

By the time our food arrived, I was cautiously optimistic. The hardest part was over. No one was at their best when they were hungry; everything was better with pancakes. Kitty took a spoonful of her grits bowl and said, "So, Jess, has June taken her portrait of you yet?"

Jess looked at her pancakes—she had taken Claire's recommendation—and shook her head. "No, and I don't totally understand it. What's the deal with the portrait?"

"It's our final assignment for our photo class. We're supposed to take pictures of people who are meaningful to us. And obviously, you're incredibly meaningful to me." The words came out much more serious than I'd intended. Maybe because I had explained this to her at least three times over the phone. I took an enormous bite of waffles to hide my discomfort.

She rolled her eyes. "Seems fake."

I laughed; I wasn't sure what else to do. But the waffles felt like cement in my stomach. She continued.

"You can take pictures of your friends anytime. That's not a class project. Or if it is, it's the easiest project ever."

Sam had been pretty quiet, but now he spoke up. "It's more than that. We've been studying portraiture for weeks now. And it's easy to take a decent photo, but it's hard to take a really great one." The table sat in awkward silence for a moment before Sam cleared his throat. "June is an awesome photographer. I don't know if she's showed you any of her stuff, but..."

"I saw some last night," Jess said. There was a tightness in her voice. "They're cool. I guess I just don't get it."

"Don't get what?" Sam asked.

Jess moved some food around on her plate with her fork. "The point. I mean, anyone can take a photo. I don't get why you would want to spend hours and hours in the darkroom, or whatever, to get the same exact thing you can have with your phone immediately."

"It's not a big deal," I said.

Sam looked at me sharply. "It is a big deal," he said. "You're really proud of this work. You've been spending a ton of time on it."

"Yeah," I murmured. "I guess." I stared at my plate, at the elaborate swirls of strawberries and cream melting into the waffle squares. I didn't want to look at anyone else. I expected Sam or Jess to say something, but when I glanced up, they were studiously avoiding each other's eyes. The silence hung in the air for a long, long time.

"More coffee?" Leah swung by our table. I pulled myself together to hold out my cup for a refill.

"June, did Sam and I tell you about the matzo incident at Passover a few weeks ago?" Claire asked, helping herself to some syrup. "It involved a squirrel."

I loved Claire infinitely in that moment. "No. Please explain."

"I honestly think it wouldn't have been that big a deal if it hadn't gotten inside the house," Sam said.

"But it *did* get inside the house, didn't it?"

I listened to their story and ate my waffles. But Jess was silent for the rest of the meal. I felt the distance between us growing greater, inches expanding into miles. I saw the way Sam and Kitty and Claire looked at me between sentences and knew that my attempt to appear relaxed was not working.

We were supposed to walk around town after lunch. I was hoping to take Jess to a park I liked and show her some of the weird old magazines in the antique stores. Then, I was going to show her the campus: the dorms and the art building and Oma's classroom.

Now, as she sat silently beside me, none of that seemed viable.

After we paid, I cleared my throat. "I think Jess and I are gonna head back to the condo," I said. Though everyone had known the original plan, no one objected. I didn't mention dinner, either; we had talked about them coming over to Oma's to cook, but now I wasn't sure.

"Sorry if I was a downer," Jess said, the first words she had spoken in ages. "I'm just super hungover."

The silence that followed made me want to disappear. Was I imagining it, or were the others avoiding my eyes?

"We'll see you later," Kitty said noncommittally as we all got up from the booth. "It was great to meet you, Jess."

"You too," Jess said. We exchanged hugs. I didn't linger. I wanted desperately to be away from Harold's, away from my friends, away from all the indefinable awkwardness that had eclipsed what was supposed to be a nice meal.

Jess and I walked without talking for a while. I kept going over the conversation in my head, trying to figure out why things had gone wrong, until I started second-guessing that anything had gone wrong at all. Maybe I was too sensitive; maybe she really was just tired.

"Are you okay?" I ventured after a few minutes.

She sighed. "I'm fine."

And I knew I wasn't imagining it.

We passed the soccer field, the grass lush and overgrown in the green chaos of spring. We passed the bakery with the old wooden table and chairs set out in front, as if waiting for a couple to sit down and have coffee. We passed my favorite of the many churches, its whitewashed walls shining in the sun, its red doors flung open to the air. I wanted so badly for her to see these things like I did, their astonishing ordinary beauty. But she kept her sunglasses on and looked at the ground or at her phone as she walked.

"What's wrong?" I asked.

"Nothing," she said.

More silence.

Without a solid plan for her portrait, I had been hoping to take a picture of her somewhere on this walk. In many ways, it was not unlike the time we used to spend together at home: alone and outside. But I wasn't seeing any locations that inspired me. I was preparing to give up and snap a picture at home when we passed by the elementary school and its playground.

"Jess, look." I pointed to the empty swing set.

"Yeah, what?"

"It's like the park at home." The setting was different, but the swing set was the same, blue metal posts and two faded red rubber seats. "Could I take a picture of you there?"

She was silent for a moment, her jaw set. "Okay," she said finally.

"Cool!" I was hoping some forced cheerfulness would make a dent in her mood. We walked around the wire fence until we came to an unlocked gate. I gestured Jess toward the swing set and held my camera up to my eye, adjusting the focus. Through the viewfinder, she moved listlessly, trailing her fingers across the chains. I snapped a shot; she turned.

"I wasn't ready," she said. "That's not fair."

"It was just a test shot," I said, setting the camera down on my chest. I tried to smile at her. "I'll make you look good, I promise. Just sit down on the swing, and I'll find the right angle."

She sat, crossed her ankles, and plastered a smile on her face.

"It's not a school photo," I said. "You don't need to smile like that."

The smile dropped as suddenly as it had come on. "Okay."

"Just look natural," I said, but I could hear how unnatural that sounded. Her expression didn't change at all. I tried to think about what had worked with other people. "Think about something nice. Something fun we did together. Like..." I racked my brain for examples. The sun was full in the sky, and sweat gathered in the small of my back.

"Like remember when we were at the pool last summer and the ice cream truck came and you got the guy to give us free ice cream sandwiches? Because you told him we were sisters and we weren't allowed to have ice cream at home?" The foamy vanilla had oozed out from between the chocolate shells and melted down our arms. Jess was remembering, too; I could see it in the way her lips curved, as if she was trying to tamp down her smile but couldn't quite.

"I was very convincing," she said.

"I think it was your tits in that bikini that were convincing," I said, and she laughed big, and I snapped.

Her smile disappeared again. I was still holding the camera to my eye, and I faltered, seeing her expressionless face through the viewfinder, not sure if we were continuing or not. Her eyes were hidden behind her sunglasses.

"Did you get what you wanted?" Jess asked.

"Yeah, I think that one was good. But we can take more." I had envisioned—hoped for—a whole photo shoot, enough so I could bring her prints of herself when I came home for the summer.

"If you got what you needed, let's go home," she said in a voice that brooked no disagreement. She got up and turned, and though I knew she wouldn't like it, I took one more picture of her like that: the swing set in the foreground, her ponytail swinging, the back of her walking away.

———

When we got back to the condo, Ellie was there, but Oma was gone—working with the Garden Club, or visiting Nadine. Jess asked if she could nap in my room, where she could close the blinds to shut out the sunlight, and I said yes. I almost asked how late she had stayed up last night, but I didn't think there was much point.

I folded laundry and washed some dishes that I had left to soak the previous night. I opened and then closed my computer; I had no homework.

It was the first weekend after testing was done, the lawns of St. Anne's were busy and happy, and if Jess hadn't been here, I would've gone down there and found Claire and Kitty or just read a book by myself, enjoying the activity around me. Or maybe I would've gone to the arts building to keep working on my photo project, which I was behind on, thanks to the chaos of the last two weeks. But I had not planned to do any of those things. Jess was here for a precious thirty-six hours, and I had planned to spend all of them with her. Instead, she was alone in a dark room, passed out.

I texted my group chat: **Jess still isn't feeling well. I think I need to cancel dinner tonight—so so sorry.**

The response came immediately from each of them: **don't be!** from Claire, **totally get it** from Kitty, **no worries** from Sam. I looked sadly at the screen. I had asked Oma to buy all the ingredients for a rice-and-vegetables dish that Claire had made us in the dorm kitchen, and now they'd sit there unused.

Kitty texted me separately: **everything ok?**

I replied, **who knows!!!!!!!!** to which she said **love you v much, here if you want to talk,** but I did not. I didn't know what I wanted. I picked up a novel I had started a few weeks ago, but I couldn't get into it. After twenty minutes of trying, I turned on the TV to find a *Law & Order* marathon. I got a glass of lemonade and sat down with it. I picked up my phone to call Oma and see where she was, but then I set it down again. My Saturday was ruined, but hers didn't have to be.

Two episodes later, my bedroom door opened and Jess came out, wearing a big T-shirt and tiny sleep shorts and looking tired but not unhappy. She glanced at me on the couch, went into the kitchen, and returned with a glass of water.

"Feeling better?" I asked.

"Yeah. Sorry for being so boring."

"You're never boring," I said. She grinned at me and raised her glass like a toast. I raised my lemonade to match her. I felt the instinctive desire to reach out and touch her—her shoulder, her thigh—and scooted away, into my corner of the couch.

We made it through half of another episode before Jess

checked the time on her phone and asked, "What're we doing for dinner?"

"Up to you," I said, trying hard to sound casual.

"Weren't your friends going to come over?"

"They were, but I canceled."

She didn't say anything for a long time, long enough that a few scenes passed and I thought she had accepted what I said. But then she spoke up. "Why?"

I shrugged. "It just seemed like you didn't like them that much."

"I liked them fine."

I wasn't sure what to say. I said, "I'm sorry," though I knew there was nothing to be sorry about. But it seemed to prompt her, because she spoke up again.

"They're fine," she said dismissively. "I don't have anything in common with them, but they're fine." She paused as if deciding whether or not to continue and then plowed ahead. "What I don't like is who *you've* become because of them."

I looked at her without understanding, the TV show forgotten.

"Like, where did this whole photography thing come from? You were never that artsy at home. At first, I thought it was just an easy class, but now it's this huge part of your life, and I don't get it. And I saw how judgmental they were when I said I was hungover. Which is fine. I don't give a fuck what they think. But I felt like you were judging me, too."

"I wasn't—"

"And you like *walking*? What does it even mean to *like walking*? You're living in the most boring town in America, and you love it. Before I got here, you lectured me about the rules over and over. You sounded like your mother." The words were spilling out of her, as if she had been tipped over and could not be set straight. Her cheeks were flushed, her eyes hard and determined. "You're different now. Even the way you talk is different. You're not fun anymore."

I looked away from her, back to the TV, and focused on breathing. In. Out. In. On-screen, a girl was crying; justice had not been served. I braced myself for Jess to keep talking, keep striking the tender spots where bruises were already forming under my skin. But a minute passed, two, and she didn't say anything else. Inside my head was white noise.

I tried to line up my thoughts to form a coherent argument. *Jess, I'm allowed to have new hobbies. I still like drinking with you. I have always liked walking. I told you about the rules because I love Oma and I don't want her to be angry at me. I can be different and still be myself.*

Or: *Jess, that was really mean.*

Or, somehow: *Jess, I am in love with you.*

Instead, what came out of my mouth was, "You're right. I'm sorry."

And a part of me believed it.

Jess muttered, "No, I'm sorry," under her breath.

My phone buzzed a few minutes later, with Oma telling me she was staying at Nadine's for dinner. So she missed me and Jess watching TV for the rest of the night, not talking, and she didn't get to enjoy any of the takeout we ordered and then barely ate. Cooking with Nadine two floors down, she couldn't reprimand Jess for pouring vodka in her lemonade. She wasn't around to bridge the gulf between us. There was only Ellie, who stretched out in the middle of the couch, trying to touch us both.

When Oma got home at nine, we had turned out all the lights, and Jess had lain down on the futon in the living room. I was in my bedroom under the covers, not asleep. I heard the key turn in the lock and the familiar creak of the door opening, the deadbolt sliding home again. Oma's soft footsteps tapped into the living room and paused, then came down the hall.

I was turned toward the wall when she opened the door. Ellie jumped down from the foot of my bed to greet her, but Oma stayed where she was; I felt her presence, waiting, watching. I thought she might come in and sit down on the bed, ask me to explain why a gaggle of former students wasn't gathered around her dining room table, why the kitchen was still spotless, why we were in bed so early. But she must have decided I didn't need comforting, because she shut the door quietly and padded down the hall, leaving me all alone.

twenty

Maybe Jess was hungover again. Maybe she was sick. Or maybe she just didn't want to speak to me. All I know is that when her mom pulled up at the condo at the agreed-upon hour of noon, she was still brushing her teeth and putting on eyeliner. She hadn't woken up in time to have breakfast with Oma or walk along the riverbank like I'd planned, and I hadn't roused her. Instead, Oma had made French press coffee, scrambled eggs, and toast for just the two of us, and we had eaten outside, each of us reading our own books, in silence I welcomed.

In the elevator on the way down, Oma said, "It was wonderful to have you, Jess. Come back any time."

"Thanks. It was nice to be here," Jess said politely.

I almost cried then—not at Jess but at Oma, her kindness. But the elevator settled onto the first floor with a ring of an electronic bell, and we stepped out, and I knew this was no time for tears.

Beside her mom's car, I hugged Jess goodbye. She squeezed me tight and clung to me as if I were the edge of a building, and I held her back in the same way, as if I were afraid to fall.

"See you," she said, pulling back, avoiding my eyes.

"Only a month."

"Yeah."

She turned to Oma. "Thanks for having me."

"You're welcome," Oma said, glancing between us. I looked at the ground.

"Ready?" Jess's mom called through the window. She was still in the car, the AC running. Jess tossed her bag in the back seat and climbed in the passenger side, and Oma and I stood there waving until the little red sedan turned the corner out of sight.

I exhaled. Oma put her hand lightly on my back, but I stepped away.

"I'm gonna go do some work in the darkroom," I said.

"Are you sure, sweetheart?" Worry pressed deeper creases in the lines beside her eyes. "It's lovely out. We could take a walk with Ellie to the bakery."

She was right; it was a beautiful day. The sky was oil-paint blue and flowers bloomed everywhere I looked, from trees and from the ground, glorying in the new warmth.

"Yeah, I've got a lot of work to do. I'm kind of behind."

"Okay. Well, let me know if you change your mind. I might get us some croissants for later anyway."

I gathered my photo supplies from the condo and took the main road to the arts building. It took longer than cutting between the dorms, but campus was buzzing with activity, everyone outside, and I didn't want to see Claire and Kitty. I wanted, more than anything, to be alone. And there was no likelier place to be alone than a darkroom on a sunny spring Sunday.

Sure enough, I was the only person in the building. I developed the roll of film I had finished yesterday and hung it to dry, then sat on the floor next to the drying cabinet to try to make sense of the work remaining. I felt as if my head were full of dense clouds, as if I were inside an airplane, looking out into the thick gray nothingness, not knowing if I was moving or staying still. Making a list forced my attention away from the window.

So: Oma, Claire, and Sam were done. I still had to print the pictures of Kitty, Jess, Ethan, and Candace and Bryan. And I still had to figure out how to take a photo of my parents without having them physically present, then develop the film and print it.

I scratched some checkmarks and empty boxes into my notebook, and even as it helped, I knew that I couldn't evade my own mind forever. I thought back to Jess yesterday—*you're different now*—and my pen broke through the page.

I left my phone in my bag when I went into the darkroom and spread my things across multiple stations, working my way methodically through the list. If I teared up a few times, if I couldn't entirely focus on the task in front of me, I was still productive. After several hours, I finished the final print of the twins and set aside the imperfect ones to hang on my wall or give to them as gifts.

When I stepped out of the darkroom and finally checked my

phone, texts and missed calls had piled up: Claire asking what I was doing, Kitty asking if I was okay, Sam asking how the visit had been, Oma asking when I would be home. Candace and Bryan were each texting me separately complaining about the other; apparently there had been a debate about chores. There was also a missed call from Jess, but she hadn't texted or left a message.

I responded to only two messages: to Oma, **6 pm?** and to the twins, **just fold the laundry together while you watch TV, you'll get it done in half the time anyway.** Then I put my phone back in my bag. The hours had fallen away from me, but it was only five. I had enough time to make a contact sheet of this weekend's film before getting back home.

I took it out of the drying cabinet and carefully cut it into lines of five images, sliding them into their protective plastic casing. I held the sheet against the light of the window when I was done. Seeing the pictures this way, reversed in shades of brown—my friends looking like ghosts and familiar landscapes like alien dimensions—I tried to guess which ones would work best as prints. This roll was half walking-around photos with my friends and half Jess, and I thought the one of her laughing at the playground might be good.

When the contact sheet blossomed into life in the developer bath, I knew it was a failure. The images stood out against the ink-black lines and edges of the page, each flawed in some obvious way. Claire half out of frame. Oma with a pole behind her head, giving her an absurd headdress. Jess, out of focus. Jess, eyes half-closed. Jess, in the middle of speaking—not dynamic, not drawing you in, just caught in an awkward moment.

There was one photo worth printing. That was easy to see. I had composed it well; the focus was crisp. It had texture and contrast and body, clean lines and graceful curves. It was the last one on the roll. The one of Jess walking alone. Even in the still image, you could see the purpose in her walk, her step quick and her shoulders slight and slumped: a girl in the obvious, inevitable process of leaving something behind.

———

I was gathering my things to leave when the door to the darkroom opened. It startled me. No one was ever here this late on a Sunday. I thought it might be Erica, getting an early start on mixing that week's batch of chemicals, or Oma, coming to find me. But Sam stepped through.

"Oh," he said. He stopped. "Hi."

"Hi."

"I just…um." He gestured to the station where he usually worked, which was currently a holding zone for some of my extra paper. "I was just here to work on my print of my mom. I didn't know anyone else was in here. But it's good to see you." He smiled.

I tried to smile back. "You too," I said, though it was not good to see him. I had come here to not see anyone. "I was actually just leaving, though."

"Oh, okay." He shifted in place as I slid my film back into its protective plastic sheet. "How was the visit with Jess?"

"Well, it was fine," I said.

"It was really great to finally meet her," he offered.

"Yeah." I tried to slide past him to get to the stack of paper I'd put on his station, but he put a hand on my shoulder. I stopped.

"June," he said gently. "What happened? What's going on?"

He was always kind to me; his kindness was relentless, consistent, and undeserved. And he was tall, solid, reliable, *there*, and his hand on my shoulder was warm and strong. Suddenly he was close to me, studying me in this unnatural light that was called darkness, and not backing away. I looked up at him. I didn't back away, either. He leaned his head down toward me, and I knew what was coming, and I didn't stop it.

The kiss was tentative. Soft. Better than I had imagined, the many times I had imagined it. But nothing like it had been with Jess. Even as his hands moved to my waist and tightened there, sending a jolt of electricity through me, I knew in my gut this wasn't the right time, and I pulled away. My hip bumped the counter and threw me off-balance.

"June?" he said, hesitant, confused.

"I'm sorry," I said. "I have to go." I frantically tried to gather the papers I had left, but my hands were shaking. I gave up and sidestepped away from him, grabbing my bag from the floor.

"Wait, what?"

"I have to go home."

"Wait, June, did I—" He reached out but didn't touch me.

"I'm sorry. I thought you wanted—but maybe I was wrong. I just—can we talk about this?"

I shook him off. "I'm late."

"But we—you can't—" He took a breath. "Can I call you?"

"If you want."

"June, come on. What the hell?"

I was at the door. I turned around to see him with his hands raised, like he was trying to surrender. I couldn't read the expression on his face.

"We have to talk."

"I don't have to do anything," I said. My voice was shaky. "I don't owe you anything."

He ran a hand through his hair. "Well, fuck you too, I guess."

I pushed open the door. From behind me, muffled through the wall, I could hear him calling me back.

"June, I'm sorry. I didn't mean that. June, come on. Come back! You left all your paper!"

———

He didn't call me. I wasn't sure if I wanted him to. I responded to all the texts from Kitty and Claire that evening: some variation of **fine, just tired** or **I had a lot of work to do.** And I didn't call Jess, though I did text her **hope you got home okay,** to no response. I knew I would have to reckon with all of them tomorrow, but after I got home, I couldn't even face Oma for dinner. I said I was feeling sick and went to my room. I lay in the dark and replayed

279

the kiss with Sam over and over again. I regretted it. I wanted to do it again. I was grateful when I felt all the exhaustion of the last two weeks finally hit me in an accumulated wave, letting me sleep, a white noise machine humming inside my head.

I managed to avoid my friends all through the next day—a feat, given that most of our class periods were now study halls that we'd normally spend together. I accomplished this by returning to the darkroom for lunch and every empty period, and in doing so, I finally finished the print of Ethan. I could have gone all Monday without seeing Kitty and Claire were it not for physics, one of the few classes that still had a final exam to come. I arrived right at the bell and left as soon as class was dismissed, pretending I had ignored their increasingly concerned glances and notes, but I could not escape them forever. They cornered me by my locker.

"What in the world is going on with you?" Claire didn't sound angry, just worried. I hoped that meant Sam hadn't told her about the kiss.

"Nothing. I just have a lot of work to do on my photo project."

"Are you okay?" Kitty was looking at me skeptically. "Did something go wrong with Jess?"

"She was fine." I could hear but couldn't stop the aggressiveness in my voice. I didn't know where it was coming from. "You were at lunch on Saturday. She seemed fine then, right?"

They exchanged glances. "Yeah," Kitty said slowly. "She seemed...fine."

"You didn't like her, did you?"

Claire looked genuinely bewildered. "I liked her. It didn't seem like we had a lot in common, but—"

"I have to go," I interrupted. "Oma wants me back home early today."

"Why?" Kitty asked before I could turn away. "Did you get in trouble?"

"We didn't get in trouble!" Kitty took a step back, and I knew it was wrong to raise my voice, but it felt so good to finally lash out. "Jesus, we were fine. I followed all the rules."

Claire put an arm around Kitty protectively. "Okay, that's not what—"

"I know what she meant. Jess is a bad influence, right? That's what my parents think. That's what everyone thinks. I should've known you wouldn't like her. And guess what? She didn't like you, either. She thinks you're boring. And I fucking agree."

"June, what the hell," Kitty protested, even as Claire's eyes widened, but I turned and fled. I felt all my horrible words trailing behind me, but I couldn't turn around, couldn't stop. I weaved my way through the groups of loud, laughing girls until I got to the doors, and then I ran until my shoulders started to hurt from the bouncing of my bag. Claire and Kitty didn't follow.

Once I was finally free of the campus, I stopped, breathing hard. I felt a buzz in my pocket, and I pulled it out, but it wasn't Jess. It was just Candace, asking **do you know what day you're going to be home for the summer yet?** I didn't respond. I looked at the condo building. Oma wouldn't be there, I knew, but I still didn't want to go home. I didn't want to sit at the table doing my physics homework, didn't want to pace around the rooms where Jess had stood only a few days before. And I certainly didn't want to go back to the darkroom. Instead, I turned left and walked aimlessly for ten minutes, twenty, thirty, and then I stopped at my favorite park bench and sat down. I took out the book I had been trying to read, but the words were illegible, written in a different language.

I hated this, all of it. My guilt about Sam, about fighting with my friends, was an overwhelming wave. But the worst part was fighting with Jess. It required muscles I had never used. Hard as it was to believe, we had not fought before; we had been annoyed with each other, but we had never had real problems, never stopped talking. Back in North Carolina, we were around each other so constantly that any frustrations were worn smooth by proximity, like sandpaper on the splintered edge of a table. She had never looked away from me like she had on Sunday. I had never felt like I absolutely could not talk to her. And I was adrift.

My phone buzzed again, Candace asking **hellooooo?** Irritation flashed through me. **not sure**, I responded. **ask Mom.** She didn't reply, and I could feel—or was I imagining it?—the hurt in her silence. I sat there for a long time, rereading the same page of my book over and over again, while the trees and their fresh new leaves whispered unintelligibly around me.

When I was drunk with Jess, there was always a fraction of my brain that stayed reasonable. The more I drank, the smaller it got, but it was always there, my sober, sensible self. I would be about to do or say something stupid, and that part of me would speak up: *Don't do that. Come on.* If it was early in the night or if the stakes were high enough, I would listen. The words would stay put on my tongue; the dare would be laughed off, untaken; the shot would be a single, not a double. That voice was the reason I had never blacked out, or gotten into a car with a drunk driver, or told Jess how I loved her.

But other times—later nights, lower stakes—I heard the voice and shoved it away. *You know better,* that voice would say, and I would tell myself, *It's fine. It doesn't matter,* and do it anyway. I always regretted it later. In the moment, though, the mistake held a rich, electrifying satisfaction. *Fuck you,* said my sober self; *fuck you,* said my drunk self. And the two halves met in mutual loathing.

I'd had this exchange before, so it wasn't wholly shocking that over the next two weeks, that rational, reasonable voice spoke up over and over again in the back of my head. Every time I turned around in the hallway to avoid Claire or Kitty, it asked, *When are you going to apologize?* When I brushed off Sam's questions in photo class and ignored his texts, when he called and left a message, asking, "June, can we please talk?" and I didn't call back, it said, *You're about to lose something important.* And as I went day after day speaking only the bare minimum to Oma, it said, *Why are you locking her out?*

I quashed it down, every time. I moved through each day feeling smaller and smaller with the effort of being horrible, handling chores and homework with the hopeless efficiency of someone with nothing better to do. I did not talk to Jess. I talked to my parents only long enough to take my portrait of them, their two pixelated faces pressed together in the phone screen propped on the windowsill.

The sun shone yellow and sweet outside, and I tucked myself away in the darkroom every day until dinner. I finished, mounted, and framed every portrait, attempting as I did so to focus on the technical work—the grain of the image, the crisp white mat—rather than the subjects themselves.

———

For two weeks, I ignored everyone I loved and skipped every school event, with one exception. Claire's piano recital was on a Saturday, marked with a clumsy drawing of a few musical notes on the calendar in the kitchen. Every time Oma brought it up, I shrugged or changed the subject. I spent the day of the recital curled in bed napping and reading. At 5:30, Oma knocked on the door.

"Yes?"

She opened it, stuck her head in. "I'm going to Claire's piano recital. Do you want to come?"

I bit my lip. Despite my best attempts to not think about it, it had been on my mind all day. Claire had spent so many hours learning and practicing and memorizing; when she told me pianists had to memorize all the music they played in recitals,

I had hardly believed it, it sounded like so much work. She had done it, and she was about to show it off. But...

"I'm not feeling well," I said. "Sorry."

I turned away from her as she hovered in the doorway. For a few seconds, I thought she was going to push back, tell me, correctly, that I was being a horrible friend. But she just sighed sadly and said, "Well, June, I hope you feel better soon." I heard her leave, and the room was quiet.

It was better for everyone, I told myself, *that I wasn't there*. I had only been friends with Claire and Kitty for a few months, and I had hurt them, and if I came, they would probably assume I was there to hurt them again. This was Claire's big night, the culmination of a whole year of work. It was, she had told me, the first recital she was holding entirely by herself. I didn't want to distract from that.

But I felt so sad and so lonely, curled alone in my bed. I wanted to hear the music.

I looked at my phone. If I left right now, I would be able to sneak in just before it started. Claire had told us she expected a big crowd—not because of her talent but because every music student had to attend at least two other students' recitals, and Claire's was the very last one of the semester. There would be plenty of folks to hide me; I didn't have to be a distraction. I didn't have to talk to anyone. No one even had to know I was there.

I jumped up, startling Ellie at the foot of the bed, and threw on a black dress that could pass for formal. I hadn't shaved my legs in too long and my hair looked awful, but no one was supposed to see me anyway. I got to the auditorium, out of breath, at 6:02, and snuck in the door at the back of a small group of girls who were similarly late. As Claire's piano teacher introduced her and described the pieces she'd be playing, I found a seat in the far back corner. I spotted Oma in the middle next to a few other teachers, and Kitty and Sam together in the very front row.

"And now," the piano teacher said, beaming, "the young woman you're all here to see: Claire Isaac!"

Claire walked onstage and waved with uncharacteristic shyness as the crowd applauded. She looked stunning. When I last talked to her, she had been debating between a blue floor-length gown and a silver cocktail dress. She had chosen the blue, and she looked nothing short of regal, a gold headband nestled in her hair and a thin gold necklace resting on her collarbones. She sat down and rested her hands on the keys. The crowd quieted. She took a breath and started to play.

I didn't know anything about classical music. Or anything about the piano. But thirty seconds in, I knew Claire was good. Under her hands, the music soared and thundered, whimpered and wept. I heard triumph and heartbreak and sorrow and joy, and I saw the same emotions move her body, the slight jerks of her head, her body leaning toward the instrument and away. She filled the room. I sat captivated for the entire hour, and when she finally rose, glowing, from the bench, I slipped out the door.

I got home before Oma and changed out of my dress, got in bed again. I sat holding my knees close to my chest and looked out the window for a long time.

I wanted to text Claire **congratulations!!!!!**, to run back to campus and tell her in person how in awe of her I was, to celebrate. The music had moved something inside me. For the first time in weeks, I felt restless.

I had burned a bridge with Claire. She and Kitty wouldn't want to see me. But even if I had lost them, maybe I didn't have to lose everyone.

Two weeks was the longest time I had ever gone without talking to Jess. Before I fell asleep that night, I resolved: I would text Jess in the morning. I would do my best to cross the river between us and find her on the other side. If there was nothing left, at least I would know I had tried.

———

But as it turned out, Jess texted me first.

The text was a picture of a large McDonald's iced coffee, cream swirling down into its depths, and the words **can't wait until you're back, summer coffee = best coffee.**

It was morning and I was still in bed, too warm under the covers, my tongue dry from sleep. I curled on my side, away from the window, holding my phone in front of me. When I had seen her name pop up, I'd almost jumped to a reply right away. It was a casual message. She was asking me to forget that weekend and go back to normal, making it as easy as she could, and I was tempted.

But it was the coward's way out, and I was tired of not being brave.

I texted her: **can't wait for McDonald's with you. can I call?**

It took a few minutes before she responded, long enough that I thought maybe she would go back to silence. That this had been a fluke or meant for someone else. In the end, though, she called me.

"Hi," I said.

"Hi," she said—and with that one syllable, oh, how I had missed her.

"How's the coffee?"

"Perfect. As always."

"Are you out with Patrick?"

"Nah." A pause, and in the distance behind her, the white noise of traffic. "I just walked to the one near my house. Now I'm headed back."

"Oh. Cool."

Silence for a moment. "So—"

"How have your last few weeks been?" I interrupted accidentally, but I didn't apologize. I wanted to acknowledge that we hadn't talked.

"Pretty shitty," she said frankly.

"Me too."

"Listen," she said, "I'm sorry for blowing up at you. It was... I was..." She coughed and the ice in her coffee rattled as she took a sip, swallowed. "It was mean. I'm sorry."

I sat up and pushed the covers off me, crossing my legs underneath me. "It's okay." It wasn't, but what else could I say? "I just don't get it. Why you were mad."

She exhaled hard enough for me to hear it like a stiff breeze into the phone. "I recognize it's not rational. But—okay, again, I am sorry for what I said, just to make sure that's clear. Especially about your friends. I don't think I really mesh with them, but they seem wonderful. I'm glad you have them. So if you could apologize to them for me, that'd be great."

"I will." If I ever spoke to them again.

"Okay, good. But what I was going to say is, some of it is true. You are different now."

Thirty seconds passed, maybe a minute.

"Maybe." I ran my fingers along the edge of my quilt. "Not in a bad way, though."

"Yeah, but it doesn't matter whether it's a good difference or a bad difference. It's different."

"But you're different too," I pointed out, and she laughed, kind of sadly.

"Honestly? I don't think I am. I just want everything to stay exactly like it used to be. Perfect. I know you're coming back for the summer, but it's not going to be the same. Which I have to be okay with. People grow, I guess. But I don't have to like it."

And I knew two things then. First, that I would never tell her I had loved her, and second, that I didn't love her anymore. Not like I used to.

"You're still my best friend," I said.

"Same," she said.

We talked for another hour, and slowly the awkward edges fell away and left us with something like our old easy rhythms. We talked about summer jobs and Patrick and parents and school. At the end, I said I love you, and she said I love you, too.

But after we hung up, after I ducked across the hall into the bathroom, after I started the shower and climbed in, I cried. It had taken me so long to understand that my leaving—no one's fault but mine and hers—had made a crack in our friendship that let in enough light and dirt and space to finally split us down the middle. The enchantment that had held us together, the love I had sanctified, had finally snapped, and I could see her as she was, gorgeous and ugly and compassionate and lazy and, according to her, straight. We couldn't have a deeper friendship without my telling her how I felt. So we wouldn't.

She could offer an apology, and I could accept. She could explain herself, and I could understand. We could repair ourselves, but Jess was right: I was different. We were different. We wouldn't be the same again.

I cried until the water went cold. Then I dried myself off and stared at myself in the mirror, eyes swollen and red, hair dripping onto my shoulders. I took a deep breath, watched my chest rise and fall. If I was different, let me be different. Let me be better.

twenty-one

There was no one way to apologize. No simple place to begin.
I got dressed, made two sandwiches, poured two glasses of
lemonade, and walked out to the balcony, where Oma was
reading. I set the plates and glasses on the glass table beside
her—carefully, because I'd tried to carry too much at once—
and sat down in the other chair. She looked up from her book
in surprise.

"What's this?"

"I thought I'd make us lunch."

Oma looked at her watch and smiled, just a little, like she was
trying not to. "It's only eleven."

"Oh."

"But I'm sure I'll enjoy this later." Eleanor Roosevelt stood
and sniffed at the table, clearly interested in enjoying it now.
"Thank you."

"I'm sorry, Oma." It burst out of me, too loud, and she looked startled again.

"Why?"

"I haven't been talking to you. I've been a bitch."

She leaned forward to put her hand on my leg, her eyes gentle. "Don't use that word."

"Sorry."

"You have not been…unkind," she said. "It seemed like you were just sad, and you wanted some space. That's nothing to apologize for."

I looked at her hand on my knee, wrinkled and lotioned, the emerald on her ring finger sparkling in the sunlight. At home, when I wanted space, I didn't get it. The twins were everywhere all the time; Mom always wanted to know what was wrong, wouldn't stop asking. Dad assumed my mood was due to a mistake I had made, a situation I had mishandled, and it was something we could fix if I would just explain where I had gone wrong.

"So you're not mad at me?" I asked.

"No," she said.

"I haven't done anything around the house for the last two weeks," I pointed out. She had to have been frustrated at this, at least as frustrated as I was with myself—I did my own laundry, and I was on my last pair of underwear.

"True," she said, her smile broadening. "You seemed so down that I thought I'd give you a break. But now that you've cheered up a little, you can join me in spending the rest of the day doing some good old-fashioned spring cleaning." She picked up the sandwich I had made, inspecting the clumsy stack of cheese and vegetables. "After lunch, of course. Or brunch, rather."

"Can I tell you something, Oma?"

"Of course. Anything."

She meant it, and I could tell.

"I'm bisexual." I said it before I could be afraid.

She didn't look away. "We love who we love," she said after a long pause. "Thank you for telling me."

I looked out at the river, glowing blue in the sweet spring light, and felt so grateful for her that I couldn't say anything.

In the periphery of my vision, Ellie sniffed my plate with great hope, and before I could reach down to stop her, her nose slipped over the edge and her mouth opened, but the plate had been balanced precariously, and the weight of her snout flipped it over, showering her head in the disassembled remains of my sandwich. She looked utterly bewildered, a slice of Swiss cheese atop her head and some lettuce hanging from the corner of her mouth, and Oma and I couldn't stop laughing.

Claire and Kitty always walked to class together in the morning, always stopped at Kitty's locker before Claire's, and always left themselves at least ten minutes for Claire to sort through her things—inevitably she had lost notes or a textbook—before class. On Monday, I got to Claire's locker fifteen minutes before the first bell, sweating and breathless after the long walk from Harold's to school. I'd had to wake up before sunrise, but it was worth it. At least I hoped it was. I stood there holding the brown paper bag, leaning against the lockers, until they walked up.

They were talking until they saw me, and then they stopped, Kitty in the middle of her sentence. Claire looked surprised, Kitty wary.

I stepped forward and held out the bag. "Pancakes for you." I nodded to Claire. "And waffles for you." I looked at Kitty. Then I looked down at the ground. "I'm sorry I said what I said. You're not boring. You're the most interesting people I know. And I'm sorry I ignored you for two weeks. I still went to your piano recital, Claire. You were fucking incredible. I just didn't—" I took a breath. This was getting away from me. "Sorry. And Jess says she's sorry, too, and I'm also sorry if Jess was shitty to you, I honestly couldn't tell if she was actually mean or—"

"June," Kitty interrupted. I chanced a look at her but couldn't read her expression. "Are you okay?"

"I am now. I really am sorry. I just needed—" I remembered my conversation with Oma. "Some space. To figure things out. But I've done a lot of thinking, and you two are my best friends. I never should have called you boring or shut you out. Every day I spent not talking to you was a mistake."

"You are forgiven," Claire said. She smiled, not the big, rambunctious grin I was used to, but something smaller.

"We were really worried," Kitty said softly. "And hurt."

"I'm sorry," I said again.

"Well, thanks. I really appreciate it. And I forgive you." Kitty took the bag from me. "We're still friends."

"Me too," said Claire. "Pancakes help."

"Yeah, seriously." Kitty glanced at her phone. "Shit, we only have eight minutes to eat."

They sat down under their lockers, and after hesitating a moment, I sat down next to them as they pulled all the boxes out of the bag. "Ooh, coffee too," Claire said, grabbing the drink tray. She looked at the two cups, then at me. "None for you? Did you drink it on the way over here?"

I shook my head. "As penance."

"You idiot," Kitty said. "Split mine with me."

I leaned against the wall and took what they offered to me, a sip of coffee, a bite of waffle that, in spite of all my best efforts, had gone a bit cold. They told me what I had missed in my time alone, and I tried my best to explain the conversation with Jess, and I listened to their laughter. I could have listened to it all day. It was like my favorite song.

And then there was one person left.

All day Sunday as I vacuumed and dusted, I thought of ways to apologize to Sam. I thought of showing up at his house with a gift of a new pack of film or meeting him near his school Monday and inviting him on a walk. But then I remembered I had never been to his house, and I didn't know which of the many exits he took from school. I imagined more elaborate ideas, like taking a picture of the words *I'm sorry*, making a print of the picture, and leaving it at his normal seat in photo class on Tuesday. But again, when I thought about the logistics, it didn't seem like a great idea. In fact, the more I thought about it, it seemed like the kind of thing a serial killer might do.

Instead, on Monday night, I called him. Maybe it would've been braver to talk in person after class on Tuesday, but I couldn't wait. I sat outside on the balcony, my legs hanging off the edge, and I bit my lip as I listened to the phone ring. Once; I leaned my head against the railing. Twice; the metal was cool and hard, iron and rust. Three times; below, the condo had finally opened the pool, and the water shone like a sapphire in the moonlight. Four times; the lights in students' dorm rooms flickered off and on. He wasn't going to pick up.

The fifth ring was cut short. His voice, wary: "Hello?"

I sat up straight. "Hi."

"What's up? Do you…" He cleared his throat, and in the background, something rustled. "Do you need notes for the photo quiz or something?"

"I just wanted to talk to you," I said.

"Oh."

This was the third apology I had made in the last forty-eight hours, and somehow it still wasn't easy. "I wanted to say I'm sorry," I said. "For not talking to you these past few weeks. And not responding to your texts. And…for what happened in the darkroom. I was being a bad friend."

"No," he said, his voice low and sad. "I'm sorry. In the darkroom, I misread the situation. I shouldn't have done that. And I shouldn't have cursed at you. That was really shitty of me."

"I forgive you," I said. "You didn't exactly misread anything. I just… I was really confused. But I'm better now, I think."

"Well, I was a huge asshole, so that's kind of you," he said. He cleared his throat again. "If that's what upset you so much, I understand. But is there anything else? Claire told me you kind of blew up at them. Before…the darkroom."

I grimaced. "Yeah. I apologized today."

"Claire also told me that. Apparently she and Kitty got break-fast breads. It made me think maybe buying you pancakes would get me back into your good graces."

I laughed. "Well, I was actually trying to apologize to *you*, so maybe you can buy me pancakes and I can get you breakfast in return. We'll have the best brunch Harold's has to offer."

"Deal." I could hear the grin in the word, but then he went quiet. "So, if it wasn't the kiss, what happened? You don't have to tell me if you don't want, but not talking to you for so long was weird. And bad."

"I know. I'm sorry." I picked at the rust on the railing; a flake came off and floated five stories down to the ground.

"I don't mean to make you feel worse. I just don't get it. I could tell it had something to do with Jess, but…"

This was the moment. I had to choose. It would be the easiest thing in the world to tell him that Jess hadn't gotten along with him, Claire, and Kitty and that this clash had made me doubt the depth and importance of my new friendships. It was true, which made it even easier. But it wasn't the only truth, and that meant it wasn't enough.

"Jess is my best friend," I said slowly. "And she's really different from y'all. I was worried you wouldn't get along, and as it turned out…things didn't blow up, but I could tell that she didn't really fit in. And she could tell, too.

"But over the past few months, I've kind of been realizing that I was feeling a lot more for her than you're supposed to feel for your best friend."

Silence. I listened hard to hear his breathing, anything, any reaction, but there was nothing.

"I wanted it to be this perfect weekend. With everyone just being absolutely happy together. And then she got mad at me for…well, for nothing, really. We didn't talk after she left," I finished, "until yesterday."

"Did she apologize?"

I was too nervous to distinguish his tone, and I nodded even though he couldn't see. "Yeah. She knew she was being awful. She's got her own insecurities."

"Did you tell her…how you feel?"

This time, I could hear him clearly. The easy smile that he'd given me earlier was gone. He was guarded again, cautious, maybe—was I imagining it?—a little sad.

"No."

He murmured something, and I pressed the phone closer to my ear, feeling the heat of it. "What?"

"Sorry. I said, why not?"

I looked out at the river. It was a clear night, the moon vivid and shining overhead, and I could see all the way across it to the bank on the other side. It could have been a mile wide or more. Behind the trees, there might be houses or shopping malls or an equally quaint downtown with a boys' boarding school, our mirror. In all my time here, I had never crossed the bridge to find out.

"Partly because it already messed things up with us, me moving here," I answered. "And I didn't want to make it worse. But mostly because I don't think I still feel that way. And if I told her and she somehow felt the same way about me—which I'm positive she doesn't, but still—I don't know if I'd want to be with her like that." I paused for a long time, kicking my legs absently against the side of the balcony. "I don't know if we're good for each other, in the end."

He was quiet for a minute, and I wondered if he was going to ask more. If he was going to ask me: *Do you feel that way about anyone else?* Or if he would be bolder: *Do you feel that way about me?* We weren't just friends. He deserved to know.

But I didn't have a good answer. I felt a spark with him where with Jess it had been a blaze. Thinking back on those long, sunlit weekends with her, I was amazed at myself, ashamed of myself, that I had failed to recognize my own ferocious desire. Maybe I didn't love her exactly that way anymore, but I knew what it had felt like. I missed it, kind of.

He didn't say anything, and I asked what I wanted to know: "Do you think we can still be friends, Sam?"

"Yeah, we can be friends," he said. There was silence on the other end of the line. Then he repeated himself, his voice stronger. "We can be friends."

"Can I sit next to you in photo tomorrow?" I had been sitting in the corner next to Maya.

He laughed, and the tension eased a little. "Yes. Of course. As long as you help me finish my prints."

"God, yes. It's the least I can do. I'm done with all mine."

"Already? We still have a week left."

"What do you think I was doing for the last two weeks?"

"Moping. Making plans to never see me again."

"I slept a lot."

"I always sleep a lot. That's why I'm not done with my photo project."

We talked for over an hour, until my phone battery ticked into the red and an exhaustion headache spread across my forehead. By the end, we were both laughing. I hung up and closed my eyes.

Absent my voice, the quiet of the night settled in all around me. The light wash of the river against the shore, the occasional faraway rumble of a car crossing over the bridge. Frogs somewhere. Cicadas. The things we said and didn't say to each other.

twenty-two

On the last day of school, I woke up early to make coffee for myself and Oma. When she walked into the kitchen, still wearing her bathrobe, and saw me carefully lowering the French press beside the two waiting glasses, she smiled and shook her head.

"You don't have to do that, you know," she said.

"Yes, I do." I poured the coffee, filled the glass the rest of the way with ice, and held it out to her.

"But it's cold!" She looked at me, indignant. "Why is there ice? Did you use cold water? You know it won't work if you use cold water."

"I made cold brew," I corrected her. I had prepared it last night after Oma went to bed after watching several YouTube videos on proper technique. I forced the cup into her hand and poured myself one. Oma's nose wrinkled.

"Coffee should be hot," she said.

"Just try it."

She took a sip, closed her eyes, considered.

"Coffee should be hot," she repeated, "but this is good."

I tried it myself. It was great. "You're welcome."

She left to shower without another word, but she took the cup with her. "Victory," I murmured to myself as I started cleaning up.

We walked to school together, earlier than normal for me, later than normal for Oma. Technically, she still had class to teach. In contrast, my only non-AP classes were in the afternoon, and with our exams having wrapped up earlier that week, all my teachers had given me permission to skip so I could hang my work for the photography show at 3:00. I didn't really need to be anywhere until lunchtime. But I had walked to school with Oma that first morning, back in January, and I wanted to do it again now that we were at the end. The sun was dazzling and warm; I was wearing a dress with straps that just barely passed the dress code. Everything was green.

I spent the morning as I had spent every other morning for the last week, outside with Claire and Kitty. All the juniors and seniors had the same idea, and the lawn was a quilt of brightly colored towels and picnic blankets, girls talking and laughing and walking from blanket to blanket as if they were calling on the houses of their friends. I had made a second carafe of cold brew and poured it into a thermos. Claire brought strawberries from her aunt's garden, and Kitty filled a tote bag with mini blueberry muffins from the cafeteria's end-of-year breakfast buffet.

"I wish this was all summer," Claire said, stretching on the ratty blue quilt.

"Same," Kitty sighed. She was going home for the summer, spending time with her family and working at her local library. "But your music camp is going to be great."

"It will be," Claire acknowledged. "But still." She had gotten into the kind of summer camp that was really more like school—hours and hours of practicing and lessons with well-known instructors. It sounded way too intense for me, which meant she would love it.

"I'm gonna miss you," I said to the sky. Claire rolled over to hug me, and Kitty squeezed my hand.

Like Kitty, I would be going home. My parents were arriving tomorrow to pick me up. Unlike her, I didn't have a job lined up, but on Monday, I had an interview with a new coffee shop near my old school. I was excited about it; if I could learn how to be a good barista, I might be able to do the same work once I got to college or even find a part-time job here next year. As far as I knew, Jess hadn't submitted any job applications.

"It's only three months," Kitty said.

"Not even," Claire said.

"And then we'll be back here." The thought of returning for another year, which I had once found depressing and scary, was now a great comfort.

My phone buzzed. Sam: **where are you??** The timestamp said 12:33.

"Shit." I jumped up.

"What?" Claire squinted up at me. She had lost her sunglasses again.

"I was supposed to be in the arts building three minutes ago." I grabbed my bag and started running up the hill, dodging groups of girls as I went. From behind me, Kitty yelled, "We'll see you at three!" and Claire called, "Good luck!"

By the time I reached the hallway, I was out of breath, but I shouldn't have rushed. I was far from the last to arrive. A few girls were walking up and down the stairs, carrying their framed prints in batches of two or three down to the hallway where they would hang. Erica was hammering nails and hooks into the wall, following long blue stripes of painter's tape. In Sharpie on each piece of tape, she had written a name. All of us had a section of wall and two rows of photos, four or five on top and the same number on the bottom. I found my spot at the end of the hallway, the last except for Sam's, before I went upstairs.

He was stationed on the floor in the back of our classroom, carefully resetting the mat on one of his photos. I picked my way through the chaos of girls and black frames. He looked up when he saw me and grinned.

"Finally," he said.

"I thought Erica was gonna be mad," I said, not so gently nudging him with my foot as I moved past him to where my own frames leaned against the wall. "I *ran* here."

"Oh, did I not mention that half the class still wasn't here?"

"You're a jerk." I lifted up my frames and moved them to the desk beside the floor where he sat. Below me, he shrugged, smiled, looked up, and held my gaze for a few seconds. He had gotten a haircut and traded out his T-shirt and shorts for slacks and a green collared shirt. Dressed for the occasion.

"You look nice," I said.

"You too," he said. "Good dress."

A few minutes later, having made sure all our photos were intact and set properly in their frames, we took the stairs down together. Since Erica hadn't yet made it down to our end of the hallway, we grabbed hammers and picture hangers and measuring tape ourselves.

It was the last afternoon of class, and I wanted it to go on forever. I had glimpsed bits and pieces of my classmates' work over the past six weeks, but I hadn't seen it all together like this. Sam and I barely had time to hang up our own photos before helping out the girls who had come rushing in late, and every picture took longer to hang because I was marveling at it. Not all of them were technical masterpieces—far from it—but every single image I saw fulfilled the first challenge that Erica had set us, to take a picture of a person that told you what that person meant.

I hammered nails; I lifted frames; I unfolded plastic tables and folding chairs. I ran back and forth to the cafeteria carrying trays of cookies and jugs of lemonade. At ten to three, the entryway with the drinks and snacks was starting to fill up. Erica looked around, wild-eyed, took a deep breath, and said, "Okay. I think we're ready. If you need to prepare anything else, now's your time. Be back here at three. I'm going to say a few words."

I escaped to the bathroom, where I found half my class. It swarmed with the breathless, intimate energy of girls gathered in front of mirrors. The counter was a mess of lipstick and hairbrushes dense with tangles. Megan fastened the thin silver clasp on Ruby's necklace, biting her lip. Jasmine zipped Maya's dress. Lauren swiped on deodorant and leaned close to the mirror, dabbing at her hairline with a damp paper towel. They— we—chattered. So many people, so many more than we were expecting. Were our photos good? Would our friends like how we had showed them, or would they be angry at us? What were we doing this summer? Could we believe it was the end of the year?

I put on red lipstick. I had never worn it before because it wasn't mine; it belonged to Jess, and I had found it under the futon, cleaning up after she left. Once we started talking again, I told her I'd mail it back to her, but she said I could keep it. "I only used it once, and it'll look better on you," she'd said, even though our skin tones were almost exactly the same. She was right. In the mirror, I looked new.

I took a picture of myself and texted it to her. **almost time for my photo show!**

"Two minutes," Jasmine said to nobody in particular, and I ducked out before the mass exodus could begin. As I pushed open the door, my phone buzzed with a reply: **you look AMAZING, good luck! remember me when you're a famous photographer!!!**

Back in the entryway, I spotted Claire, inches taller than everyone around her, and squeezed my way through the crowd. I gave her and Kitty one enormous hug.

"Thank you so much for coming," I said. "This is a *lot* of people."

"That it is," Kitty said. She looked over my shoulder, half smiling. "We were actually just talking to—"

"Hi, June!"

I turned around. There, beside Oma, were my parents.

Dad grinned broadly, and Mom raised a hand in an awkward wave. They both looked so wholly out of place in the crowd that my mouth hung open for a moment before I could react. The weird thing wasn't that they were parents at a student event. So close to move-out day, a lot of my classmates' families had come. In fact, Sam had told me his family was coming, too, though I didn't see him anywhere.

The weird thing was that in this building, this safe and separate space, I almost never thought of my parents. Them and their anger, their suspicion, their disappointment. My gut reaction was to turn away, certain that when I turned back, they would be gone.

Instead, I stepped forward and hugged them both.

"I didn't know you guys were coming!" I said into Dad's shoulder.

"Mom invited us," said my mother. "She said we couldn't miss it!"

"This is a big deal," Dad said, looking slightly overwhelmed—or at least surprised—by the crowd and the noise. I gave Oma a hug too, trying to catch her eye and silently communicate *what the hell*, but she just gave me a big smile and turned to talk to a student who had asked her a question.

"Did the twins come, too?" I asked, looking around, and Dad shook his head.

"They're staying with friends tonight," he said. "End of school sleepover."

"So, do y'all have baby pictures of June to share or what?" Claire interjected.

Thankfully, Erica chose that moment to stand up on a chair and shush the crowd. As everyone settled down, I felt someone grab my hand and squeeze it once, quickly, then release. I turned to my right, where Sam had appeared beside me as if by magic. He smiled. Behind him, Claire was hugging and whispering greetings to a couple who had to be his parents. I smiled back at him—those eyes, how could you not?—and then turned with the crowd to listen to Erica.

"Welcome to the first annual St. Anne's photography show!" The crowd hooted and clapped in such rambunctious appreciation that I started laughing. This was definitely the rowdiest art show I had ever attended. It was the first art show I had ever attended, too, but whatever.

"The twelve students in my class have worked very hard over the past semester to learn how to not just take great pictures but also develop and print their film—a dying art," she added, grinning at some of the parents and teachers in the audience, who were nodding in shared nostalgia. "They've spent the last six weeks making portraits of the people in their lives who mean the most to them. Those portraits will hang in the arts hallway until next January, so if you have friends who couldn't make it today, you can tell them they only missed the cookies.

"And speaking of, we have plenty of refreshments." She gestured to the back of the room, where we had set out enough snacks for an army. "So please, grab a plate as you browse, and enjoy the work. Let's give a round of applause for the artists!"

As Erica climbed down from her makeshift platform, the crowd exploded in applause even louder than the first round, and I glanced at Sam, giggling despite myself. It was impossible not to be both embarrassed and proud.

As the noise died down, people started to move into the hall. Sam and his parents had split off to talk to Claire near the table of cookies, Kitty and Oma were chatting with some of her former students, and my parents were standing still, looking baffled.

"June, we had no idea this was such a big deal!" Mom said.

"It's not a real exhibit, just a school thing." Even as I resented them for being surprised, I had to admit that I hadn't given them much information. I tried to remember what I had told them. I had definitely mentioned it, but I was pretty sure I had made it sound like the event was an in-class celebration. When they told me they were planning to come up the day after school ended, I hadn't even considered inviting them. Apparently Oma had taken it upon herself.

"School exhibits can still be a big deal," Dad said gently.

"We just met Kitty and Claire," Mom said. I braced myself for criticism, but she continued, "They seemed wonderful. Are their parents here?"

"Not yet. They weren't in my photo class. Their parents are coming tomorrow. But my friend Sam, I don't know if you met him—" I nodded to him across the room. "He goes to school in town, but he got a special exception to attend this class. He's Claire's cousin. His parents are here."

"We'd love to meet them, too," Dad said, following my gaze.

"Yes, we were thinking maybe we could take you and your friends out to dinner tonight," Mom said. "Your oma said there was a place you like. A diner?"

"I—yeah, that would be great." I had planned to spend the evening packing, but I definitely wasn't going to turn down free Harold's. And if my parents were actually going to be nice to my friends for once…

"But first, show us these photos!" Dad clapped his hands together and turned toward the hallway, now swarmed with people.

"Yeah, sure. Mine are way down at the end."

As I threaded my way down the hallway, Mom grabbed my hand, Dad holding her hand behind her. I was reminded of when we used to go to the state fair when the twins were younger and I had been the middle link in the chain, Mom in front, then Candace, then me, then Bryan, then Dad, the five of us weaving our way like ducklings through the crowd.

The area in front of my and Sam's photos was still open; he wasn't there, and the crowd hadn't gotten this far. "Here they are," I said, gesturing to the wall. I felt suddenly self-conscious, and I leaned against the door to a supply closet, looking at the portraits that signified the last five months of my life as my parents stepped closer to inspect them.

I had ended up with eight pictures. On the top row, I had hung the portraits of people from my life here. There was Claire in her bedroom, cheeks puffed out and laughing, eyes wide open, fairy lights tangled in a bokeh shimmer behind her. Kitty at Harold's looking down, smiling, her short hair curling around her ears in need of a trim, golden hour soft on her cheeks.

In Oma's portrait, she was paused on the beach, the gentle tide washing up to her ankles. She was looking out toward the horizon so you could see her profile more than any details in her face; I had tried my hardest to balance the light, but she was still more outline than anything else. Beside her, Ellie paused on the rocks and looked out in the same direction, as if hoping for a stick she could chase.

Last on that line was Sam, standing in the middle of a wide landscape of parking lot and hill, holding his camera up to his eye. He might have been the only person in miles. He was barely identifiable if you didn't know him. But I knew him.

On the bottom row were the pictures of people from home. Ethan looked out his car window at the camera lens, his face in shadow but his eyes still sharp, wearing the wry expression that appeared just before he smiled. Raindrops blurred the air between him and the camera. The twins' portrait, too, was one I had taken at home: both of them in the corner of our L-shaped couch, the place they had claimed as theirs for as long as I could remember. Bryan held a book, and Candace was playing a game.

Their faces shared the same concentration; their bodies turned toward each other in perfect, unconscious symmetry.

My parents' photo made me wince, but there was nothing to be done about it now. On spring break, every time I had raised my camera to take a picture of my mom, she had noticed and thrown her hand in front of her face as if the photo were a bug to swat away. My dad had kept making goofy faces, which might have been fine, but I had never gotten the composition right, so I had never taken a picture.

The image I had finally printed was of my phone propped up on the windowsill at night, in the middle of a video chat, glowing so brightly that the world outside the window had been reduced to flat black. I had turned off my camera so they wouldn't see me taking the picture, so the rectangle that should have showed me was dark, too. They were waiting for me to speak, both of their faces crowded in the frame of the phone. Dad's left ear and half of Mom's cheek were cut off.

And then, finally, Jess. Hers was the eighth in the series, far right on the bottom row. I had given her the last word, like I always did. The print was the one of her walking away from the playground, the swing empty in the foreground, with the chain-link fence and the road beyond. I had made maybe a dozen prints of the photograph, even though there weren't any major technical mishaps—the focus, framing, lights, and darks had all been in order from the beginning. It had been clear from the first moment I saw the negative that this was the image I would choose, and if the symbolism was a little too on the nose, maybe that was what I needed. I think I made so many prints because I was always hoping that in the next one, when the picture appeared on the page, she would have turned around.

My parents took several minutes to look at the pictures, during which a bunch of other people wandered down the hall, glanced at my photos and Sam's, then turned around again. It gave me time to look over Sam's collection. I had seen a lot of his pictures because I had helped him with last-minute prints, but I hadn't looked at them all together like this. They were, as I had known they would be, very good. Lines and curves, black and white met each other in crisp, intentional contrast.

It was funny to see his portraits of Kitty and Claire next to mine. He had taken the picture of Claire at the Shabbos table at his parents' house, her hands in the middle of tearing a piece of challah and a rare serene expression on her face. In Kitty's photo, she was lying down, apparently asleep, on a blanket on the grass. I remembered that day. The lawn had been crowded with winter-sick girls desperate for the sun, but Sam had found the angle that made it look as if Kitty were alone.

The picture of me was the only one I hadn't seen, and though it made me feel horribly self-absorbed to admit, it was the one I liked best. Like my picture of Sam, his image of me showed me alone in a wide landscape. Unlike him in my photo, though, nothing shielded me from the camera. I was smiling a little, leaning protectively against the gate to the condo, as if guarding it from intruders. My bag was nowhere near me—I remembered him taking it away—so it was just me and the wall and the river and the sky. My hair was blowing in the wind. I looked beautiful.

Finally, my parents turned around. My heart sped up. I couldn't read their expressions.

"These are really lovely," Mom said. She stepped in to hug me tightly, and when I started to pull away, she didn't let go. "I'm so impressed."

"I'm very proud of you," Dad said, joining the hug, and I felt Mom nod. "This is great. Really, really great. And all As on your report card, too!"

"Thank you," I said. My voice was muffled by their bodies, and I was thankful they couldn't hear the waver in it. I couldn't remember the last time my parents had said they were proud of me without a "but." I had not expected them to think very much of the photographs. And I hadn't particularly expected praise for my grades, either. At the very least, I had thought they'd call out the A minus in AP Spanish, which I couldn't pull up to an A despite hours of studying. But they hadn't said anything bad at all.

When they finally pulled away, Mom's eyes were wet, though she quickly wiped the back of her hand across them. "I wish I had known more about this exhibit," she said. "I would've made sure you had time to take a nice picture of me."

"At spring break, I didn't know about it, either," I said honestly. "My teacher hadn't told us yet."

"I'm sorry about that." I turned and saw Erica, who had appeared beside me out of the crowd. "I've heard it from a lot of parents who are conspicuously absent from these collections.

Next year's class will know before they go home, but this year, I didn't get permission for the exhibit until after break. My fault!" She held up her hands and smiled. My parents introduced themselves, and she shook their hands, beaming.

"Your daughter is incredibly talented," she said, putting her arm around me.

"She's exaggerating," I said.

"I'm not," she insisted. "It's been a joy teaching you this semester, June."

"We're very proud," Dad said again, smiling.

I was feeling wildly uncomfortable, if happy, when Kitty and Claire broke through the crowd, Sam and his family in tow and Oma bringing up the back of the group.

"Oh my God, these are amazing," Claire said immediately. "Way better than anything else here."

"You haven't even had a chance to see them," Sam said.

"They feature me," Claire said, rounding on him. "Therefore—oh my God, June, you got the one with my cheeks puffed out!" She posed next to her photo in an uncanny imitation of herself.

I leaned against the wall again, Sam beside me, while everyone looked at the pictures and my parents talked to Erica. This time, I grabbed his hand.

"We did it," I said to him. "Good job."

"You too," he said. He leaned down and placed the lightest, briefest kiss on the top of my head.

We probably stood there for half an hour, chatting in different groups. I met Sam's parents, who said warmly, "We've heard a lot about you," and Sam met my parents, who pretended they had heard a lot about him, even though I had told them almost nothing. Mom raised her eyebrows at me when no one else was looking, and I knew I would have to answer questions later, but I resolved not to worry—not today, at least. I had all summer to decide how much I wanted to tell her and Dad, about Jess and Sam and my whole life for the past five months. Sam and I answered questions about our photos, and as self-conscious as I felt, it was nice, to have done all this work and have almost all the people I loved there to see it, showing real interest.

By four, the hallway had almost cleared out, and my parents had gotten friendly enough with everyone to invite the entire group to a celebratory dinner. I had no idea how we were going to fit nine people in a booth, but I trusted that Harold's would provide.

"What time is it?" Dad checked his watch.

"We have a few hours until dinner," my mother said. "Mom, can we go get settled at your place? We drove straight to the school. Traffic was worse than I expected."

"Oh yes, of course, I'll go with you. June—great job, again," Oma said, giving me another big hug. "Want to come?"

"I need to finish up some stuff here. But I'll be back home before dinner."

"We should get going, too," Sam's dad said. "Sam, we're giving you a ride home, right?"

"Right," Sam said. He hugged me, too, as our parents said

goodbye to each other. "See you at dinner," he said. "I'll give you a proper goodbye then."

"Deal," I said. "But it's not goodbye forever. Just for a while."

"Deal," he said, smiling as he pulled back.

Finally, Kitty and Claire and I were left alone in the hallway. We looked at one another in the sudden silence, and I started laughing.

"God, that was a lot."

"Congratulations," Kitty said, giving me one last hug

"Congratulations to you," I said. "You finished your junior year."

"We all finished our junior year," she pointed out.

"Congratulations to us all," Claire said. "What do we want to do now?"

"I was supposed to pack," I said.

"I should pack, too," Kitty said.

"Yeah, I guess so," Claire said. "Where do we—oh!"

She looked startled.

"What?" I asked.

"I had a New Year's resolution to spend more time on and near water."

"You did that," Kitty said.

"Yeah, but I said at the beginning of the year that I was going to take us out on the river on a kayak, and I never did."

"You're supposed to check those out at the athletics office," Kitty said, frowning. "I don't think they're even open now."

"The office is closed, but the kayaks are right there. No one's going to get mad at us for taking one without filling out a form."

"I don't know—"

"We'll put on life vests," Claire said as if making a great compromise. "It's the safest way of breaking the rules I can imagine."

Kitty stayed silent for several long seconds before she broke into a grin. "Fine. Okay. I will be a rebel in this one specific way."

Claire turned to me. "June?"

"Yes," I said immediately. "You promised, right?"

"I did."

Claire led us out of the building and into the bright, hot sun, splitting into a run as soon as she hit the grass. Kitty and I chased her down the hill to where the faded red kayaks and life jackets stood, stacked neatly in covered racks. Together, we pulled out a boat—"These are two-person kayaks, right?" Kitty asked, to which Claire said dismissively, "Two to three people, I'm sure"— and kicked off our shoes. Kitty draped life vests over our shoulders and tightened the straps like a camp counselor, and after some splashing, we made it into the boat: Claire at the front, then Kitty, then me, squeezed in tight. We used our paddles to push off from the muddy edge. Before I knew it, we were way out from shore, floating in the river.

The school was spread out like a postcard on the riverbank. I thought I could see Ellie on the balcony of Oma's condo, but I couldn't tell for sure; at that size, she would have been just a dot, one tiny part of a pointillist masterpiece. Kitty sighed happily,

Claire leaned back—and with that miniscule shift in weight, the boat flipped over.

The life vests kept us on the surface, but I still shrieked.

"Shit!" Kitty yelled.

"Oh no, I'm so sorry!" Claire screamed, but that was that: we were swimming, and now—

Now here we are, the water cold and singing with sunlight all around us, our home close enough for comfort but far enough away for adventure. We are kicking off from the boat and looking up at the sky, and I can feel this moment from the edges all the way into the middle, the sky so far above me and the river so deep below.

Claire dives and rises laughing, pulled by her life vest back to the surface. She says, "It feels good, try it," so we all do. We get our hair wet and our eyes wet and the world blurs into water and light. We go down, and then we come up.

acknowledgments

For me, writing a second book was significantly more difficult than writing a first. Between *The Goodbye Summer* and *Any Place But Here*, there were almost three years of daily writing that occasionally felt pointless, and I'm grateful for everyone in my life who helped create the conditions—support, stability, joy—that enabled me to keep writing.

More specifically, thank you to:

Nell Pierce, for advocating for this book and believing in me as a writer. Also, for making me start outlining (even if that wasn't something you intended to do). I hate outlining, but it turns out it's popular for a reason. It really helps!

Annie Berger and everyone at Sourcebooks who worked on *Any Place But Here*, for turning it from a Word document into a real, and much better, book. Working with Annie is a revelation. It is a wild, wonderful feeling to have someone read your work, know precisely what you were trying to do, and offer good ideas to improve it.

Claire Sorrenson, for her thoughtful, sensitive read and critique at a time when she had plenty of other things to attend to. Read her short stories!

All the places where I spent time writing this book: Austin, Texas; Orlando, Florida; London, England; Durham, Boone, Pittsboro, Holden Beach, and Topsail Island, North Carolina; Florence and Camporsevoli, Italy; Washington, DC; and New York City. Special gratitude to Cocoa Cinnamon, where I wrote the last few pages, and Bean Traders, where I wrote quite a bit of the rest of it. Everywhere I went, I never had a better cup of coffee than at Bean Traders, and I never will.

Lemon Tree House, for creating a perfect cocoon in which to do my first editing pass on this book (and start the next one). Those two weeks at Camporsevoli were a world unto themselves; I don't think I've ever been anywhere more beautiful. Thanks in particular to Jason for thunderstorm gnocchi; to the entire evening karaoke crew (Lynn, Dana, Tierra, Jill, Jacquetta, Nicole, et al.) for the songs and the laughter; and to Julie Jolicoeur, for building and sustaining it all.

My training partners and instructors at the Coalition, who kept me safe, sane, and strong while I was writing this book, and still do. Thank you in particular to DC, for heel hooks and rhythm, and to Jaimie, who taught me that anger is a gift.

DYWC—Barry and Julia especially—always.

The dog park: Jaret, Alissa, Chloe, Xander, Clare, Carter,

Allie, Alex, all of the babies, and all of the dogs. I would fight about food with you any day. Thank you for all your support and your unwavering agreement that summer is the best season.

Bethany, for bad television recommendations, conversations about fitness and relationships, and always answering my stupidest texts.

Melissa, for every time we were talking across a twelve-hour gap and had the same thought at the same time; for Mr. Brightside.

Nathan, for your willingness to do the literal act or emotional equivalent of cooking a five-course pasta meal any time it's necessary. And, also, for Mr. Brightside.

Chloe, for your jokes and your love, for garage podcast listening parties, for always being the second person to read everything I write.

Lucy, for poetry, Paris, and the saying "two things can be true."

My married-into-family, the Azevedos, for green bean casserole and earnest puns.

My first family—Mom, Dad, Allyn, and Scott—for everything, everything. I cannot narrow it down.

And Ben. You're the best person I've ever met. I love you infinitely.

about the author

Photo © Ben Azevedo

Sarah Van Name grew up in North Carolina and attended Duke University. She is the author of *The Goodbye Summer*. She lives and works in Durham with her husband, Ben, and her dog, Toast.